# SOME DREAMS FOLLOW
## :MILLENNIAL ASSIGNMENT

### SCOTT R. FORREST

rockhousepublishing
charlestown • indiana

Unless otherwise indicated, all Scripture quotations are taken from the *King James Version* of the Bible.

*Some Dreams Follow: Millinnial Assignment*
ISBN: 978-0-9837453-2-7
Copyright©2012 by Scott R. Forrest
138 Downing Court
Bossier City, LA 71111

Printed in the United States of America. All rights reserved under International Copyright Law. Contents and/or cover may not be reproduced in whole or in part in any form without the express written consent of the Publisher.

# :ACKNOWLEDGEMENTS

First of all, I would like to thank my beloved wife Trish. She has been at my side for almost 30 years now, through the highest of the highs, and through the lowest of the lows. She is a wonderful woman and has been a wonderful wife to me! Thank you babe for your continued love and support, especially during the writing of Millennial Assignment! I love you so much!

I would like to thank my mother Rita who always taught me to dream big when I was growing up. Aside from her steadfast love, it has been her greatest legacy to me by far. I love you mom!

I owe a tremendous debt of gratitude to my college best buddy Murray Kartanson who painstakingly conducted a thorough copy edit of my original manuscript and did it as a ministry to me. His inputs were well reasoned, always germane, and always appreciated. Thanks Murray! You're the best!

Special thanks to my college roommate and good friend Rick Fincher who made some excellent inputs to the manuscript concerning operational considerations for long range space missions at near light speeds. Many years ago, Rick and I spent many a late hour in our apartment at N.C. State discussing such things. Thanks Rick! You are a true American hero!

Special thanks to my truly anointed and talented daughter Alicia, who once again captured the essence of this project with an awesome book cover. Thanks Alicia! Great things are in store for you as your gift continues to make room for you!

Heartfelt thanks to a veritable army of proofreaders, at Word of Life and at other places, who provided valuable inputs concerning the story line and the tenor of the emerging manuscript. Thanks to Mike Arkless, Cory Brown, Don Bussey, Jenny Garing, Dixie Giddens, Laurie Giddens, Linda Goodpastor, Dave Ivey, Patty Kasomo, Titus Kasomo, Rajeana Munn, Ron Munn, Zachary Munn, Ethan Pease, Randy Pease, Terri Pease, Shane Prestridge, Larry Scott, Jon Shows, and Boyd Wheeler. And if I forgot anyone, I humbly ask for your forgiveness.

Finally, humble and hearty thanks to the folks at Rock House Publishing who embraced the Some Dreams Follow project and went above and beyond the call to help me along this new journey. Special shout out to Reverend Shaun Garing! Your leadership and humility are truly inspiring and I thank the Lord for the gifts he has placed into you. I have definitely been a beneficiary!

After reading an early manuscript of Millennial Assignment, the talented young artist Ethan Pease produced this amazing rendition of what he had read. I love it because of its retro nature and because it reminds me of the Robert A. Heinlein novels that had such a profound influence on my life as a young man. I offer it as a tribute to Heinlein's Juveniles which lit the fires of my imagination like no other books I can remember.

# :PREFACE

I thought it would be worthwhile to write a few paragraphs explaining the motivation that led to the creation of the Some Dreams Follow Trilogy. I am bold in declaring that I felt strongly led of the Lord to write these books, especially the first one, Millennial Assignment.

First of all, for those familiar with Christian eschatology, I have written these books from a Pre-Tribulation Rapture Pre-Millennialist perspective, a belief that I hold very deeply after many years of studying the Bible. Accordingly, I believe in the literal return of Jesus Christ to set up his Kingdom on the Earth, and that we as church age believers will rule and reign with him, beginning with a one thousand year period known as the Millennium. Although much of the book is speculation, I can say with confidence that I believe it to be informed speculation, having taken all of the major concepts from scripture.

With this in mind, my primary motivation for writing this book was to illustrate my belief that some of the dreams that God places in our hearts will inevitably follow us into the next life. Furthermore, the assignments given to us by the Lord in this life are designed to prepare us for the assignments we will be given in the next life.

Finally, as a life-long science fiction fan, an equally important motivation was to offer encouragement to generations of believers who have been made to feel at times that our love of such things was contrary to or out of step with the tenets of our faith as Bible believing Christians. Nothing could be further from the truth. In fact, if what the Bible predicts is true, and I believe with all of my heart that it is, the future world that awaits us is more fantastic and wondrous than any science fiction or fantasy novel could ever hope to capture.

# :TABLE OF CONTENTS

## SECTION ONE
## :FIRST LIFE

PROLOGUE    13

**CHAPTER ONE**
    *CHILDHOOD DREAMS*..........................................25

**CHAPTER TWO**
    *PURDUE: CRADLE OF ASTRONAUTS*......................35

**CHAPTER THREE**
    *HOG PILOT*........................................................47

**CHAPTER FOUR**
    *TEST PILOT*.......................................................65

**CHAPTER FIVE**
    *HANNAH BROOKS*..............................................77

**CHAPTER SIX**
    *TUMBLE FROM THE SKY*.....................................89

**CHAPTER SEVEN**
    *RECOVERY*......................................................103

**CHAPTER EIGHT**
    *NEW DIRECTION*..............................................113

**CHAPTER NINE**
    *CONFLICTING DREAMS*....................................123

**CHAPTER TEN**
    *SUN SETTING DREAMS*....................................141

## SECTION TWO
## :NEXT LIFE

PROLOGUE    151

**CHAPTER ELEVEN**
    *RECONSTRUCTION*..........................................159

: SOME DREAMS FOLLOW

CHAPTER TWELVE
*TECHNOLOGY ADVISOR........................175*

CHAPTER THIRTEEN
*SOME DREAMS FOLLOW....................181*

CHAPTER FOURTEEN
*THE CREW..........................................191*

CHAPTER FIFTEEN
*THE PROVIDENCE..............................211*

CHAPTER SIXTEEN
*SPACE TRIALS....................................221*

CHAPTER SEVENTEEN
*HIDDEN PLANET................................237*

CHAPTER EIGHTEEN:
*TERRA PRIME.....................................259*

TECHNOLOGY APPENDIX   267
ABOUT THE AUTHOR   271

## SECTION ONE

# :FIRST LIFE

# :PROLOGUE

The first thing that struck him about the ship was its sheer size. It suggested that it was designed for interstellar, not just interplanetary travel. It appeared to be a starship, a thought that immediately intrigued him.

He couldn't stop staring at the massive vessel. It was simply breathtaking; the largest craft of any kind he had ever seen. Its sleek metallic sheen was captivating, giving it a surreal aura that was difficult to quantify. Oh, it was real all right, but it was such a fantastic sight that it seemed like an apparition; a dream that had suddenly leapt out of the depths of his imagination and into reality.

It reminded him of the first time he had seen the southern rim of the Grand Canyon. It too had seemed surreal in its breathtaking beauty, its magnitude, and its awesomeness. But there, he had seen pictures ahead of time that prepared him somewhat for what he would eventually see in person. Here, there *was* no such preview, no advanced warning, nothing that could have prepared him for the sight of this ship. Spellbound, he immediately determined to learn as much as he could about the mysterious craft and began to pore over detail, every inch of her that he could see.

Looking at the top of the large two story observation window, he could see a sword like projection attached to the front of the craft. It looked like a fencer's foil which gave the ship a slightly menacing yet graceful appearance. She had beautiful lines which curved out smoothly from the hilt of that sword to form a spoon shaped bulge. He could tell that this bulge housed the bridge along with the ship's functional decks and living quarters.

Aft of this bulge, the lines tapered quickly into a boom like inner fuselage that fed into a trumpet shaped scoop of some kind. The trumpet scoop then tapered into an outer hull that appeared to run the length of the ship. Although he couldn't tell for sure from his vantage point, he deduced that the outer hull must have been part of the main engine and probably had some kind of nozzle attached to the back end. "A Bussard Ramjet?" he wondered briefly. Had they finally figured out how to build one that really worked?"

Immediately aft of the trumpet scoop he saw what appeared to be fuel tanks. He could not see them all, but he deduced that there were six oblong fuel tanks attached to the outer hull in symmetric fashion. Aft of the fuel tanks he saw two toroidal shaped containers that surrounded the outer hull and were attached to it by support struts, one behind the other.

"Those look like Tokomaks," he thought; "the ship's power source perhaps. The tanks probably store fuel for the reactors."

Immediately aft of the Tokomaks, if that's what they were, he saw what appeared to be six more oblong fuel tanks. They were at least four times longer than the previous ones and were also attached in symmetrical fashion to the outer hull. He could just make out a nozzle attached to the end of one of these longer tanks and figured that it was not a just a tank. It had to be a rocket booster of some kind. He was pretty sure if he could see the other side of the ship that there was another one just like it on the other side.

"So she has one main engine and two boosters," he surmised. "Wonder what kind of thrust they put out, and how far it could take you with onboard fuel?"

## : PROLOGUE

From what he could tell, the business end of this spacecraft took up a full three quarters of its length, and it appeared that much of it was for fuel. "But wasn't that the point of a Bussard Ramjet?" he thought. "Why all the extra fuel? Perhaps they store fuel for the boosters," he reasoned.

The front end had the look of a classic rocket ship right out of the pages of a 1950's era sci-fi novel, but the back end looked strictly functional, designed to get you where you needed to go…and fast!

He could tell by looking that this vessel would never rise through or reenter the atmosphere of a planet. It was just too big. "So why the smooth lines at the front?" he wondered. With this vessel, there was no real need for aerodynamic design.

As he continued to gaze intently at the magnificent starship, the sight of her, indeed the very notion of her existence, triggered something on the inside of Flynn. From deep within his heart he felt a surge of vivid emotions together with a collage of distant memories and long, lost dreams. Caught off guard by the suddenness of it all, his mind raced with a flurry of rapid fire thoughts: What's going on here? This looks like something I used to dream about as a young boy! Is someone playing a cruel joke on me? What's the matter with me? I thought I left those dreams behind long ago! Long, long ago! Why did they bring me here?"

With his mind still racing, he struggled in vain to fight back the tears. As he wiped them from his eyes with his left hand, Flynn reached toward the vessel with his right hand as if he could possess her somehow. He just stood there … trembling, gazing, reaching and wondering … until a sudden tap on the shoulder snapped him out of his immobilized state.

He was startled, as he had been left alone momentarily with his thoughts. Turning to see who it was and struggling to regain his composure, he realized that this was the first time he had looked away from the ship since the moment he had entered the observation deck.

"It's time to go Dr. Roberts. Our party is waiting for us on the command deck."

His escort was a familiar face. He was an Angelic, a Guardian that Flynn had come to know well after the transformation. His name was Magan Flynn which meant "Shield or Protector of Flynn." Though he remained at his side to serve, he was more of a partner now than a Guardian since Flynn had become one of the Many Brethren. Still, Magan insisted on using the formality of "Dr. Roberts," instead of just plain "Flynn," something he had never quite gotten used to. Magan was dressed in a white suit, was about Flynn's height and build, and had short cropped auburn hair like his own.

"She's beautiful, isn't she Dr. Roberts?" he said with a big grin. As they both turned to look at the ship, he continued, "They call her the Providence, HMSS Providence to be exact; 50 years in the making you know!"

Flynn didn't know how to respond because he didn't want to let on that he had no idea that such things were being built. He knew that the Kingdom had taken an active interest in a revitalized space program, and he knew they had been building some sort of advanced space station, but he had no idea that they were building a ship like this. He had always figured that man would return to the moon or maybe even make it to Mars one day, but this ship looked *way* over the top. It was clearly designed to go much farther than that.

"Why was this thing built?" he thought, "and why was *he* here? And how is it that Magan seems to know what's going on here and I don't? I've known him since the transformation; about a hundred years now, and he's never kept secrets from me before."

: PROLOGUE

Magan asked, "Has anyone told you why you are here, Dr. Roberts?"

"No," Flynn responded, "but I get the feeling I'm about to find out!"

Magan seemed to be brimming with excitement at the prospect and turned to escort Flynn down the corridor.

As they walked along the corridor from the observation deck toward the command deck, Flynn began to reflect on the sheer enormity of such a technological accomplishment and on the recent summons that had led to this new journey. First, there was the trip into low Earth orbit which he and Magan had accomplished via conventional means to even get here to see the Providence.

They had taken a Starliner from the Air-Space Port at Ben Gurion to the orbiting Bethel Space Station. The Starliner space plane got its namesake from the old Lockheed Starliner of AD 1958 and was formally referred to as the Starliner II. Starliners were everywhere now and the fact that they had become such a common form of transportation was something that Flynn took great pride in. His first assignment in the Next Life had been to help integrate the revolutionary craft into the transportation infrastructure of his region, and he had worked for the first 50 years of the Millennium to make that happen. Although he knew that they were designed for flight in air *and* space, he had never taken one this far out of the Earth's atmosphere and had never had occasion, or need, to enter low Earth orbit.

During that first century on planet Earth after the invasion, Flynn had employed a fierce dedication to his duties and a laser like focus that left him little time to think about anything else. In fact, he had been so focused on his millennial assignments that he had almost completely forgotten about his childhood dream of one day flying in space. It had burned deeply in his heart for so long but he had buried it once and for all near the end of his First

Life. At least that's what he thought he had done; now he wasn't so sure.

It almost seemed pointless to him now since he was one of the Many Brethren. After all, he could transport himself *anywhere in the universe* he wished to go, provided it was within the will of the Creator. He would simply concentrate for a moment, slip into the Second Dimensional Sphere, transit to the desired location and rematerialize in the First Dimensional Sphere. Furthermore, his new body could function in any environment; with or without gravity; with or without a breathable atmosphere, and could withstand the rigors of the extreme temperature ranges found throughout the cosmos. These extraordinary powers were not exclusive to the Brethren. Indeed, the Angelics possessed similar capabilities. But the Brethren were asked to use them sparingly in front of the Children: only in times of emergency, to save a life, or to prevent a crime from being committed. Displays of their superhuman capabilities for no good reason were considered a form of pride and were discouraged for that reason.

The Brethren had been placed on the Earth by the First Born to help lead, guide, and benevolently rule over Jacob's Children, the ones who had survived the Time of Jacob's Trouble. The Brethren's rule was recognized by most of the world as the most nurturing, loving and protective reign in the history of mankind, and Flynn was determined to do his part to keep it that way. His only motivation was to faithfully serve the Firstborn by promoting the Children's prosperity, safety, and welfare. He was completely committed to watching over and caring for them and had done so faithfully for the first hundred years of the Millennium.

The trip to orbit had served to jolt him out of that routine, one he was familiar with and one he had grown comfortable with. He had served the First Born in the establishment and governance of his Earthly Kingdom. Now, he had flown in space, as he once dreamed so passionately that he would do one day. Yet, oddly, it had barely registered at all on his emotions. Over the years since his First Life ended, that desire had become just a fleeting thought, a distant and unfulfilled dream that he had long ago put to rest. That is, until he saw the Providence!

The Bethel Space Station was enormous in size although surprisingly simple in design. It was essentially a long, hollow cylinder with the Providence tethered in the center. Because of the Starliner's approach angle, Flynn was unable to get a glimpse of her and thus, was unaware that she was even there. It wasn't until he entered the observation deck immediately adjacent to the airlock that he saw her for the first time.

During the ascent to Bethel, one of the Starliner crew members had told him about the basic layout of the space station. The living quarters and work stations were stacked in rings that ran from the designated "north" to "south" ends of the cylinder with observation decks placed strategically along the inner side. There were four equally spaced elevator systems that ran along the inner length of the cylinder to transport you from deck to deck. Numerous docking stations were placed on the outer side of the cylinder to accommodate the constant flow of personnel and equipment.

Flynn noticed that once they were inside Bethel, there was exactly one g of gravity. Among their many abilities, the Brethren also possessed an awareness of where they were in physical space and time at any moment using any place or time as a reference. They could sense the environment as well. Temperature, humidity, atmosphere, and gravity, among other things, could be sensed with a high degree of accuracy.

He asked one of the technicians in the docking station about the gravity and was told that it was artificially produced by the station's field generators. "Gravity field generators?" Flynn asked. "Yes," replied the technician.

He went on to explain that gravity field generators were a relatively recent technology that had been developed and manufactured by Graviton Technologies, a large North American conglomerate. Flynn was no stranger to technology; he had advanced degrees in engineering from the First Life and had been there on the Earth when the Knowledge Seas were loosed in the Next Life. Indeed Earth's technology had taken enormous strides in just a hundred years. As the Chief Technology Advisor for his region, Flynn had witnessed first-hand, the quantum leaps of applied knowledge and the wonder of the resulting technological transformation. He had to admit though, he had never heard of gravity field generators.

Magan and Flynn turned their heads in unison each time they passed one of the interior windows that lined the corridor just to get another look at the Providence. She was simply magnificent, and Flynn began to wonder what she looked like on the inside. Before he could explore those thoughts any further Magan led with a sharp right turn and the ship disappeared from their view behind them. They walked down another corridor about 50 feet until they came to a door on their left. There was a sign over the door that read "Main Observation and Command Deck."

There were two guards stationed at the door who looked as though they were expecting their arrival. They were Angelics, large and fierce in countenance, and wore the typical fighting tunics of the warrior class to which they belonged. Magan spoke to them briefly in Angelic, and the door swished open a few seconds later. Flynn wondered what occasion had prompted them to become visible for all to see, especially the Children. Normally, they were not so conspicuous.

As they entered, Magan walked to the center of the room, turned to the left, and headed down an aisle between a series of neatly organized consoles. Flynn followed as he surveyed the large and spacious room. He was immediately taken by the efficiency and beauty that characterized the command deck. Form and function seemed to flow together effortlessly creating an air of harmony that immediately set him at ease. All the control consoles and instrumentation were perfectly streamlined, and were organized in a manner that funneled toward the natural focal point

## PROLOGUE

of the room, the large interior window with accompanying large multifunction visual displays placed all around it.

The main observation window in the command deck offered the best view yet of the Providence, and Flynn was again mesmerized by the sight of her. As they walked toward the front of the room, he could tell with peripheral glances that the multifunction displays offered both external and internal views of the space station. On one monitor, he could see the Starliner he had just arrived in preparing for its return trip to Earth. On another, he could see technicians in space suits busily working on the backside of one of the ship's engines, in zero g, and in an area not visible from the observation window. But before he could absorb anything else, they had reached the forward quarter of the command deck where their party was waiting for them.

There were four individuals facing the observation window with their backs turned to Magan and Flynn. As they surveyed the Providence, three of them seemed to be taking turns talking to the one who was clearly the leader of the group. He wore a familiar looking burnt orange robe adorned with a sash, a ceremonial sword, and a regal looking hood. "Could it be?' Flynn wondered. As Magan and Flynn approached the group, the leader turned around to greet them followed by the other three. Flynn immediately fell to his left knee. He stretched out his arms toward the floor with his palms facing forward and bowed his head and shoulders in reverence.

"My Lord and my King! I am honored to once again be in your presence! As always, I am at your service!"

It was the First Born himself and Flynn responded with the traditional greeting rendered by the Many Brethren.

*"Greetings, Brother Flynn! So good to see you! Rise and give me a hug!"*

Flynn rose up and embraced him, still adjusting to the unexpected rendezvous, but nevertheless glad to see him and eager to oblige him with a hug. He was his Lord and King, but he was also his close friend.

"It's good to see you as well", replied Flynn. "We last saw each other in the Great Hall at the Centennial Celebration in Jerusalem, one month ago today, as I recall."

*"Yes, Flynn, I remember it well! Was it not an awesome time we had together?"*

"Yes, my Lord, it was truly awesome."

The First Born then turned to Magan and said, *"Magan, as always, thank you for your faithful service to Flynn and to the Brethren, it's good to see you too!"*

Magan had risen as well from his bow of reverence and was smiling ear to ear, "Yes your Majesty, it's good to see you! We await your instructions with great anticipation!"

Flynn looked at Magan and again wondered what he seemed to be hiding and why he seemed to be so animated.

The First Born then turned his attention to introductions: first there was Dan Steele, commander of the Bethel Space Station, then Mike Johnson, Bethel's chief engineer, and Nadia Habibi, chief architect and original design engineer of the Providence. Flynn knew instinctively that all three were normal humans, from Jacob's Children, something he thought to be significant, but was not sure why at this point.

After the few moments of brief conversation that followed the introductions, the First Born turned to Flynn and said, *"A private room has been prepared here in the command deck. Please come with me. You and I have some catching up to do."*

: PROLOGUE

He turned to the rest of the group and said, *"Gentlemen, Nadia, if you would please excuse us, Flynn and I must speak to one another alone. Magan, you can wait outside the door."*

Magan followed the First Born and Flynn as they walked side by side toward a door at the back of the command deck. Before they reached the door, Magan strode ahead, turned and stood at the left side of the door facing outward.

As the door opened, the First Born turned to Flynn and said, *"You first."* He and the First Born entered the spacious cabin and the door closed behind them. Flynn could tell from the holographic images and the HD photos placed around the room that this was the commander's suite. Apparently he had graciously agreed to lend it to the First Born for this private meeting. At the rear of the cabin, there was a large portal through which he could clearly see the Earth, over 200 miles below. What a beautiful sight, he thought, as he finally began to enjoy his trip into space.

*"Please sit down Flynn, and make yourself comfortable. We're going to be here for a while."*

Flynn settled into the comfortable chair in front of him. The First Born sat directly across from him with a small round table between them. He started speaking immediately and said, *"Flynn, I have been waiting a long, long time to speak with you about something that is very important to me and something that is very near and dear to your heart as well. But before we do that, I need to take you on a journey of remembrance.*

*"I am going to take you back through the significant seasons and events of your timeline that have prepared you for and brought you to this time and to this place; for a special purpose, for a special assignment. Some of these memories will be painful. Some of them will be joyous. But they all need to be remembered before you receive your new assignment. Are you ready?"*

Flynn responded calmly, but resolutely, "Yes, my Lord, I am ready."

The First Born answered back, *"Very well then, we will begin with your First Life."*

As those words left his lips, Flynn felt himself drift into a trancelike state. Images of his life, in amazing clarity and detail, panned before him rapidly, going backwards in time. In just a few moments, he saw his whole life flashing before him in reverse, until the images slowed, and he saw himself as a young boy in the middle of the 20$^{th}$ century. He was able somehow to view these things as a spectator and as a participant at the same time. As he would discover throughout this amazing vision, he would relive each key moment and experience every emotion exactly the way he did when these things actually happened, all with the First Born at his side.

# :CHILDHOOD DREAMS

Sean Flynn Roberts was seven years old when Virgil "Gus" Grissom became the second American to fly in space. He watched the news coverage of the story with a heightened fervor that was obvious to his parents. Steve and Elaine Roberts had known their boy had a deep seated fascination with space, even at an early age, but nothing in Flynn's short life thus far had so captivated him as this event.

When Yuri Gagarin became the first human to fly in space it had certainly commanded young Flynn's attention. And when Alan Shepherd followed as the first American, the degree of intensity had ratcheted up a notch for sure. But now it was much closer to home.

Gus Grissom was an Air Force pilot from his home state of Indiana, had learned to fly at an airport in Flynn's hometown of Bedford, and had graduated with an engineering degree from nearby Purdue University. All these things seemed to ignite something powerful on the inside of him. That day, a dream was born in the heart of young Flynn Roberts.

His father's full name was Steven Sean Roberts so Flynn was glad they had decided to call him by his middle name. For one thing, he thought Flynn Roberts sounded like an astronaut's name, one syllable followed by two, like Gus Grissom. But he was also fiercely independent and having his own unique name was something in which he delighted. No one else in his family, as far back as they could verify, was called by that name. In any case, both his first and middle names would reflect his Irish heritage, something his father was extremely proud of.

The dream that was birthed that day was raw and undeveloped, but from that moment on, nothing else mattered in the heart and mind of young Flynn Roberts. He decided he would do whatever it took to see to it that one day he would fly in space just like Gus Grissom. He was so enamored by Grissom that when he later died in the tragic Apollo launch pad accident, Flynn slipped into a fit of depression, missed three days of school, and wept incessantly. Although he never had a chance to meet him, he would never forget that it was Grissom who had lit the fire on the inside of him that would be the driving force for most of his adult life.

Flynn's father, Steve, was born in Ireland and raised in England after his parents had moved there to find work. He served as a pilot with the Royal Air Force at Bushy Park during the years after World War II and met his mother who was stationed there as a nurse with the US Air Force.

So it was not surprising that Flynn developed an early fascination for flight. He became enthralled when his father would tell of his flying days and of how he wished he had been a little older so that he could have flown during the war. Most of his father's older squadron mates were all war veterans with a chest full of medals dating back to the Battle of Britain.

After Steve had finished just one tour with the RAF, he and Elaine decided to move to America and start a new life there. Steve had grown discouraged and felt that if he could not fly in combat, he would rather not fly at all. Furthermore, he had lost his parents when he was only 14. Their home in suburban London had taken a direct hit from a V-2 rocket while he was away in the country with the rest of the school age children.

After that Steve was raised in Dublin by his grandmother. He finished school and started college while the war was still raging, hoping to finish in time to join the RAF and get into the fight as a pilot. Much to his chagrin, he had gotten his wings right as the war was ending and by the time he got to his first assignment at Bushy Park, the war was over.

Since his grandmother had passed away while he was still serving in the RAF, he felt there was nothing left to hold him in the UK. He and Elaine decided to move to Bedford, Indiana where she could be close to her family. She took a job as a nurse in a nearby hospital, and Steve put the accounting degree he had earned from University College Dublin to good use. He took the steps necessary to become a Certified Public Accountant and started a small accounting business near the Lawrence County Courthouse there in Bedford. They were not rich by any means but they lived a comfortable life, especially since Flynn ended up being their only child.

After he was born, Flynn's mother was never able to conceive again, something the doctors were never able to explain, and a fact that proved awkward and painful for them as a family during his mother's childbearing years.

Steve and Elaine had determined that they would raise Flynn in the same devout Catholic tradition in which they had been raised when they were kids. Consequently, his mother's barrenness was a source of gossip and rumor from time to time in the relatively small community of Bedford and the Catholic Parish to which they belonged. There would be the occasional cruel and thoughtless person, almost always a woman who happened to be producing plenty of offspring at the time, who would say that Elaine was secretly using contraception so that Flynn could remain an only child. This was especially painful for his mother. He knew for a fact that she yearned; indeed she ached, for more children, and spent many a tearful moment in prayer asking the Lord why he would not grant her the desire of her heart.

The walls were thin in the Roberts' household and he was privy to many of her tearful pleadings during those times. He could hear her crying from her bedroom and often wondered why the Lord seemed so intent on not answering her prayers. It pained him to no end to hear his mother suffer through such emotional turmoil. Often times, it would bring him to tears, and he would end up leaving his bedroom for the backyard and imploring God under his breath, "Why don't you just answer her prayer, don't you see how much she is suffering?"

He was never sure who he should be the maddest at, God, who seemed impervious to her cries, or the idiot woman who happened to be spreading the latest gossip about his mother.

When his dad would get home and find his wife crying in the bedroom, he would always seem to know the right things to say to soothe her pain. He could hear his father say to her, "Now, now, my love, these folks don't know what they are saying; we love them and forgive them anyway," and "I don't know why God hasn't answered our prayer for other children. All I know is that he loves us and cares for us very much."

Flynn loved his parent's deeply. They were thoughtful and loving and always seemed to put his needs and desires above their own. They seemed equally dedicated to preparing him to be as successful in life as possible.

His mother was a registered nurse and a full time housewife with an amazing work ethic. She would get him ready for school in the morning, fix his lunch, drive him to school, and then head to the hospital for a full day's work. After work she would come home and fix dinner for the family. She never complained once, that he ever heard, and she was always ready to listen to him talk at the dinner table about the latest sci-fi novel he was reading; the latest Star Trek episode he had watched, or about the latest space launch.

She knew of course about Flynn's dream and always took the time to encourage him to hold on to his dream and to pursue it with all of his heart. If she ever, at any time, thought it was impossible for him to achieve, she never breathed a word of it to him. She would simply say, "If the Lord is with you in your dreams, you can do the impossible!"

His father was equally supportive but added a pragmatic dimension that seemed to add balance to his mother's encouragement.

"Son, it's OK to dream, as long as you are willing to put legs to your dreams. You got to work hard, take the right steps, and be disciplined in everything you do if you're going to achieve those dreams."

He led by example on this score, as Flynn watched his father build his CPA business from a one man show into a thriving enterprise with 25 full time employees and with clients all over town and all over the state. Flynn was raised to dream big. And dream big he did.

Spiritually, his parent's lived pious and devoted Christian lives. He watched time and time again as they walked in love toward those who treated them shamefully, a fact that made a lasting impression on young Flynn. His father had related many times how he had struggled with forgiving the German people for the death of his parents. It was the forgiveness he found in the arms of Jesus Christ that had finally set him free to walk in love toward his fellow man, no matter what. Although Catholic in tradition, they always taught him that no matter what denomination a person attached themselves to, it was what they *did* with Jesus, the Son of God, that determined whether or not they were a Christian.

He grew up believing in Jesus and believing the Bible, but never really felt he could grasp the reality of a personal God. Flynn's heart was filled with only one thing, and that was his dream. There was no room for anything or anyone else. It was the only thing that seemed real and alive to him on the inside. Thus, a personal relationship with a God he couldn't see, and who apparently wasn't responding to his mother's pleas, was something that he pondered and struggled with throughout his childhood and well into his adult years.

Throughout his junior and senior high school days Flynn was an avid reader, especially when it came to science fiction. To him, this was the stuff of dreams, dreams that might one day come to pass in some way. Although he read Clarke, Bradbury, Norton and other prominent sci-fi writers, his favorite author was Robert A. Heinlein. Flynn devoured what came to be known as Heinlein's Juveniles. They were filled with adventure and with futuristic imagination like no other books he had ever found. To top it off, they were all written with young people as their main characters. Tunnel in the Sky, Time for the Stars, and Starship Troopers were his all-time favorites.

But Flynn's dreams were not confined to the pages of the sci-fi books that he read. Flynn followed all the NASA programs faithfully from the early days of Mercury and Gemini through the Apollo program. He could recite by memory every crew member of every launch right up until Gene Cernan became the last man to walk on the moon during Apollo 17. After the Apollo program was abandoned, he went through a profound period of depression. The Shuttle program was fine but rather limited in scope, he thought, even with a planned space station. He considered it to be the wholesale abandonment of *real* U.S. space exploration programs, confined to earth orbit only; something he attributed to short sighted politicians and government bureaucrats.

Where were the leaders like JFK who had set a national agenda for us to follow? Where was our sense of adventure as a nation? Did they not realize that the space program lit a national fire under America that produced an explosion of technology like no other time in our history, which benefited all of humanity, not just Americans? Because of this, Flynn developed an early distaste for politics of any kind. It was something he would learn to loath, especially when he came to realize that politics was not confined to government alone.

## : CHILDHOOD DREAMS

Flynn excelled in grade school, junior high, and high school as he had determined it necessary if he were to eventually get into engineering school at Purdue. He drew on an inner discipline that others found hard to comprehend, but one that was driven by the dream that was ever present in his heart. He never made anything less than an A in any of his classes and was active in sports as well. He was a star baseball player, with an amazing ability to both field and hit, and was a champion wrestler as well.

"A great pilot was one who had a sound mind and a sound body," his father had told him.

It was advice that he took to heart, always mindful to place priority on his studies but not to neglect the physical discipline which also characterized young Flynn. He was not very tall, growing to only 5 foot 9 by his senior year in high school but a rigorous weight training regimen that he relentlessly pursued through his high school years produced a powerfully muscled body that served him well in his athletic endeavors.

Flying was never too far from his mind and heart, and Flynn was able to take lessons on the weekends and in the summer at the same airport where Grissom had learned to fly. His father Steve encouraged the flying bug but tempered his encouragement by making him work to pay for the lessons himself.

Flynn would work at his dad's CPA office after school when he did not have a sports practice to attend. It was mundane work, filing and typing, but Flynn didn't mind because he knew that each day he worked was only a means to an end that would allow him to once again take to the air when the weekend hit.

Flynn adapted to the air as one who was born to fly, amazing his instructors with a steep learning curve. A flight procedure only had to be demonstrated one time and he would master it almost immediately. His stick and rudder skills were second to none and his ability to think well ahead of the aircraft made him a cut above the average student. He soloed the day he turned 16 in the same beat up Cessna 150 that he had used for the majority of his lessons. By the time he finished his senior year in high school he had amassed over 500 hours of flying time, most of which was by himself.

He loved to go flying after a hard week of practice and school work. To him it was a solace like no other place he had ever found; a place where he could set aside the frustrations of life and dream of nothing but flying; flying other airplanes, and one day, flying into space.

Flynn was boyishly handsome, affable, outgoing and had lots of friends, both girls and boys. Yet he was so focused on his goals that he couldn't honestly say he had a "best" friend with whom he spent most of his spare time. In fact he spent what little spare time he had with his baseball or wrestling buddies, but never doing anything that he considered to be risky behavior.

He avoided alcohol and drugs, though they were prevalent; not necessarily because he was a "good" Catholic boy who attended mass regularly. It was more that he considered the pursuit of such things to be a threat to his future and to the attainment of his intermediate and long term goals.

He attracted his share of female attention and dated a few girls from time to time, but he never allowed such things to progress into a full blown relationship. He simply did not have time for a girlfriend as much as he might have wanted one. It was a luxury he felt he could not afford if he was going to get an Air Force ROTC scholarship at Purdue. Completing his engineering degree and becoming an Air Force officer and pilot were paramount to him and no girl or any other distraction was going to keep him from achieving those goals. After that there would be test pilot school and then maybe, he thought, he might have time for a relationship with a woman. Time would tell he told himself, but for now he had bigger fish to fry.

## : CHILDHOOD DREAMS

Flynn graduated from high school with high honors and missed being the class valedictorian by a few decimal points; a fact he attributed to his athletics and his aviation pursuits. Had he concentrated solely on academics like the girl who beat him out, he knew he could have easily won that distinction. His consolation was that he had built a strong mind *and* a strong body for a purpose and for a reason that was higher than just being the class valedictorian. He was headed for space, and if he had to take second place for some reason; to him, that was a worthy reason.

*"You were a pretty focused young man, Flynn. It was something that I greatly admired about you. But I was really concerned about your lack of spiritual hunger. I beckoned you many times but you would not answer,"* said the First Born.

"I just didn't know my Lord. I just didn't know how vital it was at this point in my life," Flynn replied.

*"Yes, I know. It would be some time before you came to that realization. Let's continue."*

# :PURDUE: CRADLE OF ASTRONAUTS

**CHAPTER 2**

Flynn briefly flirted with the idea of applying for the Air Force Academy. He had figured out early on that the folks at NASA seemed to favor pilots who were service academy graduates and so he pursued the idea for a short while as he was finishing up his junior year in high school. But every time he would speak of it to his mother, she would go all misty-eyed at the prospect of her only son moving all the way to Colorado Springs to attend the Air Force Academy. A few of those sessions with his mother was enough to turn him back to his original plan of qualifying for an Air Force ROTC scholarship at Purdue University. Besides, his father had said that since Purdue was not that far from Bedford, he would buy him a car so he could come home regularly on the weekends.

He and his parents set up a meeting with the school guidance counselor and they helped him put together an application for Purdue. With his SAT scores and his grades well above average, Flynn got his acceptance letter from Purdue a little over a month after he had mailed it in. After that, the same guidance counselor helped him put together an application for an Air Force ROTC scholarship at Purdue.

Although it took longer than he expected, no one was surprised when during the middle of his senior year, Flynn received a letter which awarded him a four year full scholarship to Air Force ROTC Detachment 220 at Purdue. The thing that thrilled Flynn was that the scholarship would pay for all his tuition, books, and lodging, but also would provide him a monthly stipend for groceries and living expenses. He was excited because he quickly calculated that if he worked during the summers for his dad, and was frugal, there would be enough money for him to live off during the school year and to fund his now fully developed addiction to flying. All this he could do without having to work a job during school, allowing him to devote his full attention to his studies and his ROTC duties.

High school had been relatively easy for Flynn. But he knew that academics at Purdue were going to be a great deal more challenging, especially in the Aeronautics and Astronautics curriculum offered within the School of Engineering at Purdue. His goal was to graduate with a perfect 4.0 grade point average and that was going to take every ounce of diligence he could squeeze out of his mind and body. Although he felt he could probably make the wrestling team at Purdue and perhaps even start as a walk on, he quickly dismissed the idea in favor of devoting his full attention to his academics. He would continue to lift weights and run to keep himself in shape, but college level sports were something that he deemed to be far too demanding.

By the time Flynn entered his freshman year at Purdue, the Apollo program had been phased out and it seemed there was a national pause in the great race to space that had characterized his younger years. Plans for the Shuttle program had begun and plans were being made for an International Space Station but nothing much seemed to be going on space-wise at the time. No matter, thought Flynn, this would give him time to catch up with the other astronauts, and when the Shuttle program began, he would be primed to be a vital part of it. Maybe we wouldn't be going back to the Moon anytime soon but at least it was a shot at flying in Earth orbit, and maybe even taking part in the building of that space station.

"An orbital spacewalk with the whole earth lit up right in front of you, just like Ed White had done…now that'd be cool!" Flynn sighed to himself.

That fall, his parents followed him in his new car as they all drove to the Purdue campus early one Saturday morning in late August. Well, it was a new car to him; his father had followed through with his promise and had bought him a used Ford Pinto with a faded yellow paint job. It had no air conditioning and only an AM radio but at least it ran well. His father had insisted that one of his clients, who knew cars well, check it over thoroughly before he had purchased it. Flynn didn't mind. He was not out to make style points with anyone but had one thing on his mind and in his heart continually, the pursuit of space. If he had to drive an old Ford Pinto for a few years at Purdue, so be it. It was all a means to an end he thought, all taking him one step closer to his dream.

His parents helped him move into his dorm room that Saturday morning which didn't take long. He could fit all of his belongings in the trunk and the back seat of his Pinto. The move in consisted of a trip to the Residence Advisor's office to check out a room key, and then a few trips upstairs to unload his clothes and his boxes of sci-fi novels. After that there was a brief tearful goodbye, mainly by his mother but to a lesser degree his father and they were off. They said it was so they could get back to Bedford in time for mass, but Flynn knew it was to spare his mom a long, drawn out emotional farewell. Even though he was relatively close to home, sending him out on his own like this was something she was having difficulty adjusting to.

Flynn was not sure why, but his roommate had not yet arrived. He was alone with his thoughts. He decided to take a stroll around the campus as a brand new freshman. When he was in high school his dad had taken him to as many of the Purdue home football games as he could, and they would always come early enough to take a walk around the university grounds before game time. Although he was somewhat familiar with the campus, now he was viewing it through new eyes. He was now an officially enrolled student at the university and on the inside there was a stir of excitement at what the next four years would bring for him at this place. He was a "Boilermaker"!

But even more so Flynn was now a part of what had become known as the *Cradle of Astronauts*. As he walked around the campus he was taken by the air of history that he sensed, especially when it came to the space program. After all, Purdue boasted such iconic names as Neil Armstrong, Eugene Cernan, Roger Chaffee, and of course, Gus Grissom among its graduates. Just to be walking where these men had once walked and taking classes in the same classrooms where they had once sat was a constant source of inspiration that was never too far from his mind during his years at Purdue. In a way, he felt a kinship with these men, as if he knew on the inside that one day he would be counted among their ranks. He thrived off of that energy until it became a part of the inner drive that constantly motivated him to achieve and succeed in his goals.

His roommate finally arrived the following Sunday afternoon and had to scramble to get his key from the RA and get ready for registration the following Monday morning. His name was Jimmy Barnes, and he was there to major in sociology.

Jimmy was from a tiny little town in rural Virginia called Hillsville. His dad was a Boilermaker and had encouraged his son to apply to Purdue. So Jimmy was there to follow in his father's footsteps and that was about it. To him Purdue was just one of many colleges he could have attended. He thought the space program was a complete waste of time and money and felt like the money we were spending on space could be better used to feed the poor and shelter the homeless.

He also had the annoying habit of always being late and always waiting till the last minute to do things that needed to be done, something Flynn could not relate to at all. He would even sleep in from time to time and skip his classes. Consequently, Flynn was respectful and courteous, but he was never able to develop a genuine friendship with Jimmy though they shared a room together for two years. They were just too far apart in their constitution and in their outlook on life. Flynn was passionate and driven, and Jimmy was aimless and floating; at least that's the way Flynn saw it. In the universe of purpose and motivation, Jimmy was the epitomy of the anti-Flynn and although he never saw him again after college, Flynn determined early on that he would never, ever be a person like that.

After he completed registration, Flynn reported to Detachment 220 at the appointed time. As a four year scholarship student, an interview with the detachment commander, Colonel Jim Sikes, was required. Colonel Sikes was a no-nonsense, hardened type of officer who seemed to resent the fact that he was charged with playing "nursemaid" to young ROTC cadets.

When he interviewed Flynn, he asked him to share his intermediate and long term goals as a cadet and as a future Air Force officer. That was all the invitation he needed and Flynn unloaded his always at the ready vision, complete with near term, intermediate, and long term goals, all the way through test pilot school and on to astronaut training. Colonel Sikes seemed a bit taken aback and listened with a half smirk, half smile on his face until Flynn was done.

"Do you realize how many of your fellow cadets share the same dream as you and what the odds are of your success in these endeavors?" he asked.

Flynn was visibly shaken. He could feel the back of his neck and the tips of his ears getting hot and red as they did when he was either very angry or embarrassed. He was not expecting this kind of response and it was the first time anybody had ever challenged him in this way.

He sat there for a moment and then replied, "Sir, I don't have time to worry about what anyone else says they are going to do, but I know what I am going to do. Mark my words, one day I will fly in space!"

Colonel Sikes replied, "Let's just see if you can get through engineering at Purdue with a B.S. from the School of Aeronautics and Astronautics, and keep your scholarship intact. Dismissed!"

Flynn rose, saluted the Colonel, did an about face, and got out of there as fast as he could. He simmered with anger and brooded for days over what the Colonel had said to him. Even though it made him angry, he worked through it mentally and decided he would add *this* to the list of things that motivated him to succeed. No one had ever told him before in his life that he could not do something he dreamed he would do. He determined from that day forward that he would make it a practice to ignore any of the naysayers he would encounter and press on toward his goals in spite of them. One day, he thought, he would prove them all wrong.

He found out later from one of the cadet officers that Colonel Sikes was a Purdue grad and had been a test pilot. He had flown with many of the famous Purdue grads that went on to become astronauts. He had applied for astronaut training himself, on numerous occasions, but was never accepted. After that, Flynn could sort of understand Sikes' disappointment and bitterness, and his anger toward him dissipated somewhat. He would have to be more careful about what he said to him in the future.

Flynn put the blinders on when classes began and he never looked back. He was a fiercely devoted student and soon developed a reputation amongst his peers and his instructors as a young man to be reckoned with; someone who was pursuing life with laser like focus and unflinching determination. If you put him up against some of the top students in the School of Aeronautics and Astronautics, there were definitely students that could compete with him academically, but none of them could match the inner drive and absolute intensity that characterized young Flynn. It would prove to be the edge that always seemed to put him over the top in whatever he applied himself to do.

Flynn's one respite from the seriousness with which he approached his studies was his flying. Again, he preferred to fly solo, many times on out and back cross country flights, so that he could be alone with his thoughts and ponder his dreams. Though he flew primarily single engine light aircraft while he was at Purdue, he often wondered how it would feel when he finally got his hands on a powerful jet aircraft like the ones that the Air Force flew. He wasn't necessarily enamored with fighter jets the way some of his fellow cadets were, but saw flying fighters as another means to an end because it seemed to be the aircraft type that the majority of the astronauts had flown.

When he found out that the Shuttle was going to be essentially a 200,000 pound glider, he wondered why NASA did not take a more common sense approach and recruit a few guys who had flown heavy jet aircraft with the military services. After all, many of them had gone on to become test pilots as well.

"Oh well," he thought. "If fighter pilots were what they were looking for, then he would become one so he could reach his ultimate goal of one day flying in space."

Despite his mother and father's admonition, Flynn had stopped attending mass soon after he started his classes at Purdue. Another thing that concerned them was that Flynn did not seem to want to come home that often. He tried to explain that it was because of his dedication to his academic pursuits but they weren't buying it. In their minds, Flynn's dream was rapidly becoming an obsession that tended to shut everybody else out of his life. It was interfering with his relationship with his family and with the Lord.

Flynn didn't have the heart to tell them that he never really had a relationship with the Lord, so nothing had really changed. He was too busy working toward his dream to think about the heady things that his parents were increasingly talking to him about. Whenever he *did* come home on weekends, there would always come a time, usually at the dinner table, when one or both of his parents would say things to him like, "Mankind has a void, a need that only God can fill. A relationship with him is the only source of true happiness and fulfillment in life. Flynn, you need to submit your dream to God and to his higher purposes!"

Flynn would respond by saying, "I believe in my heart that flying in space *is* what he has called me to do! How else do you explain the way I feel about these things? Who else could be driving me like this on the inside?"

*"Your parents were very concerned about you during your time at Purdue, and they were right to be. Your dreams were beginning to cause you to lose sight of the truly important things in life: love, family, relationships. And equally as important, you had yet to learn that a relationship with the Creator is the life blood of any true God given dream. Without it, there is no real meaning or purpose to any dream; to any pursuit,"* said the First Born.

"My Lord, this is becoming painful to watch," said Flynn.

*"Yes, I know, but we must continue."*

When it came to making friends at Purdue, Flynn followed the same pattern from his high school days. He developed a circle of friends, mostly male, but some female, that were either his fellow cadets or fellow students in the School of Aeronautics and Astronautics. Yet, as before, he did not have one friend that he could consider a "best friend".

The majority of his free time, which was much scarcer than his high school days, was spent flying, and that was usually done alone. His fellow cadets nicknamed him "The Machine" because of the way he attacked his studies, and anything else he did for that matter. If you wanted to know what Flynn was doing at any given time, there weren't that many choices. He was either studying, flying, working out, eating, or sleeping - in that order of importance.

Although he was amiable and personable to all, his intensity was an order of magnitude higher than was the case when he was in high school. This time round there was no dating at all. Any girl who tried to get close to him, soon found out that he had no time for them. At this point in his life, his heart was filled with the pursuit of *space*. He just didn't need the distraction of a relationship if he was going to accomplish his goals one step at a time.

Flynn's years at Purdue passed quickly and his summers were filled with working, flying, and his required ROTC summer training. He would put in a full day's work for his dad and then hop over to the Bedford Airport to log at least an hour of flying each day.

By the time he was ready to graduate he had saved a good chunk of money and had logged an accumulated total of 1,000 hours of flying time. This was one of his goals, of course, and in typical fashion, Flynn had calculated just how much he would need to fly, on average, during the school year and during the summers, to reach that goal.

When it came to his GPA goal, Flynn suffered his first set back since he had narrowly missed being his class valedictorian in high school. He had made a B early on in his studies which seemed to him like a giant wrecking ball that had crashed into his all-important short term goal. That B had been earned in an English composition class his freshman year and was a constant source of irritation for the rest of his time at Purdue.

He remembered working hard at writing his papers to meet the standards set forth by the pretty young graduate student who had taught the class, and he would seethe whenever he thought about it. He had the distinct impression that she had singled him out and had decided ahead of time that she would not give him an A, even if he deserved it.

She had made a passing comment one day about how she thought the university should not allow ROTC units on campus that taught young college men and women the ways of war. He had turned to one of his fellow cadets in the class and said, "Wonder what planet she's from?" They both got a quick laugh out of it but unfortunately for him, he had unintentionally said it loud enough for her to hear.

Since he was required to wear his cadet uniform one day a week for drill, and that day just happened to coincide with one of the days that his English class met, there was no hiding the fact that he was destined to be a military man. His English instructor reminded him of Jimmy, his roommate, with the same lame liberal attitudes about life and politics, only she was prettier and with a Masters in English composition.

The B flustered Flynn for a while afterwards and it took some time for him to regroup. What seemed to be a minor setback to others was nevertheless devastating to him. He made up his mind that it would only serve to steel his resolve to an even greater degree. He would do *whatever it took* to make sure it never happened again. And it never did.

Flynn walked the stage at the traditional venue, The Elliot Hall of Music, and graduated from Purdue Summa Cum Laude. He had earned his B.S. in Aeronautical and Astronautical Engineering with a near perfect 3.98 GPA. Though it was an impressive achievement, he cringed when he saw that number on his official transcript, just slightly less than the 4.0 he had imagined.

Later that day there was a commissioning ceremony in the Purdue Memorial Union North Ballroom and he officially became a second lieutenant in the United States Air Force. His mother and father were there with some of his relatives on his mom's side to see him graduate and to see him commissioned.

During the ceremony, his father took great pride in pinning the gold Second Lieutenant bars onto the epaulets of Flynn's uniform and did so with mist in his eyes, extremely proud of his son for his dual achievements that day. He initiated a brief man hug with his son but was careful not to overdo it. The Roberts family was very emotional and prone to tears at moments like these. His father didn't want to embarrass Flynn in front of his ROTC buddies with a display of affection that could cause them both to break down. He would save that for more private moments.

His mother cried anyway and hugged him tightly afterwards. She whispered in his ear, "Flynn, I love you so much and I'm so proud of you! God has been so good to you! Always remember that!"

Flynn thought about that for a moment and was tempted to quip that he was thankful to God, but he himself had put a lot of work into making these things happen. He thought better of it though and kept silent. After all, he firmly believed that God had put these dreams in his heart and that all he was doing was carrying them out to the best of his abilities.

Colonel Sikes was one of the first to congratulate him when the official ceremony had concluded. He had waited till after his parents and relatives had fawned over Flynn sufficiently to shake his hand firmly when the first opportunity arose. Flynn responded with a quick salute and Colonel Sikes responded with a crisp one of his own.

"Congratulations on graduating as the number one cadet in your class! That's quite an achievement Lieutenant Roberts!"

He pulled Flynn aside where no one else could hear and whispered, "If I was a little rough on you at first, forgive me. I hear a lot of cadets come through this place with the same kind of dreams that you have. You have done extremely well here but remember, you have a long way to go and a lot of things have to fall your way for your dream to come true. Best of luck, Flynn."

"Thank you sir," Flynn cordially replied.

He tried to put a good face on it but inwardly he was chagrinned at the awkwardness of his first ever left-handed complement. There was an element of praise but then there was that injection of doubt at the end that ruined the sentiment.

"No matter," Flynn thought. He had long ago added Colonel Sikes to the ever growing list of people and things that served as a sort of "negative" motivation for him to succeed in his endeavors. "One day," he thought, "I'll show him!"

# CHAPTER 3: HOG PILOT

Flynn had received his orders the same day that he had been commissioned. He was to report for flight training at Williams Air Force Base in Mesa, Arizona just one month later. He was one of the few that year at Purdue that had been able to secure a pilot assignment. After the Vietnam War had wound down there was a dramatic cutback in the number of pilot slots available, and only the top cadets were able to qualify. He had been one of only five that were able to keep their "guaranteed" pilot slots after the cutbacks. For that he was thankful. He had no idea what he might have done if he wasn't able to go to pilot training. That was perhaps the most important short term goal of all; the lynchpin upon which all his other goals depended.

He had a month or so before he was to report to Williams so he moved back home to Bedford with his parents while he waited. His old room still looked the same as always. He had come back to it every summer for the last four years and could still navigate every corner of it, even with the lights out.

But something was different this time; the room had a different feel about it. He knew that this was the last time he would live in this room, in this house, in this town, for the rest of his life. There was a definite sense of anticipation as if he was about to begin a fantastic journey; a journey that would take him from the four walls of this tiny bedroom to adventures of flight yet unknown. He laid on his back that first night home and pondered the wonders of flight, thankful that he lived in an era where man had taken to the air and then pressed on into space.

He stared at the ceiling which still sported an array of model aircraft and spacecraft that he had built and accumulated over the years. Each of them hung from wires that he and his dad had meticulously attached to the ceiling's wooden beams. These were the models that helped fuel his dreams many a night as a young boy, and now he was on the cusp of achieving them. It had been a long day and Flynn drifted off into a deep sleep, still in the clothes that he had worn on the trip home that day.

In the dream he was falling; falling out of the sky from high altitude. He was falling out of the sky in a flight suit with accompanying g suit, helmet, and oxygen mask. Like the mythical Icarus and Daedalus, he was falling helplessly from the sky. Only unlike the fable, it wasn't because the wax in his man-made feathered wings had melted from exposure to the Sun; it was because the aircraft he had just been flying had suddenly disappeared from beneath him.

He kept falling and spinning, falling and spinning, and wondering what had happened to him and why there seemed to be nothing he could do to stop it. As he saw the ground rushing ever closer toward him, he knew that action on his part was necessary if he were to survive. He suddenly became aware that he was wearing a military style parachute and quickly pulled the D-ring. A second or two later the canopy fully inflated and he floated safely to the ground. After he hit the ground, he collapsed and then rolled onto his back and stared at the sky, his hands clutching the grass in the field where he had landed. He was thankful to be alive. As he lay there, someone spoke into his ear but he could not see who it was.

"Did you survive your tumble from the sky?" they asked.

Before he could offer a reply, he woke from the dream. He was still on his back and was again staring at the model airplanes and spacecraft that hung from his bedroom ceiling. He had no idea what this dream meant, if anything, and tried to put it out of his mind.

"After all," he thought, "it's three in the morning and I need to get some sleep."

Flynn then mustered enough energy to strip down to his boxers. He turned off the light, got under the covers and was asleep again in minutes.

That last month in Bedford before flight training could not have gone by any slower. Even though he flew every day that the weather was good and sometimes more than once a day, the days just seemed to crawl by. When the last week finally hit, he gave himself three days to drive from Bedford to Mesa with a one day cushion. In typical Flynn style, he left four days prior to his report date in mid-June, eager to get started.

To keep his mother and father happy, he had attended mass regularly while he was home with his parents. It was the least he could do for all the love and support they had given him over the years. After the last service they attended together, they had a farewell party in the Parish Fellowship Hall. Although grateful, he felt a bit awkward since he had not attended mass regularly since high school. His parents however had always been a vital part of the Parish community and he figured it was out of respect for them more than anything else. He knew also that his parents had spent many an hour praying for him with Father Pilcher, the Parish Priest who had been there since he was a small boy.

To his dismay, Father Pilcher had made it a point at the gathering to tell Flynn, in the presence of everyone there, that he would be in his prayers continually. He was thankful for the prayers but was uncomfortable with such overtly spiritual and public displays of affection. Flynn thanked him in a respectful manner but was relieved that the party had withered rather quickly after that.

He rode home in the back seat of the family sedan, already sensing that his mother was getting emotional about his imminent departure. The very next morning, to spare his mother the long goodbye that he knew would be difficult, he hugged both his parents briefly, told them he loved them, and left for Mesa. He had packed and loaded the night before, and drove out of Bedford in the same beat up yellow Pinto that had seen him through his four years at Purdue. He was on top of the world with excitement!

He was finally going to get his hands on an aircraft that could fly faster than 150 knots! He was going to be an Air Force jet jock and the thought of it absolutely consumed him!

Flynn arrived at Williams AFB the evening of the second full day of driving and checked into the Bachelor Officers Quarters. It was very late so without unpacking he just collapsed on the bed and fell asleep instantly. He woke early the next morning, realizing that he now had two days to explore the base and the city of Mesa before he had to report for training.

Even though it was his first visit to the desert southwest, he took to it immediately. There was something captivating about the combination of barrenness and beauty that seemed to characterize the landscape. On the last day before he had to report for training, he decided to take a drive to the southern rim of the Grand Canyon, something he had promised himself he would do when he had the time. When he finally stood on the rim and looked out over the canyon, he beheld a beauty and a grandeur that would be etched in his mind and heart forever. After that day, there was no doubt in his mind that he was going to love the desert.

He would soon discover that desert sunrises and sunsets could be breathtaking, and of course the weather was almost always perfect for flying; something else that he would learn to love about the desert.

He would be at Williams for about a year and knew from the moment he stepped foot on the base that he was going to love every minute of it. Yes, he knew the training would be rigorous, but that was something he almost reveled in. He looked forward to the challenge of pursuing yet another important goal and doing everything in his power to see to it that he earned his Air Force wings with more than just distinction. As always, he planned to be the very best. He felt at home in the air by now and was confident that adapting to high performance jet aircraft was something he was more than ready for. In fact, he had been waiting for this chance all of his life and couldn't wait to get started.

When ground school began the following week, Flynn put on the same blinders that he had employed when he was at Purdue. No distractions. He focused only on the task at hand. As was the case in high school and in college, he made friends easily but had no particular friend that he spent the majority of his spare time with.

He soon discovered that pilot training was even more demanding than he had imagined. The days were long and the pace was rapid. Before he knew it, he had finished ground school and was flying the T-37 primary jet trainer, affectionately known as the "Tweet" by the instructors and students that flew it.

It was a straight wing, twin engine jet trainer that he found easy to fly. Not really fast as jets go, but one thing he found out early on was that it had a very high g onset rate. In fact, it was one of the fastest onset rates of any aircraft in the world. This meant that if you pulled back on the stick too hard or snapped into a turn too quickly you could very quickly find yourself pulling enough g forces to black yourself out. This was the dreaded G Induced Loss of Consciousness or GLOC and was an almost certain trip home if you succumbed to it on more than one occasion. It was almost as if someone was holding a large rubber mallet over your head and was just waiting to bonk you with it and turn out your lights if you made a mistake. As far as Flynn was concerned, GLOC was the only real threat that the Tweet posed. It just wasn't that hard to fly.

Adapting to the insanely rigid mindset of Air Force pilot training was a different story. It was a game that you had to master. Even if you were the best pilot on the planet, if you could not recite procedure in exactly the right manner, dotting every "i" and crossing every "t", even to the point of reciting the memory acronyms that were taught, verbatim, you were a failure in the eyes of these instructors. Flynn made sure he learned this strange new language quickly so he could play the game well. He knew he could fly but evidently that wasn't enough, you had to fly *their* way or you weren't going to make it through the program.

This was something that Flynn had never encountered before. When it was just academics, there was never any real chance of not making it through, provided you put in the effort required to pass your classes. In pilot training however, a few slip ups and a few bad days could end your pilot career rather abruptly. To Flynn, this was an unthinkable fate and he quickly pushed it out of his mind. He would not fail he told himself. He had come too far to get stopped in his tracks now.

Flynn lived, ate, and breathed procedures and flight manuals, and "chair flew" every single training sortie before he actually flew it. He would sit in his BOQ room in a chair and mentally "fly" the following day's flight all the way from takeoff through landing. This was recommended by many of the instructors, and he found it to be an excellent way to prepare for his flights.

After making these mental adjustments and employing these techniques, it wasn't long before Flynn rose to the top of his T-37 class. His previous flight experience together with his unmatched intensity and personal discipline proved to be a powerful combination and helped him claim the number one spot in his class before it was all said and done. His instructors were impressed, and word spread through the squadron quickly that Flynn Roberts would be *the* student to beat.

After an outstanding showing in the T-37, it was on to the advanced jet trainer, the T-38. "Now this is more like it," thought Flynn, "a twin engine, tapered wing, *supersonic* rocket of an airplane!" In fact, he had been salivating at the prospect of flying the T-38 ever since he saw one in the pattern the day that he had arrived at Williams.

After he finished ground school for the advanced phase of training, Flynn finally made it to his "dollar" ride. That was the first training sortie, and was considered "no threat" because the instructors just took you up and let you get the feel of flying the T-38. As Flynn would find out, it would prove to be the calm before the storm because after the dollar ride it was "game on" with an even faster pace and blazing intensity.

The first thing you had to get used to was the speed and the acceleration of the T-38. It could get away from you quickly if you weren't careful and required a lot more finesse than the T-37. Because of its speed, you had to learn to think miles ahead of the aircraft if you were going to be successful flying it. Flynn found it strange but he actually adapted more rapidly to the T-38 than he had to the T-37. Thinking ahead of the aircraft was one of his strong suits from his early flying days; he just had to dial it up a few notches. Consequently, he quickly rose to become the number one student in his T-38 class. He kept that ranking right up until it was time for his flight commander to recommend him for a particular aircraft in preparation for the upcoming assignment night.

Unbeknownst to him, Flynn was about to suffer a setback that was entirely out of his control, something he had never experienced before. He had put his top aircraft choices down on his "dream sheet" in the following order: F-15, F-16, F-4 and A-10. He figured since he was number one in his class that an F-15 was his for the taking.

But one of the things the training wing commander had emphasized to his class during orientation was that the factors affecting your aircraft assignment always stress the needs of the Air Force over the desires of the individual pilot training graduate. For Flynn that meant that if there were no F-15s to be given out on his assignment cycle, then even as the number one student in the class, he would not get an F-15 for his first assignment.

In fact, it was worse than he could have imagined. There were only five fighter assignments available for his graduating class, two A-10 assignments, and three RF-4 assignments. His flight commander pulled him aside one afternoon to break the news to him.

"Think it over Flynn", he said, "I have the commander's word on it; you can pick whichever one of those you want."

Flynn was deeply disturbed. He thought to himself, "You mean I busted my butt for a year to make sure I was the top graduate in my class and I still don't get my first choice of aircraft? Or even my second or third choice? What's up with that?" It wasn't that he was dead set on the F-15, the F-16, or the F-4. It was that F prefix that seemed to be important to NASA and thus, to him. It was just a fact of life that fighter guys had the best shot at becoming mission pilot astronauts.

The A-10 looked like a real hoot to fly, with plenty of firepower and impressive maneuverability. But perceptions being what they were, he knew that flying the relatively slow, straight wing attack jet, dubbed by its pilots as the "Hog" was not the aircraft that would best position him for a shot at the space program. NASA had its own particular brand of snobbery and it was something he knew he would have to deal with when the time came.

His only other option was the RF-4, an unarmed photo reconnaissance version of the classic Vietnam era F-4 Phantom. Nicknamed the "Lead Sled", it was a heavy aircraft with lots of power and plenty of speed.

After agonizing for an entire weekend, he finally settled on the A-10. It was a brand new aircraft and the close air support mission appealed to Flynn more than the recon mission of the RF-4. If he ever did fly in combat, he just liked the thought of being in a direct position to help the guys on the ground that were toting the rifles and doing the real fighting.

Flynn's parents came alone this time to see him graduate from pilot training. His father proudly pinned the shiny set of Air Force pilot wings on his uniform during the graduation ceremony and of course, his mother cried. Flynn had been awarded the commander's trophy for finishing number one in his class and once again felt on top of the world. The other milestones he had achieved before this were important, but now he was an Air Force pilot and would soon be entrusted to fly one of the worlds most advanced and deadly fighter aircraft. It was a feeling that was absolutely exhilarating. He knew his life would never be the same again.

After spending the weekend with his parents, they left to head back to Bedford. There were the inevitable discussions which ended with the usual comments he had come to expect at moments of triumph like this.

"Remember to seek the Lord with all of your heart Flynn. It's the only path to true happiness and fulfillment. Achievements alone are no substitute for a relationship with God; they have to be submitted to his will and to his purposes."

*"Your parents were genuinely proud of you but were still concerned that you were basing your acceptance in life on the number and magnitude of your achievements. They wanted you to know that the Creator loved you and accepted you independent of these things,"* said the First Born.

"Yes Lord, I had yet to learn that truly great accomplishments flow out of true service, and true service flows out of relationship with the Creator," Flynn responded.

Flynn was given one set of orders the day after he graduated from pilot training, but the orders would send him to two different locations. First, he was to report to Holloman AFB in Alamogordo,

New Mexico to attend Lead in Fighter Training and then he was to report back to Arizona to Davis Monthan AFB in Tucson to train in the A-10. All totaled, it would be about a nine month process. He would start by flying the AT-38 at Holloman for an introduction to fighter aircraft fundamentals and tactics. After that he would finally get his hands on an A-10.

He would learn to fly it and learn to employ its lethal array of weapons; foremost being the already legendary GAU-8 Avenger 30 millimeter Gatling gun. He got chills just thinking about pulling the trigger on that big gun.

He was quietly amused at the thought of the aircraft's official name, the Thunderbolt II. No one called it by that name, ever, except perhaps some geek model aircraft builder.

"No," chuckling as he thought of it, "the public knew it as the Warthog, but the pilots who flew it called it the Hog."

"How fitting," he thought.

Although the Hog was extremely good at what it was designed to do, it was ugly as fighter aircraft went. Heck, it didn't even have an F prefix but an A which stood for attack. With its blunt geometry and "tomato can" looking, externally mounted engines, it did not conform to the Air Force's vision of the sleek, pointy nosed, extremely fast fighter jet. Consequently it was never popular with a lot of the Air Force brass, and members of the Hog community had to constantly fight the ever present threat of cuts to the A-10 fleet.

Although he was looking forward to flying the A-10, and knew that he had been number one in his pilot training class, he was already concerned about the image of the Hog when it came to his NASA aspirations. He was even more certain now that it would be something he would have to contend with as long as he flew the aircraft.

Lead In Fighter Training, or LIFT, as it was called back then, was a short but extremely demanding introduction to fighter fundamentals. When he got to Holloman, Flynn again loved everything about the familiar desert southwest. He didn't lose a single sortie to weather during the 10 weeks that he spent at Holloman. The pace was quick, like pilot training, but the training was completely different.

Here they would bend the AT-38s around in much more aggressive fashion than when he was flying the "white jets". The AT-38s sported a sexy, blue-gray camouflage that was a stark contrast from the pristine looking, white T-38s. Because of this, the students and instructors that flew it often referred to it as the "Smurf Jet".

While he was at LIFT, Flynn received what felt like a crash course in fighter formations, basic fighter maneuvers, surface attack tactics, and other fighter specific training. It was hard, it was intense, but it seemed like it was over before he realized it. Again, Flynn's intensity had set him apart from the rest of his peers, especially those who were destined to fly an air to ground, or close air support aircraft like the A-10. As it turned out, he had a real knack for air to ground weapons delivery and ended up finishing number one in the Air to Ground Top Gun Competition. It would serve him well in the A-10.

When he finally made it to Davis Monthan and began his training in the Hog, it seemed almost like a vacation compared to the rapid pace of pilot training and the super high intensity of LIFT. The biggest challenge with the A-10 was the fact that you were flying a single seat attack jet. There was no one else in the back seat to help you.

Although relatively easy to fly, the combination of flying, navigating, employing weapons, and performing other vital cockpit tasks, all by yourself, could be quite demanding. Task saturation was something that you had to constantly guard against. It might not have been a fast jet, but it was certainly challenging to employ effectively. And the big gun had been everything he had imagined.

He would always remember the feel of his first trigger pull on his first trip to the weapons training range. To him, it felt like he was sitting on top of a giant McCullough chain saw and had just pulled the chord to crank it. He remembered the vibration, the loud and distinct grinding buzz and the smell of ozone as the hot gun gases were discharged and the large cannon shells left the barrels of the GAU-8. He knew that if he were using the depleted uranium rounds rather than the required training rounds, a two to three second burst from a mile away would deliver enough energy to completely demolish an enemy tank.

Six months later he was finished and was officially designated a combat ready A-10 pilot. He was only a wingman, but immediately set his sights on becoming a flight lead and an instructor in the aircraft as soon as possible. He had once again finished first in his A-10 class at Davis Monthan, but with Flynn there was only time for a short celebration, then it was on to the next goal that needed to be accomplished. He had already read the Air Force Instruction on test pilot school and knew that he would have to be an instructor in his designated weapons system, the A-10, to submit an application. So on went the blinders again.

Flynn volunteered for overseas duty for one reason and one reason alone. He figured that being deployed overseas would minimize the distractions that life in the US might pose. A foreign country would offer the perfect type of isolation that would allow him to turn on the burners and excel in the A-10 above and beyond his peers. He asked for an assignment to Korea but felt like his plan had gone awry when he got the news that he had been given orders to RAF Bentwaters in England. Not exactly what he was hoping for. In England, after all, they spoke the same language and he didn't think he would get the kind of isolation he was hoping for.

His dad, of course, was delighted that his son would be stationed in the UK. Flynn would be just down the road from where Steve had grown up and not too far from where he himself had flown in the RAF. After hearing the news, his dad told him that it would give him and his mother an excuse to come and visit Flynn more often, and give him a chance to return to his boyhood roots. Since his parents had been killed during the war, Steve never really felt like he had a reason to return to the UK. Now that Flynn was going to be stationed there for the next three years, he had a renewed interest in returning to his homeland.

Flynn left for England after a month of leave that crawled by just like when he was waiting to go to pilot training. He had a goal he was aiming for and every minute where he sat idle, was, in his mind, time wasted. He felt like he couldn't really rest until he at least finished test pilot school. So whether it was wise or not, he pushed himself constantly to achieve; to do better than the best, and held himself to a rigorous and relentless personal timetable.

After arriving at Bentwaters, he spent his first night in the BOQ trying to get to sleep. He had flown the last leg of his trip on a KC-10 out of Charleston AFB and had slept a few hours on the plane. Then there was the bus ride from RAF Mildenhall to get to Bentwaters and he had slept once again. Thus, when he finally got to bed that night, he found himself wide awake at one o'clock in the morning. Plus, he knew it was barely dinner time back home.

All he could do was lay there thinking about his new surroundings and his new assignment. Tomorrow, he would report to his squadron and begin his duties as an A-10 pilot on the leading edge of theater deployed NATO forces. The A-10s were there to help stop the huge onslaught of tanks and armored vehicles that would surge through the Fulda Gap when Warsaw Pact forces began their likely invasion.

But the fact that Flynn could suddenly find himself flung into the mother of all wars between Eastern and Western world powers was not the thing that kept him up that night. Indeed he relished the thought of employing the considerable firepower of the A-10 against the foe for which it was designed: Warsaw Pact tanks and armor. His biggest fear was not that World War III might actually start on his watch, but that the start of World War III might interfere with his shot at test pilot school and astronaut training. This sudden surge of worrisome thoughts tired him emotionally and finally brought about the deep sleep that had previously eluded him.

In the dream he was falling; falling exactly as he had the first time he had the dream. Everything was the same from the moment he realized he had lost his aircraft to the moment he sensed the ground rushing up to meet him. He pulled the D ring and deployed the chute the same as before and again ended up on the ground on his back, clutching the grass, staring at the sky, thankful to be alive.

Once more, he heard the voice say, "Did you survive your tumble from the sky?"

He woke abruptly and wondered what in the world the recurring dream might actually mean. The fact that it had repeated itself exactly as before troubled him, and it began to dawn on him that there was significance to the dream that he was yet to discover. After thinking about it for several minutes, he could not settle on an answer that made any sense. Was it some sort of premonition of things to come? This time he focused on the fact that he was falling in full flight gear, a detail that seemed particularly menacing. Also, the only way he could imagine that an airplane would literally seem to disappear beneath you was after an emergency ejection. With no answers forthcoming, his thoughts faded quickly and he drifted back to sleep again.

Flynn adapted well to his new assignment at Bentwaters. As always, his amiable, soft spoken demeanor helped him to make friends quickly, and his relentless work ethic made him a favorite amongst the squadron leadership. He was the first to volunteer for any unwanted task or assignment and had told the operations officer that he was available to fly any sortie that no one else wanted to fly.

When there was an airshow that needed an A-10 static display, he was first in line to volunteer to fly to that location and to man the aircraft all weekend if necessary. When one of the "seagulls" dropped a sortie unexpectedly, he was always hanging around the ops counter waiting to take that pilot's sortie. He had not heard the seagull moniker before he had arrived, but soon found out exactly what it meant. Seagulls were those pilots, young and old, who for whatever reason, were always looking for an excuse *not* to fly. There were like seagulls, it was said; you had to throw rocks at them to get them to fly.

Flynn could not relate to the seagulls on any level as he was always eager to get into the air, especially in the Hog; it was a sheer joy to fly. He loved the feel of being strapped into the cockpit of the A-10, spacious by fighter standards, but still cramped by most. Once he was strapped in with his g-suit plugged in and had begun his prestart checklists, he felt he was in his own private world. Though he rarely flew alone, it was almost always a formation of two; he still felt the cockpit of his aircraft was his domain and his domain alone.

He loved the tightness of the g-suit as it automatically inflated in response to an aggressive flight maneuver and he loved the feeling of rolling the aircraft on its back to visually acquire the target on a popup bomb delivery. He loved the feel of the big gun as it fired 50-60 rounds a second on a strafe attack and the sound of white phosphorous rockets as they left the rails of his aircraft and sped toward their targets. After the gun, rockets were his next favorite thing to employ. Unlike the BDU-33 practice bombs which had to be spotted by a range officer, rockets offered immediate feedback as to the accuracy of your shot. As soon as a rocket left the rails, you could tell by the smoke trail whether it would be short or long, left or right of the target.

The air in England was cold more often than not which was always good for maximizing performance out of the Hog. If the temperature was really low, as it often was, you could even get 400 knots out of the Hog at low level. He loved the feel of the potential energy that accompanied each pulse of the stick as you ripped through the cold, clear air of many an English morning.

Though the training ranges in England were somewhat limited, and the weather was not always the best, the countryside was beautiful and he usually got to see it from the standard low level altitude of 500 feet. His favorite training route was the vaunted "castle tour"; a low level sortie which took you from range to range along the English coastline and featured historic villages and majestic seaside castles along the way.

"What was there not to like about flying the Hog," he thought, "especially in England."

Flynn was nominated for flight lead upgrade training by his flight commander even before he had the minimum required flight hours. The operations officer had flown with him many times since his arrival and recognized his great potential and his extraordinary flying abilities and was eager to upgrade Flynn as soon as possible. The squadron was in need of instructors and the sooner they made him a flight lead the sooner they could upgrade him to instructor. Flynn was told that he would start his training as soon as he had accumulated the required minimum hours.

As always, Flynn put on the blinders during his flight lead upgrade training and was always striving to improve his skills and his abilities in the A-10. Flynn quickly upgraded to two-ship flight lead, and not too long after that to four-ship flight lead. All of this was to his delight, and in his mind was inching him ever closer to the next important goal in his quest for space. He only had one more goal to achieve before he could qualify for and apply for test pilot school. As before, there was little time in his mind for celebration. His next goal was to upgrade to instructor as soon as possible so he could qualify to apply for test pilot school.

Socially, Flynn again restrained from engaging in any sort of behavior that he considered risky, including alcohol consumption. If he went to the pubs with his buddies, he would drink a Tab or a Diet Pepsi while the others drank their favorite English beer. This discipline, along with the fact that he always avoided female entanglements led to his being the only member of his fighter squadron that was given two regularly used call signs.

When he flew the Hog they called him "Irish", but when he went out on the town with his flyboy buddies, they would call him "Church Boy". He didn't mind the Irish nickname because of his obvious heritage, but the Church Boy name really bothered him, especially since he had not attended church regularly in years. He felt they should know the reason why he was like this. He was never shy about his ambitions and would make it clear to anyone who would ask him why he practiced such rigid discipline in his flying and in his social life.

Besides, Flynn enjoyed hanging out with the opposite sex, and actually found himself attracted to some of the young British women he had met out in town and on the base.

"It simply was not time for such things though," he would say to himself. He had bigger fish to fry."

One thing he did notice while in England was that female attention seemed to be on the increase. Maybe it was the fact that he was a reasonably good looking American fighter pilot stationed in a country that still harbored a romantic nostalgia for such things. Perhaps it was his Irish heritage, or the fact that he seemed so unattainable to those who had tried to get close to him. Or it could have been a combination of all of these things. In any case, he knew one thing for sure; the heavy dose of male hormones he was experiencing as he moved from his mid to late twenties was making it harder and harder to fend off female attention.

During the beginning of his third year in England, Flynn upgraded to instructor and soon afterward turned his attention to putting together his first application for test pilot school. He was a flight commander by then, and so he scheduled an appointment with his operations officer to let him know of his intentions. Of course, it came as no surprise to anyone; everybody knew this is what Irish had always wanted to do.

His first application left the base with sterling recommendations from his squadron commander and from his wing commander. If anyone deserved a shot at test pilot school, it would be Flynn, and there were none of his peers and there was no one in his chain of command who thought otherwise. It was now a waiting game. He was told it would be a few months before he would hear anything.

Soon after he launched his test pilot school application, his parents showed up for their yearly visit to England. He would always book them a room on base so they could be close to him and he could look out for them while they were his guests. He was always glad to see them, of course, but dreaded the inevitable talk that would come before the visit ended.

How many times had he heard one or both of them say: "Flynn, remember God loves you and obviously his favor has shined on your path, but remember, truly great achievements flow out of service and service flows out of relationship with the Creator."

*"Flynn, your parents were very wise and were trying to help you put your achievements in their proper perspective,"* said the First Born.

"Yes Lord," replied Flynn, "I just wish I had listened to their counsel more closely at this critical time in my life."

# :TEST PILOT

# CHAPTER 4

Flynn did his best to put the test pilot application out of his mind but he was never fully successful as it was usually at the forefront of this thinking at any given time. The only exception being when he was flying; he was always able to compartmentalize when he flew. There were just too many things that could go wrong with a lapse of attention, even in the relatively slow flying A-10. Task saturation was very high at times, so keeping your mind focused on flying and employing the aircraft safely and efficiently was always his top concern. He wouldn't allow himself to think about other things until after he had landed and could afford the luxury of day dreaming.

About three months after he had submitted the application, the test pilot school selection board sent their results through his chain of command. It was on one of those early cold mornings that Flynn loved so much and he had just led a new guy on the castle tour. After they landed, bedded down the aircraft, and walked back to the operations building, they found the squadron commander waiting for them at the ops desk. There was a small group of fellow flyers there as well.

His commander pulled him aside and quietly told him, "Congratulations Flynn, you have been accepted for test pilot school. You report to the 6510th Test Wing at Edwards in three months!"

After that, he turned to the others around him and shouted, "Everyone to the pub this evening and drinks are on me! Irish is going to be a test pilot!"

Everyone began shouting accolades and Flynn was suddenly surrounded and smothered by handshakes, high-fives, and some serious back slaps. Some of them were a bit rough but he never felt a twinge of pain. All feeling seemed to leave his body as he began to process this news.

"Another hard fought and sought after milestone," he thought to himself, "every minute has been worth it. My dream is becoming more and more a reality."

He struggled to hold back tears that would always come to him at times like this. It would simply not be in keeping with his image to let emotions like that escape, especially at this time. Suppressing his emotions, and with the crowd thinning, he debriefed the flight with his wingman, stowed his flight gear, and headed to his Q room to call his parents.

When Flynn left England, it had been almost three years to the day since he had been in the US. He couldn't wait to get back but it wasn't because he had missed home, it was more the anticipation that was building at the prospect of actually stepping foot onto the legendary Edwards Air Force Base in the California desert. Names like Scott Crossfield, Chuck Yeager, Neil Armstrong, and of course his personal favorite, Gus Grissom, were among the roster of Who's Who at this historic base.

It was there that the sound barrier was first broken by Glamorous Glennis and then after that the X-15 rocket plane became the first aircraft to fly over twice the speed of sound and reach the fringes of space. It was there that Bob Crippen and John Young had completed the maiden voyage of the new Space Shuttle.

His mind was filled to overflowing and he tried in vain to think of something else just to calm himself down a bit before the C-5 transport landed at McGuire AFB in New Jersey. After landing, he was scheduled to take a commercial flight out of LaGuardia to Indianapolis where his parents would pick him up and take him to Bedford for a few weeks leave. It would be just enough time, he thought, for him to trade in his Pinto for something a little nicer. He couldn't very well show up at Edwards in a beat up yellow Pinto. Not that he needed to buy a brand new Corvette or anything like that, but at least he thought he should be sporting some decent looking wheels when he got there. He had left the Pinto in the care of his dad who faithfully cranked it and drove it every once in a while so it would be running good when he got home.

In England, Flynn had amazed himself at how well he had gotten by using only the buses, trains, and subways in the highly developed mass transit system of the UK. But now, it was time to reward himself for his self-imposed austerity. As long as he didn't go too crazy with his choice of car, he had saved up enough money so that he could use the Pinto as a trade and make up the difference with cash.

When Flynn and his parents got home from the airport, his father told him he had a surprise waiting for him. Before unloading his luggage from the family car, his dad pressed the automatic garage door opener.

Flynn responded with, "When did you install that, dad?"

"I put it in just a few months ago so I could show you this in more dramatic fashion," came the reply.

The door rose slowly but methodically until he saw a car sitting in the garage that he recognized immediately. It was a candy apple red 1976 Triumph TR-6 with spoke wheels and a black roll bar.

"Whoa dad," shouted Flynn, "whose is this, and where's my Pinto?"

"Didn't you always tell us when you were in college that one day you would own one of these? Well, I hope you don't mind, but I took the liberty of trading in the Pinto and bought this for you instead. It's over ten years old but still considered a classic. It took me a while to find a red one with a black roll bar but I'm glad I found it. Son, you've earned it and I want you to have it as a gift from me. Congratulations on being selected for test pilot school!"

Flynn was quickly overwhelmed. He looked at the car and then looked at his dad and did not even try to hold back the tears. There were none of his flyboy buddies around, just him and his parents, and the display of generosity and affection was just too much for him. It provided a release of pent up emotions that he had stifled in England when he had gotten the news about test pilot school. There would be no man hug this time; he embraced his dad tightly as he too burst into tears.

His mom came over and put her arms around both of them, tears now flowing from her eyes as well. "Flynn, we didn't want you to think that we weren't proud of you," she said. "We just feel like we may have been a bit heavy handed in the things we've said to you over the years. Please don't ever forget that we love you and are proud of what you've been able to achieve in such a short period of time."

After that, they stood there for a while, soaking in the moment and enjoying the fact that they were together again.

Flynn went to bed that night with visions of driving onto Edwards AFB in his classic TR-6 with the top down and taking in the desert scenery he loved so much.

"This is all so perfect," he thought, "just perfect!"

In the dream he was falling … and every detail was exactly as before. He deployed his chute and ended up on his back, clutching the grass, and staring up at the sky.

"Did you survive your tumble from the sky?" the unidentified person once again asked him.

When he woke this time though, he got angry at the thought of the dream ruining the end of such a perfect day.

He blurted out loudly, "What the hell is going on here Lord? Are you trying to tell me something? If so, why don't you just come out with it instead of playing games with my mind with this ridiculous dream?"

It was the first time that he had spoken to the Lord since he had been in high school and it was hardly what you would call a prayer. It was an angry rant and a demand for answers that hadn't come, though he had had the dream now more times than he could remember. But he heard no reply that night. He was frustrated and angry and it took him a long time to get back to sleep.

Flynn drove onto the base at Edwards after the long trip from Indiana. As he had envisioned, he had the top down on the TR-6 which was recently washed, waxed, and detailed with Armor All. He had been driving for three days and was tired but his spirits were high. It was a beautiful day when he arrived and he was taking in the familiar desert environment that had so captivated him when he had gone to pilot training at Williams.

He got there a few days before he was scheduled for his flight evaluations; just enough time to get acquainted with the base and get snapped into his Q room. He would report to the school commandant the next day and set up for the flight evals, a formality in his mind but an occasional stumbling block for some. Once he passed the evals, he would be admitted to the school and would begin his training as a test pilot candidate. The school itself would last for about a year during which time Flynn would fly up to 30 different aircraft and endure a rigorous combination of academics and flight training. He relished the thought of it all and couldn't wait to get started.

When he got to the housing office he was eager to get checked into the Q and get settled. The sooner he started, he thought, the sooner he would finish. Then at last he would be able to relax for a few years, build his experience in the test community and start firing off applications for astronaut training. He knew that almost no one got accepted their first try, and considering the competition he would be facing, he did not presume to think that he would be any different on that score. It was almost considered a rite of passage to have submitted at least three applications before finally being accepted into the program.

Flynn gave the clerk at the housing desk his orders and waited patiently for him to verify that he was a single student at the test pilot school and would be housed in the Edwards BOQ. As he waited, a tall young man with jet black hair came and stood next to him at the counter, waiting for his turn to check in. He guessed him to be about 6 foot 2 and maybe 185 pounds. His lanky build contrasted sharply with Flynn's shorter, more muscular frame. He assumed that he was another incoming student, even though he could not know for sure since they were both dressed in civilian clothes.

"The name's Matt Parker," said the stranger with his right hand extended toward Flynn.

"Flynn Roberts, glad to meet you," he replied as he gripped his hand firmly and cracked a friendly smile. Matt grinned back and asked, "Test pilot school?"

"Yea," said Flynn, "I just finished a three year tour at Bentwaters in the A-10."

"Three years for me too; F-15s at Tyndall," he shot back. "Where'd you go to school Flynn?" "Purdue, how 'bout you?" he asked.

"Air Force Academy," said Matt.

With those last words, Flynn felt a twinge of angst rise up on the inside and knew at that moment that Matt Parker was going to be his main competition for the top spot in his test pilot school class. He didn't know how he knew, but he just did.

After exchanging pleasantries, they parted ways and went to their respective rooms.

"No matter," thought Flynn, as he started unloading his gear out of the back seat of his Triumph, "I can handle some competition, especially from an F-15 guy."

He had packed lightly and was able to put everything he needed in the back seat and the small trunk of his classic car. It took less than 20 minutes for him to get settled in his room. After that he fell back on his bed and drifted off to sleep. He had done a lot of driving in the last three days and even though it was only the afternoon, he took the liberty of surrendering to a much needed nap.

As the year at test pilot school began, Flynn put on the blinders as was his normal custom when starting an important new endeavor. No unnecessary distractions had been his inner mantra and this would be no different. This was the one of the last steps in a long progression of short term, intermediate, and long term goals, and he was not about to goof things up now by letting his guard down.

This time, however, he developed a rapport with Matt Parker, a significant departure from his usual friendly, yet detached manner. It surprised him a bit that he would even want to befriend the guy who was his chief rival but there was something about Matt that seemed to draw people to him. The relationship was something he would have to keep an eye on, and the minute it got out of hand, he had decided he would pull back as necessary so that his ultimate goal could be achieved. He was going to finish at the top of his class and that was all there was to it.

Nevertheless, Flynn became closer to Matt than any of the other classmates. And before long, Matt became the closest thing to a best friend he had ever had. Even though there was an undercurrent of quiet competition between them, they had developed a friendship that was borne out of mutual respect and a recognition that they had more in common than not.

Matt was from Columbia, South Carolina and had always wanted to fly for the Air Force. It was his childhood dream to attend the Air Force Academy and to go on to fly as a combat fighter pilot, test pilot, and then one day as an astronaut. Matt was the first person Flynn had met that had a similar internal drive to his, and he felt like he was finally able to relate to someone who shared his level of intensity and desire. Flynn shared his story openly as well, and the two became closer and closer as the year of training progressed.

There was one thing different about Matt though that stymied Flynn somewhat. He was very open and honest about his faith in God and about his Christian walk. He came from an Assembly of God background and was raised in church just like Flynn. But Matt had an air about him; it was clear from the way he lived his life that he relied on a higher power that was the center of everything he did. And everything he did, according to Matt, was because he felt "led by the Lord" to follow a certain path. He did nothing without first covering it in prayer, and everything he did, he did with all his heart, mind, soul, and strength. Once he had gotten what he called "the mind of the Lord," he went after every goal, after every assignment with a tenacious ferocity that was all too familiar to Flynn. In short, Matt was motivated internally very much like he was, but there was a spiritual component to his drive that Flynn knew he did not have.

Matt attended church regularly while he was going through test pilot school, even on weekends when important reports were due and critical academic exams were forthcoming. This was the thing that Flynn couldn't seem to get his arms around. Having a spiritual life was OK he thought, but letting it interfere with your chief goal in life, well that was something different altogether. But in spite of what Flynn considered an unnecessary distraction,

Matt still proved to be a worthy competitor, as both he and Flynn traded turns as the number one student in their class throughout the program.

Flynn loved the fact that each hour in the classroom had practical application as he flew the many aircraft that were made available to the students. He flew helicopters, turboprops, heavy multi-engine aircraft, and high performance jet aircraft of all kinds. It was quite a treat in his mind and one of the most rewarding things about test pilot school.

Performance, handling, stability and control were all measured for a variety of aircraft and recorded on a test card; something that Flynn learned would be a staple of test pilot life. Evaluation of avionics, sensor systems and even proper functioning of communications systems, were all part of a comprehensive work-up on a particular aircraft. Then there was the report writing; something that Flynn loathed as did many other students, but he acknowledged it to be a necessary thing if he was to become a top notch test pilot. You had to be able to communicate orally and in writing what each aircraft was telling you as you flew it so that the engineers could perfect certain aircraft systems or correct malfunctioning components or subcomponents. After a thorough scrubbing, an aircraft or aircraft systems report had to be written and submitted to school officials. It was one of the most important metrics used to evaluate each of the test pilot candidates that attended the school.

Because of his background in aeronautical engineering, Flynn soon discovered that he had a knack for explaining the feel of an aircraft to the engineers. He could translate how an aircraft was behaving into the technical jargon that they were more familiar with, and he did it with ease. One thing the engineers liked about him was that he never treated them like second class citizens just because they weren't flyers. It was a skill and an attitude that would be a significant asset both in the school and in his future endeavors.

When the end of the school term was at hand, Flynn was positioned to take the number one spot in the class. As long as he didn't make any mistakes in the last couple of weeks, he felt he had it wrapped up. Matt was working hard to overtake him but was in a position where even if he made no mistakes, the top spot was Flynn's to lose. When the final grades and evaluations were tallied at the end, Flynn indeed edged out Matt by the narrowest of margins for the number one spot in the class.

For Matt, it was a disappointment that he soon recovered from, but for Flynn, it was a huge weight off of his shoulders. The final step in Flynn's progression of goals had been accomplished. He had been number one in his class in every flight training course he had attended, even the rigorous and demanding test pilot school at the legendary Edwards AFB. Now, at last, he thought, he could relax a bit and enjoy the life of an Air Force test pilot.

When the graduation ceremony had concluded, Matt was the first to come and firmly shake his hand with a hearty and sincere "Well done!" "I'll get you next time," he told Flynn in jest.

The two had become good friends and had the highest of respect for one other.

After the graduation ceremony it was off to the Officers Club for the reception. Flynn and Matt's parents had both attended and he was eager for everyone to get to know one another. When they all arrived at the club, Flynn noticed that there were two young women with the Parkers. Since they had not met until after the ceremony, he had not seen them before. He thought they might be Matt's sisters or even friends of the family, but was surprised when Matt introduced them to him.

"This is Emma Mills, an old friend of mine from my Academy days," he began. Emma then glanced at Matt disapprovingly but said nothing.

Shifting attention away from his obvious gaffe, Matt turned toward the other girl and said, "And this is her friend Hannah Brooks."

Flynn took one look at Hannah and felt something grab him on the inside. There was a quickening sensation as he surveyed her pretty face and her petite but curvy frame. Emma was cute, but a little too tall for his taste. Hannah, on the other hand, was an absolute vision! He fought to maintain his composure as she spoke to him softly,

"Congratulations Flynn on being the number one student in your class."

"Thank you," he replied with an awkwardness that he hoped was not that noticeable.

He was so taken by Hannah that he suddenly realized that he had barely spoken to his parents since arriving at the club. He turned quickly to them and helped with the introductions then hugged them both and thanked them for driving all the way from Indiana.

"We wouldn't have missed this for the world!" exclaimed his dad. "Congratulations Flynn, you did it again!"

Flynn turned to find his mother busy talking to Hannah, and noted that there seemed to be an immediate bond that formed between them.

# :HANNAH BROOKS

As Flynn had suspected from Emma's reaction to their introduction, Matt had significantly understated their relationship. He later told Flynn that he had met her at a campus Bible study group when she was a student at the University of Colorado, Colorado Springs. They had dated pretty steadily his last year at the Academy and had fallen pretty hard and fast for one another. So fast, in fact, that both of them were concerned that they might be, as Matt put it, "getting ahead of God in the timing."

They decided to put things on hold for a while but to stay in touch as they went their separate ways.

Emma had grown up in Colorado Springs and wanted to stay near her family when she graduated. She finished her teaching degree and took a job in one of the area high schools. Matt graduated from the Academy and left Colorado Springs to enter pilot training at Sheppard Air Force Base in north Texas. They had kept in touch over the years as planned, but rarely saw one another, and it seemed there for a while that they might not end up together after all. It was only recently that they had decided to see if they could make a go of it again. Neither of them felt like they wanted to spend the rest of their lives apart, and they both felt like the Lord was drawing them back together again.

Matt told Flynn that he had regretted the decision to put things on hold and if truth be told, it was more him than her that had made that decision. She was devastated when the time apart grew into months and then into years and had just about made up her mind that she would seek the Lord to see if there was another man that he had in mind for her. After they left each other that summer, Matt said that hardly a day had gone by that he did not think of her and miss her and wish that they had not parted ways.

Now that he had graduated test pilot school, he felt that he could yield to those inner yearnings and begin to once again cultivate their relationship. Emma had agreed but was determined to take it slowly. She did not want to get hurt again. In fact, she later confided in Matt that when he had offered to fly her out to see the graduation and meet his parents, she almost said no. It was her best friend, Hannah Brooks, who had convinced her to go and see what the Lord might have in store for the two of them.

"If you don't go," Hannah had said, "you will never know for sure if he's the one the Lord has for you."

Emma had agreed with her but was in need of moral support.

"I will go if you will come with me," she stipulated.

Hannah and Emma had gone to high school together and had both gotten their teaching degrees from UCCS. And both had taken teaching jobs in the Colorado Springs area. Hannah taught tenth graders and Emma taught ninth graders just across town from one another. The two were able to coordinate their schedules and take a few days off to attend the graduation.

After the reception, Matt asked Flynn if he would like to give the girls a tour of the base the next day. He jumped at the chance to spend some more time with Hannah. She was smart, funny, and easy to talk to. And she was the first girl he had ever met that he thought he could potentially have a relationship with. The timing wasn't exactly what he had in mind; he would have preferred to have flown for a year or more as a test pilot.

"But never mind that now," he thought, "she is here and she is amazing!" There was something distinctly different about her. Perhaps it was the way she had connected so effortlessly with his mother, or maybe it was just the way she seemed to look at life. She seemed to be full of purpose and full of joy, all at the same time. Not to mention the fact that she was drop dead gorgeous. He made up his mind then and there that he would get to know her better and would get to the bottom of some of these things.

He found out very early on that she was a committed Christian, like Matt and Emma, and was very open about her faith. She seemed to sense that Flynn struggled spiritually so she was not too overt in talking about spiritual things; at first, that is. As he was to discover, she had a soft and gentle manner about her but there were moments when she could display a disarming boldness. Most of the time though, she was able to weave her faith into her conversation effortlessly but in a way that was not threatening to the listener.

As they toured the base the next day, they talked to one another in an honest and relaxed way, careful not to reveal too much about their initial inner feelings, but revealing just enough to get to know one another a little better. Flynn was honest and open about his faith, or from his viewpoint, the lack thereof. He explained in the course of conversation that he had grown up Catholic but still struggled with the concept of a personal relationship with God. His parents were different, he explained. They had always been able to talk about God in a personal way, like they knew him. They had always encouraged him to seek God for himself and to pursue a relationship that transcended organized religion. For whatever reason though, Flynn confessed that he was never able to do so.

Hannah explained that she had grown up Baptist but her family started attending non-denominational churches when she was in junior high. She told him that she grew up maintaining a close personal relationship with God, having given her life to Jesus when she was just six years old. She had known nothing else her whole life so she found it hard to relate to Flynn and others who struggled the way he did.

## : SOME DREAMS FOLLOW

When Flynn told her about his dream of becoming an astronaut, she told him she had known that about him. Emma had given her the scoop on Flynn before they left Colorado Springs.

"You know," she said, "I can relate to having a vision, but the vision I have was long ago committed to the plans and purposes of God."

"I'm not sure I know what you mean by that," said Flynn, "but now that you mention it, what *is* your vision?"

"Well," she said, "I want to teach young people to pursue their God given destiny; to take the dreams that God puts in their hearts and run with them with all their might."

Flynn fell silent for a moment and felt a pang, a stirring on the inside. He fought back all too familiar emotions. Isn't that what he had been doing his whole life, he thought? Isn't it enough to just pursue what is in your heart? Doesn't that mean it was ordained of God?

She seemed to sense that he was troubled and asked him, "Flynn, have you ever submitted your dream to God; to his plans and purposes; his timing?"

"Well no, not exactly. I have always felt like I was pursuing the dream that God put in my heart, but to be honest, I have never really talked to him about it."

"Flynn," she replied softly, "spend some time alone with God and start talking to him; he will help you know for sure what you're supposed to do with your life."

"Maybe I will," replied Flynn, "maybe I will ... Don't you just love the desert, there's just something alluring about it, isn't there?"

A bit taken aback by the abrupt change of subject, Hannah replied, "Why yes … I do … I find it both stark and beautiful at the same time."

After they said goodbye that weekend, and Hannah and Emma returned to Colorado Springs, Flynn and Hannah started writing letters to one another. At first, it was maybe one every couple of weeks but it quickly ramped up to two to three letters a week, even if they weren't that long. They would speak on the phone from time to time but being the disciplined individuals they both were, they kept these times to a minimum to keep the phone bills manageable.

During his first year as a line test pilot at Edwards, Flynn found that he was starting to long for her. He wanted to be with her as much as he could and that was something he was quite unfamiliar with. He had pushed away these kinds of feelings for so long that now it was a bit of a shock that he was falling so fast for Hannah Brooks. He could only hope that she felt the same way about him. It seemed that she did, but she was very guarded in her conversations along these lines, something that he had not quite figured out.

As line test pilots at Edwards, Flynn and Matt could check out in up to three separate aircraft simultaneously, consistent with their duties and any special projects they were involved in. Flynn checked out in his primary aircraft, the A-10, and got chase qualified in the T-38. Matt checked out in the F-15 and was also chase qualified in the T-38. Chase aircraft duties were something that the junior test pilots had to get used to. There was a hierarchy that had to be climbed and one of the things you had to do was fly chase for some of the senior test pilots and the more important aircraft test projects that they honchoed.

That first year, both Flynn and Matt flew primarily as chase pilots and did not get to fly their primary aircraft very often, only what was necessary to maintain their qualification. This didn't bother Flynn at all. He loved the sleek, fast T-38, and got reacquainted with its capabilities in rapid fashion. He had reveled in its speed and sleek lines every minute that he flew it in pilot training, and was loving it even more now. He got to fly his favorite pilot training aircraft but without some instructor trying to tell him what he could and could not do with the aircraft. With the pressure off, he could learn the aircraft better than ever. Soon, he felt he could fly the T-38 as well or better than anyone.

Matt on the other hand, kept complaining to Flynn that the T-38 lacked the power and the g capability of a true high performance aircraft and wished he could fly the F-15 more often.

Flynn told him one day, "I guess it's a matter of perspective. Coming from the Hog, the T-38 is like a rocket by comparison!"

After finishing their first year as line test pilots, both Flynn and Matt put together their first applications for the astronaut program. Both of them applied as Mission Pilot candidates. As Flynn already knew, active duty military pilots had to apply through their respective services. This meant that Flynn and Matt had to apply to an Air Force astronaut board, and then the Air Force would decide which of those applicants would be sent to NASA for further consideration.

Flynn thought this was patently unfair since civilian applicants did not have this extra hoop they had to jump through. But then again, he thought, how many of them had access to the kind of training and equipment that was available to an active duty military test pilot. He knew that most of the civilian applicants that were competitive would have PhDs in an applicable field and would be applying as Mission Specialist candidates.

"No," he thought, "I want to *fly* in space, not just *ride* in space!"

Both of them knew that those who got selected for the astronaut program, whether Mission Pilots or Mission Specialists, averaged at least three application cycles before they were selected.

Nevertheless, they both secretly harbored the faint hope that they might be the lone exception.

"That only happens if you're a female pilot!" Flynn blurted out one day when he and Matt finally discussed it.

"Better keep those kinds of feelings to yourself!" Matt had said. "NASA has a real reputation for being politically correct about such things."

Flynn thought long and hard about his statement after that day. If there was a woman out there somewhere who had this dream burning in her heart the way that he did, why shouldn't she be allowed to pursue it? Although he didn't like the fact that the quest for female astronauts seemed to give them a leg up in the selection process, he couldn't fault them for pursuing the same dream that he had. No, he couldn't fault anyone for pursuing the dream of one day flying in space. He could only fault someone for not giving it everything they had to achieve it.

Flynn got his rejection letter a couple of months later. He knew ahead of time it was a rejection letter because it came way too soon. After reading the contents he was dismayed to find that he had not even made it past the Air Force board. NASA had not even seen his application! He quickly called Matt, who was at home in his Q room and asked him if he had gotten a letter.

"No," Matt had replied, "no letter yet."

A couple of days later, he heard that Matt had gotten a letter from the Air Force board informing him that his application had been one of the ones selected for consideration by NASA. It was late fall, and NASA would convene their selection board soon so that selectees could report to Houston the following summer for astronaut training.

Flynn fumed as he thought for sure it was because Matt flew a pointy nosed fighter and he did not. He *knew* that being a Hog pilot would end up putting him at a disadvantage one day. The Air Force brass hates the Hog but they are enamored with the F-15 and the F-16. Had the board not noticed that he was number one in his pilot training class and was only given the option of an A-10 or an RF-4? Maybe he should have taken the RF-4. At least then he could say he flew a supersonic capable platform.

"I would have told you straight away," said Matt when they finally ran into each other, "but I was told by the wing commander to keep it to myself for a few days. Unfortunately, somebody at wing headquarters leaked it before I could tell you."

"That's OK Matt; congratulations. Please keep me posted as the selection process moves along. You know I'm rooting for you."

He wrote a long letter to Hannah that night and told her the whole story. For some reason, he couldn't bear to talk with her just yet; he needed time to calm his raw emotions. After he finished her letter, he called his dad and gave him the news. Characteristically, his father encouraged him never to give up but to also consult the Lord about his future. When he got the reply letter from Hannah about a week later, he read it with great anticipation and was pleased to see that she attempted, in her own gentle way, to console him.

"Maybe it just wasn't God's timing Flynn," she had written, "it's certainly not because you're not qualified. There will be other selections, and you will gain more experience between now and then. Perhaps it will give you some time to talk to God about it."

That was the only part of the letter that he didn't particularly like. She was beginning to sound a bit like his mother in that respect. Nevertheless, he was thankful that Hannah seemed to genuinely care about his feelings at a time like this, and if his girlfriend didn't know him well enough to know how much this bothered him, she wouldn't have been much of a girlfriend.

About a week later, Matt called him on the telephone to tell him that Emma was planning a trip to see him over the Thanksgiving Holidays. "See if you can get Hannah to come too so they can travel together like last time."

After Flynn hung up the phone he called Hannah immediately and asked her if she could make it."

"I'll have to beg out of our traditional family Thanksgiving," she said, "but I'll see what I can do. I really want to see you again."

A few days later he came home to a red message light on his phone in the Q and listened intently as Hannah told him that she and Emma would be there for the long Thanksgiving weekend. His thoughts turned immediately to how two single guys in the middle of the desert could muster up a turkey dinner worthy of their two special ladies!

They decided to use Flynn's Q room since it was a little larger and nicer than Matt's to prepare and serve the turkey dinner. They spent quite a few days gathering groceries and looking up recipes for the occasion. Neither of them had done much cooking but they felt like they could pull it off if they teamed together. In the end, the girls showed up and the meal, while not the best, was at least acceptable. The important thing to Flynn, and he was sure it was the same for Matt and Emma, was that his beloved Hannah was finally here in the flesh.

She looked great, he thought; she had cropped her hair shorter which framed her face in a particularly attractive way. Her jet black hair was contrasted by her smooth milky white skin. Oh, she could tan quickly in the summertime but quickly lost it in favor of her natural coloring as the summer melted into fall. Her captivating blue eyes seemed hypnotic at times and he was always complementing her about their color and beauty.

"You've got some pretty blue eyes yourself Flynn," she would say in return, "I like the way they turn green when you wear your flight suit."

Although the girls were aware that Matt's astronaut application had advanced to NASA and Flynn's had not, they carefully avoided the subject for the duration of the weekend. Flynn was grateful for that and for the fact that Hannah's presence there would keep his mind focused on other things. The long weekend whizzed by as Flynn and Hannah squeezed out every moment of alone time that they could. Except for the turkey dinner and a few hours watching football together, Matt and Emma, and Flynn and Hannah had gone their separate ways for most of the weekend. The girls were only reunited the morning that Matt and Flynn met them in the parking lot to drive them to the airport to catch their plane back to Colorado Springs.

But for Flynn there was something different about this sendoff that permeated the atmosphere of the car as they drove the girls to the airport that morning. Flynn knew that the time they spent together that weekend represented a significant escalation of their relationship. He knew that it would never be the same again between them. Although Matt and Emma seemed liked a couple of chatterboxes in the front seats of Matt's car, Flynn and Hannah hardly spoke and sat quietly in the back seat.

They were both thinking about how their relationship had changed; they just weren't talking about it. Flynn was genuinely sorry to see her go and he could tell that Hannah felt the same way about him. She sat on his right and he folded the fingers of his right hand over the top of hers and clasped her hand gently. It was his way of conveying the steadfastness of his new found love for her. Everything was going to be all right, he wanted her to know, and it was the only way he could think of at the time to communicate that to her. As he embraced Hannah and kissed her goodbye that day at the airport, he knew in his heart of hearts that he wanted to spend the rest of his life together with Hannah

Brooks. And if he could somehow take her into space with him one day… well, then "that would be awesome!"

# :TUMBLE FROM THE SKY

## CHAPTER 6

After the girls left, both Matt and Flynn felt a bit of a letdown emotionally but had determined that they would dive back into their work and bolster one another as the best friends that they had become. During that first year together at Edwards, Flynn had spent a lot of time with Matt and had gotten to the point where there was almost nothing that he couldn't discuss with him. He knew that anything of a sensitive nature that he shared with Matt would be treated with the utmost respect and confidence and it was gratifying to have a true friend like that.

For his part, Matt knew also that he could expect the same from Flynn. They both shared a kindred spirit and a common dream. A dream that burned in Matt's heart as intensely as it did in Flynn's. Consequently, they spent many hours talking about their future and how it might play out when it was all said and done. Matt was always quick to point out that the only reason he had pursued the vision of one day flying in space was because he felt "led" to do so by God.

One night when they lounged in his Q room, Flynn asked Matt to explain what he meant by that as completely as possible. He had heard things like that from his parents his whole life and was now hearing that from his girlfriend as well.

"Well Flynn, it's like this: I came to the realization while I was at the Academy that if the dream in my heart wasn't planted there by God, it was most likely doomed to fail. So I spent the better part of my senior year seeking the Lord and asking him to confirm that this was not just my dream, but his dream *for* me. If

I was supposed to do something else, I wanted to know so I could pursue that instead. Flynn, I don't expect you to understand this just yet, but the Lord spoke to me one morning in prayer and confirmed in my heart that this was what I was supposed to pursue with my life. This was what he had planned for me before the universe was formed. The only reason that I do things as well as I do in the classroom and in the air is because I feel energized by God when I do them. He makes me better than I could ever be in my own strength, in my own abilities. Flynn, I just don't have the natural talent and abilities that you have; I realized that a long time ago. I have to have God working with me or I can't do anything well. I am completely dependent on him to help me achieve the things that I feel called to achieve in my life."

Flynn pondered all this for a moment. His thoughts turned to all the things that his parents had told him about God; about how wonderful he was and how you could have a relationship with the Creator of the universe, and how he would lead you and guide you, and plant his desires into your heart - all because he had an unconditional love for you. And now both Matt and Hannah had come into his life confirming the same things.

Suddenly God became *real* to Flynn and all of his defenses melted. Tears had begun to trickle down his face as Matt had shared his heart in the most intimate way that Flynn had ever heard. The tears quickly turned into sobs, and before he knew it he had broken down in front of his best friend like never before in his life. Not even his mother and father had seen him like this, with the possible exception of when Gus Grissom died when he was just a kid. But even then, there was no comparing the depth of emotion he was experiencing now. Matt moved closer to Flynn and put his hand on his shoulder to comfort him the best way he could.

"I've just never been able to talk to God like that. I believe in him … I believe he is working in my life … but I've never been able to talk to him the way you and Emma and Hannah and my mom and dad talk to him ... like you know him personally! Help me learn to talk to him like that, Matt.

"I need to ... I want to ... get this straight with God before I take another step in my life!"

Matt waited until Flynn's emotions had subsided somewhat and gave him some tissue paper from the desk in his Q room.

"Flynn, have you ever made Jesus the Lord of your life? Have you ever just surrendered your life to him?"

"I can't honestly say that I have, even though my parents have urged me to do this all my life."

That night Matt led Flynn in a prayer of salvation and for the first time in his life, Flynn felt like he was connected to God in a way that he had not been before. It was something he was going to have to get used to, he thought, but he would now be able to approach the Lord and broach a subject he had been avoiding all his life. Had he really been called of God to pursue his dream of one day flying in space or was he just pursuing a dream of his own making? It was something he was determined to find out before he submitted another application for the astronaut program. If he was not called to do this, he thought, he had no business applying for the program.

That night he called Hannah to share what he knew would be good news for her to hear. She had told him before they had gotten serious, that there was no way she would even consider marrying someone that was not a born again believer. He knew this would effectively remove the last remaining barrier between them.

"Oh Flynn," she exclaimed as she burst into a torrent of grateful sobs, "that's ... so ... wonderful!"

After those few scant words, the phone went silent for such a long time that Flynn thought they had lost their connection. He was about to hang up and redial when she began to speak to him again. Her words were sniffled and halting at first, but soon she fell into the graceful and gentle rhythm of speech that Flynn had come to love about her. They spent over an hour on the phone that night as Flynn gradually realized that his conversion had opened a whole new dimension to their relationship.

There were things she could talk to him about now that she could not discuss with him before.

"Nothing too heavy at first," she had said to him.

He needed to grow in his relationship with the Lord, and she could open up more and more to him as he did.

He found out later that Hannah had been praying for him that very morning. She had told God that she loved Flynn with all of her heart but could not and would not consider taking the relationship any further until he had submitted his life fully to the Lord. In fact, she had felt herself falling deeply in love with Flynn and had determined that she would break it off to spare her the agony of an unequally yoked relationship.

She had said to the Lord, "You have to send someone to him that he relates to; that can minister this vital truth to him, and the only person he will listen to right now is Matt."

When Flynn had called her to tell her that Matt had led him to the Lord, it was all Hannah could do to maintain her composure. After her first few emotional words in response, she had clasped the phone in her hand and had wept uncontrollably for almost a full minute.

"Lord … you are so thoughtful, so giving, so wonderful," she had whispered to him in between breath-taking sobs.

And indeed there was a flood of grateful emotions on the phone that night as Flynn and Hannah connected more deeply than ever before.

Flynn called his parents and had an equally long conversation with them. His mother was as overcome with emotion as Hannah was, and his father was finding it hard to choose his words when he spoke at first.

"Flynn!" his mother exclaimed. "You have no idea how long your dad and I have been praying that this day would one day come. We are so overjoyed; we cannot even put it into words. I knew there was something special about Hannah the moment I met her. It does not surprise me that the Lord used her to help bring you into the Kingdom. I know now for sure that the Lord has brought you two together and you have a bright future together. Now you can seek the Lord together as you pursue your God-given destiny as individuals, and as a couple."

For the first time in his life, these words did not sound strange to Flynn.

"I know mom. God is good."

"All the time!" she exclaimed.

When he finally drifted to sleep that night, he had the dream again. As always, he was falling, and had no idea what had happened to him or his aircraft. He was falling and spinning, falling and spinning, until he knew he had to take action to prevent his certain death. He pulled the D ring and deployed the chute and ended up on his back, as always, clutching the grass, staring into the sky, thankful to be alive.

He jerked himself awake this time, and immediately asked the Lord what was going on.

"Now that you're my Father, I'm expecting some answers," he said.

Then for the first time in his life, he heard something like a quiet voice on the inside saying, "Don't fly the chase mission tomorrow."

But he convinced himself it was just his mind playing tricks on him.

"The nature of this dream has simply spawned an association with the next day's flight schedule," Flynn rationalized. "Surely it was not that literal," he thought, "there had to be a more symbolic, more grandiose meaning to this."

After all he had been having the same dream, over and over, off and on, for years. He was new to this "hearing from God" thing and would have to give it some more thought after his sortie the next morning. Within a few minutes, he had drifted back to sleep.

He had an early morning briefing the next morning and was excited because this was to be his last chase sortie before he would be given a flight test project of his own. He was scheduled to do the developmental test and evaluation for the AIM-9 Sidewinder missile that was to be added to the A-10's self-defense arsenal. He could not wait to get started on a project like that which he could really sink his teeth into.

"Someone else can fly chase on *me* for a change," he thought.

That morning, he was to fly chase for Matt who was testing a new advanced radar system for the F-15. He knew for sure that Matt had gotten in front of him for a choice project like this because he was being considered for the astronaut program. The wing commander wanted to get him some real flight test experience that he could talk about should he make it to the interview stage of the process. Flynn had flown several chase missions in support of Matt's project. And if he had to fly just one more before being given a more meaningful project he thought, he was glad it would be for his best friend in the whole world.

After an uneventful takeoff, Flynn settled into a loose cruise formation with Matt's F-15 for the climb to their cruising altitude. He would transition to a wider chase position when they reached the designated work area. It was a beautiful sunny day, like most of them at Edwards, but the March air was still cool and kind to the performance of their respective aircraft. As they leveled off from their climb, Flynn gave Matt's F-15 a thorough looking over, gave him a thumbs-up and then widened out to the chase position to begin their cruise to the working area.

They settled into a cruise speed of 250 knots to conserve fuel for the upcoming test runs. It was only a short ride to the test area and Matt was busy looking over his test card one more time. Flynn would eventually move from the chase position to become a "duck" for the radar tests, flying different maneuvering profiles to test the new radar's capabilities.

A few moments after Flynn had moved out to chase, he felt the stick begin to move rapidly and forcefully forward, which pitched the aircraft sharply nose down. He tried to keep the stick from moving forward but could not get it to budge.

He was able to grunt out a few words to Matt on the radio, "I think I got a runaway trim motor … full nose down."

Matt shouted back, "Flynn, get out now, eject, eject, eject!"

He watched helplessly as Flynn's T-38 went into an accelerated, uncontrollable dive. They both knew that he only had a few seconds to take action or he would be out of the safe envelope for ejection. At speeds over 400 knots, the flailing injuries he would sustain could easily be fatal. Matt blurted out a mayday to Joshua Approach Control as he turned to chase Flynn's aircraft. It was increasing speed rapidly and headed for imminent impact with the desert floor.

Inside the cockpit of his F-15, Matt felt helpless and yelled out a desperate request, "Lord, send an angel to help Flynn ... Lord, help me to help my friend!"

Flynn watched his airspeed indicator move from 250 through 300 then through 350 knots in just a matter of seconds. By the time he gave the control stick one more good pull with no results, he saw the airspeed indicator rapidly passing through 400. He got into position, straightened his spine as straight as he could and pulled the ejection handles. After that, everything went black.

Flynn would find out later that he had ejected from the T-38 at over 500 knots and should not have survived.

Matt used his Inertial Navigation System to mark and report the spot where he landed so rescue workers could get there as fast as possible. He stayed on scene over the patch of grass where Flynn lay until he was at bingo fuel and had to head back to Edwards.

Back on the Bethel Space Station with the First Born, Flynn watched all this unfold from his *spectator's* point of view. He was close enough to the aircraft to see every detail of the accident as it progressed, and much slower than real time, he was convinced.

As he watched the ejection sequence unfold, Flynn cringed at the thought of what would happen to his body as it hit the airstream at 500 plus knots. There would be no way possible to prevent his arms and legs from flailing around violently when hit by the sudden blast of near supersonic air, breaking bones, snapping joints, ripping muscles and tearing ligaments. Death was almost certain.

## : TUMBLE FROM THE SKY

Suddenly he saw a flash of light streaking through the sky toward his aircraft. To him, it looked like a combination of a flaming fire and a lightning bolt. It approached from the direction of Edwards AFB and flew in a slightly arching trajectory, reaching his T-38 in a fraction of a second. Forming a cocoon of light, it enveloped his ejection seat almost completely, leaving only his neck and head exposed, just before he hit the deadly airstream.

Flynn watched as the cocoon of light miraculously pinned his arms and legs in place so they did not flail at all. But unfortunately for him, he entered the airstream at an angle which channeled much of the resulting wind force underneath his chin. So in spite of the headrest on the Martin-Baker seat, his head was rotated upward and backward swiftly and violently. He wasn't sure why, but evidently, the light was a hair of a second late getting there. It had not gotten there in time to envelope his whole body before he hit the airstream.

Then he watched as the automatic features of the ejection seat performed as advertised while he was completely unconscious. Drogue chute deployment, main chute deployment, and man seat separation all happened in the proper sequence. There was a short free fall before his main chute deployed as the barometric sensor waited until he was at a safe breathable altitude. Flynn noticed that he was unconscious from the moment he hit the airstream till just after the parachute landing in the patch of grass where he lay. When he regained consciousness, he found himself on his back, clutching the grass, staring at the sky, thankful to be alive.

Off in the distance, he could see the smoke of his wreckage rising high into the desert sky; black, ugly, and ominous looking. It was just like the dream with a few details slightly different. But in the dream, as in its manifestation, it was clear that action on his part was necessary to give himself any hope of survival. After that, others evidently had to intervene to save his life. The broader symbolic implications of the dream, clearly sent to him by the Lord, completely eluded him at the time. As he lay there motionless, he had no idea what the extent of his injuries were, but he knew he had survived.

Magan stood next to him as he lay there, not yet visible to Flynn, and marveled at how Flynn had managed to end up on one of the few patches of grass in this area of the California desert.

He looked deeply concerned and said "Flynn … Flynn … Flynn Roberts!… Did you survive your tumble from the sky?"

"That was Magan that said that to me that day?" Flynn asked the First Born.

*"Yes,"* replied the First Born, *"and it was Magan that you saw flying through the air in his light force form. But you couldn't see him then, and you were only able to hear the last part of his plea."*

Flynn remarked, "You know, my Lord, Magan and I have gotten to know each other pretty well since the transformation. Although he *did* mention his role in saving my life that day, he has never shared any of the details. Now I know why the doctors were so perplexed at the total lack of flailing injuries. Magan saved me from death that day for sure. By the way, why did he sound so worried, didn't he know I was alive?"

*"He didn't know for sure, and was very concerned for you. As your Guardian, he had only recently been granted increased latitude to intervene on your behalf and was worried that he had already lost you.*

*"When a Guardian loses his charge, it can be very traumatic for them, even though it is never their fault; they feel the pain of it forever. A destiny altered or cut short due to an untimely death is something they dread like nothing else, especially when it is one of their own."*

As Magan put his hand on Flynn's chest to get a heartbeat, he realized that he was still alive but in critical condition.

Perceiving instantly that Flynn had broken his neck, Magan shouted, "You are alive, Flynn, but don't move!"

But it was too late. Flynn cocked his head to see if he could tell who it was that was speaking to him. As he did so, he felt a twinge in the back of his neck and then the lights went out again. Everything went black.

Suddenly Flynn found himself standing in the green field where he lay, but he appeared to be in some kind of altered dimension. He didn't even think to ask why he was able to stand if he was so severely injured. He just stood there as if he was expecting a visitor. There was a man dressed in white that approached him from the far side of the grass. He had a friendly and affable smile and sported a prominent straight nose and a neatly trimmed beard. He couldn't remember what color his eyes were but they were mesmerizing. Deep pools of love, was the only description he could muster in his mind. He didn't know how he knew, but he knew that it was Jesus, the Son of the Living God.

*"Flynn, since you have only recently come into the Kingdom, I wanted to settle a few things in your heart that I know you have struggled with up to this point in your life. I want to bring clarity of purpose and a peace to you that I know you have never known. Flynn, a man's life consists of more than the abundance of the things that he possesses ... or the things that he achieves in life."*

"I'm not sure what you mean by that Lord," Flynn replied.

*"What it means is that my acceptance of you and my love for you is totally independent of "your" performance. Do you understand that I love you completely and that nothing you achieve in life will ever make me love you more than I do right now?"*

Flynn was overwhelmed as he listened to what for him was a life altering truth. He just stood there and let it sink in. The unconditional love that was embodied by that statement and the sacrifice that was made for him because of that love became so real to him that he began to shake. Unbridled tears started to flow as Flynn was overcome with emotions ranging from unworthiness to gratefulness.

*"Your parents said it best when they told you that truly great achievements flow out of true service, and true service flows out of relationship with the Creator. As you grow in your understanding of this spiritual principle, you will be better equipped to carry out the assignments that I give you. Flynn, would you like to know what I want you to do for me in this life?"*

"Yes Lord, more than anything, I don't want to follow *my* dream anymore, I want to follow your dream *for* me."

*"Flynn, you <u>will</u> fly in space one day, just as you dreamed you would, and it will be more glorious than you can ask, think, or imagine. But before that, I want you to use your education to help people solve problems; to make life better for them. I want you to use your flying abilities to help feed and care for the people of the world and tell them about the saving power that is in my name. Will you do that for me Flynn?"*

"Yes Lord, you know that I will," Flynn replied with tears still streaming down his face.

*"Very well then, when you recover from your injuries, I want you to use the educational opportunities that will come your way, together with your aviation skills, for the purpose of which I have requested. If you are faithful to carry out your assignment, you will be rewarded."*

The next thing Flynn remembered was opening up his eyes in a hospital bed surrounded by familiar faces. His parents were there along with Matt, Emma and Hannah.

Seeing them all and recalling everything he'd been through, he teared up immediately and asked, "How long have I been out?"

After a lengthy period of shouts of joy, both exuberant and tearful at the same time, his father was the first to speak to him.

"Flynn, after the accident they brought you here to Antelope Valley Hospital in Lancaster. You've been in a coma for about 3 weeks. We have taken turns during that time praying for you and sitting by you as we waited for you to come out of it. The doctors had just about given up on you, you know, but we held an all-night prayer vigil last night and all I can say is: look what the Lord has done!"

Sensing that Flynn wanted to hear more details, his father continued.

"The initial whiplash when you ejected at such high speed snapped your neck, but for some unknown reason, there were no flailing injuries to your arms or your legs. The doctors said it was as if some unknown force had pinned your arms and legs in place and prevented further injury to your body. Whatever it was, they are almost certain that it is the reason you are alive today. Your spinal cord started to swell almost immediately and they had to act fast to prevent the shutdown of some of your vital brain and body functions. They had to repair your neck and then work fast to reduce the swelling."

Flynn listened intently and then turned to Hannah and reached out for her with his hand, "I wasn't sure I would ever see you again," he said as tears streamed from his eyes.

She rushed to his side, clasped his hand tightly and rested her head on his chest, weeping softly.

He continued, "I know I look like hell right now. But when I get myself all healed up and can go down to the jewelry store on my own, and buy you a proper ring, will you marry me, Hannah Dianne Brooks?"

# :RECOVERY

Flynn kept the vision to himself for quite some time, a little nervous about its implications for his flying career. If he was to carry out the Lord's assignment, the way he understood it, he had to get healthy again, regain flying status, and go back to school. For these things to happen, he could not afford for anyone to question his mental faculties.

He was told that his recovery was going to take a long time and most of the doctors said he would never fly again. But he clung to the words of the Lord with a ferocity that he had not known he possessed. Oh, he had been tenacious before in the pursuit of his goals, but now there was a spiritual component that he knew would put him over the top when facing impossible odds. In a way, it was invigorating because he was specifically asked by the Lord to pursue something that most people were saying would never happen.

Then there was the comment about flying in space. That too would be beyond what anyone could imagine him doing since his near fatal accident. He was thrilled to the core of his being that it had finally been settled in his heart that his lifelong dream had actually been planted there by the Lord all along. It just took him a while to figure that out, and now he had a specific path to follow to achieve that dream. He also suspected that he would not always have the luxury of a vision or a dream to guide him along the way. He would have to develop the ability to hear the still small voice of the Lord in everything that he did if he was to accomplish his God given assignment.

When he was well enough to sit up for long periods of time, Matt came to see him with a letter in his hand. It was clearly marked with the NASA logo and Flynn knew exactly what it meant.

His heart sank and he thought, "Here I am laid up in this hospital bed like some invalid and Matt is going to beat me into space! Lord, it's just not fair!"

With those thoughts, it became apparent to Flynn that his conversion had not caused his competitive spirit to wane; he would have to learn to channel it properly to keep himself from getting into trouble, he thought.

"Flynn," said Matt softly, "I wanted you to be the first to know. While you were in the coma, they checked all my references and called some of my supervisors. Next thing I know, they scheduled me for the interview process. The wing king asked me to keep it to myself so I did, reluctantly. I got back from Houston a couple of months ago and didn't hear anything for quite a long time. Two days ago, the Selection Manager called me to let me know that I had been accepted as a Mission Pilot Candidate, and the letter showed up today. I told the wing king I had to tell you first, so here I am."

For the second time in their relationship, Flynn openly wept in front of his friend, and after a few moments of struggling, he managed to scratch out the following words, "Matt you know it couldn't have happened to a nicer guy, and the great thing is, we both know that this is what you are supposed to do with your life."

He extended his hand and shook it firmly.

Matt embraced him and hugged him tightly.

"Your turn's coming Flynn, you just wait," he said with his voice cracking and tears welling up in his eyes.

Flynn replied, "I know, but for now, the Lord has given me some new direction. Some day when I'm finally walking around again, we'll have to set aside some time so I can tell you all about it. When do you report to Houston for training?"

"In August," Matt said.

"Wow, that's only a couple of months away, observed Flynn. "You must be crazy with excitement!"

"Yea, I haven't even told my parents or Emma yet."

"Better tell them now since the cat is definitely out of the bag. It won't be long before somebody in the wing leaks it to the whole world!"

As Matt left his hospital room, Flynn thought about it intently and realized that Matt's acceptance into the program was nothing short of a miracle, the hand of God at work for sure. He was barely at the halfway mark through a three year test pilot assignment, wasn't that experienced, and to top it off, it was his first time applying for the program. Yep, Flynn thought, even the fact that Matt was an Academy golden boy who flew the Air Force's top of the line fighter couldn't account for this. This was an amazing display of the favor of God!

"Lord, let that kind of favor come my way, I pray," he said out loud then shifted his thoughts to how he could get the news to Hannah before Emma told her.

Hannah eventually had to get back to Colorado Springs and her teaching responsibilities, but not before she and Flynn spent many an hour in his hospital room talking about his new relationship with the Lord and about the future of their relationship together.

One of those times she said to him, "Flynn, I want you to know what a tremendous answer to prayer it was that you were able to come out of your coma and begin your recovery.

"The others were praying that you would survive and would live out the full number of your days, but my prayers were a little different. It might sound a little strange to you Flynn, but I was taught to be straight up with God sometimes; to be bold and to be specific when you ask him for things. I told the Lord that I saw no sense in his answering my prayer to get you saved so I could marry you just to let you slip through my fingers a few short weeks later. I told him I was expecting you to fully recover and I wasn't going to take no for an answer.

"Furthermore, I told the Lord that he would have to put it in your heart for you to ask me to marry you because I was taught that's the way it's supposed to happen. That's why I broke down the way I did that day Flynn. It was just such a day of miracles. It was just all so overwhelming."

She started to cry again at the end and said, "See I can't even tell the story without getting emotional."

Flynn agreed, "I understand how you feel. It was quite a day, but since we are being so honest and open, there is something I have to tell you Hannah, but you have to promise to keep it just between you and me for now."

"I promise," she said, wiping the tears from her eyes.

Flynn then told her in careful detail how the Lord had appeared to him in a vision while he was lying unconscious in that small grassy field in the middle of the desert. She listened intently to every word, tears again welling in her eyes as he got to the end of his story.

When he was done, she looked him square in the eye and said, "Well…Flynn…I've never had anything like that happen to me but I've always believed it was possible if the Lord had a good reason for it, and it sounds to me like you and the Lord got a lot of things settled in your heart. You have new direction, and we now have a future that we can pursue together."

"I was really hoping you would say something like that," Flynn said, "Will you pray with me that we get the mind of God on our wedding day and on the next step or assignment that he has for me and you?"

"Of course I will Flynn," she replied, "you lead off and I will follow."

The most unpleasant part of this whole ordeal from Flynn's perspective was the inevitable military aircraft accident investigation. He knew it was routine but was not looking forward to answering questions from an investigator who was most likely trying to pin the whole thing on him. At least, that's the way he felt about it. But except for a few uncomfortable days of answering questions and submitting statements, it was not as hellish an ordeal as he had expected.

In the end, after a relatively quick investigation, the cause of the accident was determined to be exactly what he had suspected: the trim motor had run the stabilator trim to the full down position and put the aircraft in an unrecoverable dive. It was the opinion of the accident board that Flynn did everything he could have done before ejecting from the aircraft to save his life.

About a month before he was released, Matt came by his room to say goodbye. He was headed for Houston and wanted to say farewell to his best friend. They hugged one another and promised to keep in touch, but Matt had one more important thing he wanted to relay to Flynn before he left. He told Flynn that getting hooked into a thriving local church was vital to his personal growth as a Christian.

Matt had grown up Assembly of God but told Flynn long ago that he would attend any church where he felt led to go as long as they preached the Word boldly and the Spirit was free to move. He would always say that the Lord didn't mind being held to such a standard, and had always obliged him wherever the Air Force had sent him.

There was a Methodist church in Rosamond that fit that bill and he had attended there regularly ever since he arrived at Edwards. The church had earned a reputation for being a little rowdy because they would use guitars and drums and contemporary music in their worship services. The members were also known to raise their hands and clap from time to time during prayer and during praise and worship. Flynn had heard about this church before his conversion and had determined he would stay as far away as possible from a place like that. Thus, he found it ironic, that the first week after he walked out of his hospital room, he ended up attending the very church that Matt had recommended. It would be the beginning of a long association, and would become his home church for the rest of his stay at Edwards.

Flynn had spent a total of three months in the hospital out of an expected six, and his miraculous recovery was the talk of the hospital staff. His neck bones had fused back together with just a hint of a scar visible in X-rays and MRIs. The swelling of his spinal cord had subsided and all of his body and brain functions had been restored to peak efficiency. In all respects, he had recovered fully from his near death encounter.

Although he had lost about 25 pounds during his ordeal, he had gained most of it back when he was allowed to start physical therapy. To his doctor's distress, he was eager to rebuild the muscular body he was known for and managed to find every free weight in the hospital he could during this time. In short, he did physical therapy and then some, lifting every heavy weight he could find in the process.

## : RECOVERY

When they finally let him out, he was only five pounds shy of the 170 he was accustomed to. Flynn absolutely hated feeling puny, and the whole time he was in the hospital he felt puny, so he had determined that he would return to his normal routine of weights and running as soon he was released. And he did.

Flynn turned all his energies at that point to regaining his flight status. The civilian doctors had given him a clean bill of health but he would have to pass a Class II military flight physical to get back on flight status. Because he had sustained a serious neck injury, they had to push through a waiver to allow him to fly ejection seat aircraft again. They had done that while he was still in the hospital.

The day after he was released he checked in with his squadron commander and was ordered to report to the flight surgeon the very next day.

Knowing Flynn as well as he did, his commander knew he would not be happy until he was in the air again and he was eager to accommodate. He liked Flynn and recognized his latent talents as an aviator, but he was also aware of the tremendous financial investment that Flynn represented. And as any good commander would, he wanted to get his money's worth out of him during the time he had left at Edwards. As soon as the flight surgeon gave him a positive thumbs-up, he wanted him in the air.

It seemed to Flynn that the poking and prodding he received during *this* flight physical far exceeded any he had taken before. The flight surgeon made it clear before they started that his team was going to be a bit more thorough than usual given the fact that he had almost died just a few short months ago. Flynn decided to grin and bear it since in his mind he knew it was only a matter of time before he would be pronounced good to go.

Well, to his chagrin, it ended up being an all-day affair with an EEG and EKG and way more tests than the Class II actually required for someone his age. In the end though, it was as Flynn predicted it would be: they could find nothing wrong with him. In fact, he was as strong and healthy as he ever was before. It almost seemed to Flynn that the flight surgeon had reluctantly signed off on his Form 1042.

The flight surgeon had a smile on his face and had wished him well but something in his demeanor made it seem like he was thinking, "let's wait until his blood work comes back from the lab, surely something amiss will pop up there."

But before the flight surgeon could change his mind, Flynn took the 1042 to his commander and said, "I want to fly as soon as possible."

"Thought you'd say that Flynn. You're scheduled for your first ride tomorrow to get you A-10 recurrent. After that we'll get you recurrent in the T-38. As soon as you get back up to speed in the Hog, you can get started on the AIM-9 tests we had planned for you before the accident. I got them to slip the program to the right a few months. We've assigned you as the lead test pilot. Guess I was just hoping you would come back sooner than they said and sure enough, you did."

"Thanks skipper, I really appreciate that ... more than you know!"

Flynn took back to flight like he had never left it. It was a joy to fly the Hog again and just be in the air. It didn't take him long to complete his recurrent training and then it was on to the T-38. Except for a twinge of uneasiness that he experienced when he pulled back on the stick on his first takeoff since the accident, he quickly readapted to the aircraft he had grown to love.

For a while, he would think of the accident whenever he would trim the aircraft, something that you have to do constantly in the T-38. He had to fight off the fear that would try to come on him from time to time and finally broke through by simply dwelling on what the Lord had told him that day on the grass. He would be

OK in the air now, for sure, because flying was part of what God was calling him to do. He knew this now without a doubt. As long as he was careful to listen to that still, small voice, the Lord would keep him out of danger.

For the next full year Flynn threw himself into the AIM-9 project. He relished the fact that he got to spend a great deal more time flying the Hog and that he was heading up an important flight test project; one that he could really sink his teeth into. He worked tirelessly with the flight test engineers and with the other pilots assigned to the project, determined to complete it with excellence and with flawless data analysis and report writing. The fact that he had few distractions made this an easy task for Flynn.

After hours, there was no one to hang out with. Matt was gone and, in his mind, there was certainly no one around to replace him. Best friends like that only come along once in a life time. Except for his regular church attendance and the times that he and Hannah spent together, he had little interaction with other people outside of his work. He decided he would use his new found isolation to get to know his Bible that year.

If it would tell him more about the man he met that day on the grass, he was determined to pour over every inch of it and learn as much as he could. He read it cover to cover that year, "from Genesis to Maps," as his pastor put it sometimes, and really began to piece together the story of the people of God, starting with Abraham and the Hebrew nation, and everything that led to the Christian era that he was now a part of. He found that he loved it more than he ever imagined and couldn't believe that he was almost 30 years old and was only now discovering the treasures found in this wonderful book.

Flynn and Hannah continued their letter writing campaign and saw each other as often as they could that year. He managed to take leave and visit Hannah three times that year, taking advantage of the four day weekends which usually accompanied the numerous government holidays on the military calendar. Then she had met him at his parents' home in Indiana during the Christmas break and had spent three weeks with him at Edwards during her summer break.

Flynn had waited until his first trip to Colorado Springs to formally ask Hannah to marry him. He was old fashioned in that respect and wanted to ask her father for his daughter's hand in marriage. So after praying about it, he bought the ring he had picked out, took it with him on that trip, and popped the question in her parent's den, after Hannah's dad had given him his blessing.

She said yes, again, of course. They had decided on an August wedding which would come pretty close to the time he was expecting new orders. He had no idea what his next assignment would be but they had both prayed about it often and knew that whatever challenges lay ahead they would face them together as a married couple from that point on.

As it turned out, the date they chose would end up being a few weeks after Matt's graduation from his astronaut class and Matt had convinced them that a wedding in Colorado Springs at the famous Academy Chapel would present the least amount of travel required for their friends and relatives.

He had asked Emma to marry him at the half way point in his training and they had set a date which coincided with Flynn and Hannah's. After much discussion between the two couples, they had decided that, all things considered, it would be the perfect venue for a double wedding.

## CHAPTER 8
## :NEW DIRECTION

Flynn and Hannah and Matt and Emma got married together in a beautiful double wedding in the Chapel at the Air Force Academy that August. Despite their attempts to keep it a small affair, the in-laws made sure the guest list expanded almost exponentially, at least that's the way Matt and Flynn saw it. By the time they were done, there were no more concerns about the small wedding getting swallowed up in the huge chapel; the place was packed.

The minute the ceremony was over, Matt and Emma left for Hawaii, and Flynn and Hannah darted off to Lake Tahoe for a week of honeymooning. After that, Matt moved his new bride to Houston, and Flynn and Hannah returned to Edwards to see what kind of orders they would receive.

They moved into the temporary family quarters on base because they knew they would not be there very much longer. Flynn took the time to make sure all the loose ends were tied up on the AIM-9 project and spent quite a bit of time on his final report. "It had to be perfect," he thought. That's just the way he did things.

His commander had called him and told him he had some news and had asked him to come by to discuss it. Flynn packed up his report and left their one-room efficiency to head for the commander's office. His mind was racing. Usually you had some idea ahead of time what you could expect before you received your orders, but he honestly had no idea what he would be doing or where he would be going. He and Hannah had prayed hard and had finally left it in the hands of the Lord. They believed that he would get them where they were supposed to be at this season in their lives.

His commander shook his hand firmly as he entered his office and wasted no time getting to the point.

"Flynn sit down for a minute, I want to talk with you about an opportunity that I think would be great for your career, both as a test pilot, a manager, and a future commander.

"First off, I noticed that you completed all of your required PME for promotion to Major, via distance learning while you were in the hospital no less, so there's no issue there. Since promotion to Major is pretty much going to happen, I'd like to talk to you about something else.

"We have started a pilot program; it's an academic fellowship program that allows us to nominate exceptional individuals here at Edwards to pursue advanced degrees in engineering at the Air Force Institute of Technology up at Wright Patterson in Dayton. Now I know you have a BS in Aeronautics and Astronautics from the School of Engineering at Purdue with an exceptional GPA, and you're one of the best test pilots I know. I've discussed this with the wing commander and we'd like to exploit that rare combination of flying ability and the ability to relay actual flight experiences to the engineers on the ground in a language that they understand.

"Flynn, we nominated you for a fellowship to AFIT to get your PhD in Systems Engineering and you've been accepted. Now this is not a flying assignment, and I know you're not going to like that, but it's an opportunity of a lifetime, and we think you should take it.

"You can take your FAA military equivalency exam and get your commercial ticket with a slew of categories added on. So if you want to fly, you can do that on the civilian side. Besides, with a PhD under your belt, and as a qualified air force test pilot, it will actually increase your odds of getting selected to the astronaut program. You would be a competitive applicant as a Mission Pilot *and* as a Mission Specialist. So what do you say Flynn?"

"Sir, now I know why you asked me to get you a copy of my official transcript while I was busy with the AIM-9 project," he replied, "but how long will it take me to get this degree and what happens afterwards?"

"Well it's a three year program that is designed with a follow on assignment in mind. We're pushing to bring you back here to Edwards and prime you for a command slot but there is a chance you could end up in some other assignment; needs of the Air Force still come first you know, and there's nothing we can do about that."

"Sir, can I talk it over with Hannah and get back to you?" he said. "Not that I'm not grateful, but I need to make sure she's on board with this."

"Sure Flynn, take the weekend to talk it over with her and get back to me on Monday. But just remember, it will be an opportunity for you to help people solve problems, something you seem to be really good at."

Flynn and Hannah started packing immediately since the orders had them leaving in the next two weeks. There was no doubt in their mind that this was the assignment for them. Especially since his commander had "coincidentally" used some of the same phrases that Flynn had heard in his vision from the Lord. It was an educational opportunity that had suddenly come his way and they believed that ultimately it would be a tool that would enable him to help people solve problems and make their lives better.

Flynn wasn't quite sure how it would all work out but he and Hannah had a total peace about taking this assignment and felt like the Lord would lead them more specifically when it became necessary. He wasn't thrilled about the non-flying aspect of this assignment, but had studied the workbook and had passed the military equivalency exam. He now had a commercial pilot license with single and multi-engine ratings. He could fly any civilian aircraft within reason, provided he could meet the private insurance requirements.

When they finally arrived in Dayton, they were exhausted and decided to get a good night's rest before they struck out the next day. He didn't have to check in at the school for a few days and it gave them a chance to survey the lay of the land. They woke up in temporary housing the next morning, showered up and hit the streets in Flynn's TR-6. They had two objectives in mind, finding a church and finding a home, in that order. No use finding a home and then finding a church that was all the way across town. No, they were the types that would become totally involved in their local church and wanted to live as close as they possibly could to their spiritual sanctuary.

They found a small Assembly of God Church that seemed to be the one they were looking for. It was a Saturday when they visited the grounds and they weren't even sure anyone was there when they peered through the tinted glass door of the church foyer.

They were startled when someone opened the door and asked, "May I help you?"

"Uh ... Sorry sir," Flynn replied. "We're new in town and are looking for a church home. We were just looking around and didn't mean to disturb you."

"No worries," said the tall, lean gray headed man. "I'm the caretaker here …. Hey, I can show you around if you'd like … what do you say?"

"Sure," Flynn said.

Hannah glanced at him nervously as they entered the glass door into the foyer. The caretaker introduced himself as Mr. Ron and then took them immediately to the main sanctuary. When they entered the back of the semi-circular sanctuary with auditorium style seating, they both stopped and looked at each other with a gleam in their eyes and with smiles on their faces.

Hannah spoke first, "Flynn, I don't know how I know this, and I certainly know nothing about this church other than what we've read in the yellow pages, but I feel like this is supposed to be our church."

Flynn nodded in agreement, "I felt the same thing as soon as I walked into the room; I think this is our church."

A few days later they found a small two bedroom townhouse in a quiet neighborhood in Dayton and started settling into their new surroundings. Flynn checked into the base at Wright Patterson and then reported to AFIT then next day. It wasn't long before he was immersed into his studies and faced the first real challenge of his married life.

The absolute focus that he had employed in the past when starting any new endeavor was not going to work with a new wife in the house. His biggest challenge that first year was learning to balance the very real needs of his wife with the rigors of his academic pursuits. She had found a teaching job in a nearby high school but it was only part time. They spent a lot of time at the church and got as involved as they could, considering the demands of Flynn's studies and Hannah's part-time teaching job.

Flynn also had begun flying at a nearby airport in the small, lightweight aircraft he remembered from his high school days. It wasn't like flying an A-10 or a T-38 he thought, but it was flying, and flying was something he loved to do.

All of these activities kept them both very busy, sometimes together, but many times apart. Because of this, Flynn worked extra hard at finding ways to keep the romance sparked between them. He made it a hard and fast rule that Friday night was always *their* night and he would take her on a date unless she specifically asked to just stay home, pop some popcorn, watch a video, or just hang out or take a long walk together.

For her part, Hannah was happy just being with Flynn. Long distance letter writing was no substitute for curling up next to the man you loved, she thought, even if it was just watching an old movie with a hot cup of coffee on the used couch that you both had picked out. It was still home and they were together and very happy.

After the end of his first year at AFIT, Flynn and Hannah were asked if they wanted to take a mission trip with their church during the summer. They jumped at the chance at adventure and at the opportunity to do something for their Lord. Flynn had accumulated quite a bit of unused leave and was more than eager to use some of it for a month long mission trip in the Mohave Desert.

After he had arranged to take the time off, the school commandant pulled him aside one day in the hallway and told him that NASA was gearing up for another round of astronaut selection.

"Better get your application updated," he had said. "If you do it before you leave for the Mohave, it will be ready to launch when you get back and you won't have to worry about it while you're there."

Flynn agreed. He talked to Hannah about it and spent the next week or so getting everything together. He put it in his "special drawer" in the desk that they had bought for him that now sat in the corner of their den. He tried not to think about it too much afterward, but that was not to be the case as Matt called him just a few days later.

"Flynn, make sure you get your package ready to go before you leave on your mission trip. When you get back I'll give you a few pointers I've picked up since I've been here; things I know they will be looking for. I'll help you to emphasize them so you'll have the best shot possible. Also, make sure you put in for both the Mission Pilot *and* Mission Specialist positions; it will increase your odds of selection. And … uh … Flynn ... there's something else …"

"What is it?" asked Flynn.

"I don't know how someone as junior as me managed to pull this off, but I've been assigned to a crew as their Mission Pilot and will be training for a Shuttle launch in the fall of next year. Flynn, it's one of those Top Secret military missions and they have asked for an all military crew. The advanced radar work that I did at Edwards just happened to be the type of experience they were looking for on this particular mission. Boy, does God know what he is doing or what?"

"That's great Matt," Flynn replied blandly, "Please keep us posted; that's very exciting."

"Flynn, I know you, and I know this was tough for you to hear, but again, I wanted you to be the first one to know outside of NASA's inner circle. Oh by the way, you can't tell anyone till it's publically announced."

"You know you can trust me Matt, and forgive me for thinking only of myself, God has given you great favor, and it's wonderful to watch him work in your life. Please keep me posted. I'm really excited for you."

Flynn tried to put a good face on it but this was going to be hard for him to deal with. His best friend had not only been selected ahead of him for astronaut training, but he would be flying in space a little over a year from now. Even if he got selected on the upcoming board, he would report to Houston for training just in time to watch Matt blast off into orbit.

Yes, Flynn's life had been changed on the inside, and he had gotten miraculous and spectacular direction from the Lord, but it had done nothing to dampen the tremendous desire that still burned in his heart. To the contrary, it now burned more intensely than ever. At the core of everything else, he still wanted to fly in space more than anything. And the Lord had not discouraged this; he had only asked him to prioritize it properly. At least that's the way Flynn saw it.

That summer, Flynn and Hannah went with their church to a remote area of the Mohave Desert to help minister to some of the Native American peoples that were living there in abject poverty. Church leaders had explained to them that they were working with a coalition of churches who had found great favor with local governments and Indian reservations in the region. This coalition had raised a considerable amount of money and their vision was to begin with indigenous tribes in the Mohave and then to expand to the Sonoran and the Chihuahuan Deserts where Christian missionaries had not made significant progress for over 200 years. Most of these people were living in agrarian economies that depended on irrigating and farming the harsh land of the desert. But despite the harsh conditions, many of them were determined to stay and carry on the traditions of their ancestors.

Much of the time however, they were in need of food, medicine, and shelter. Unfortunately the reservation system instituted by the US government a hundred years or so ago, more often than not, stretched their resources to the limit, and so they needed all the help they could get. The coalition was determined to help meet these immediate physical needs but also to minister to them in spiritually meaningful ways.

They had established a base camp at a central airstrip in the Mohave, not too far from Edwards AFB; barely more than a dirt strip that eventually would be used as a distribution center to reach tribes in the desert regions above and below the U.S./Mexican border. Missionary flight organizations had donated aircraft and pilots had volunteered to help in the effort. They had staged numerous aircraft at the base camp to help distribute the supplies to the neediest areas. There were light singles and twins, but also heavier cargo aircraft, all dedicated to transporting food, medicine, and in some cases prefabricated housing components to remote areas where they were needed the most.

One of the reasons Flynn had been asked to go was because of his pilot experience and it wasn't long before he got involved in that part of the operation. At first, he flew as a copilot on various aircraft, assisting anyway he could. But ministry leaders soon realized his skills were being underutilized, and it wasn't long before they put him in charge of their small fleet of aircraft, acting as Flynn would say, as an operations officer.

Hannah worked in the little chapel that had been built by the churches as a place of refuge and worship for the locals. As she later told Flynn, this chapel was open year round, not just during these kinds of operations. It was collocated with the airport and served as a vital hub of activity during these types of operations. After several years of involvement, the affiliated churches came up with an agreed upon name for the long term missions effort. They called it, Operation Desert Reach. Flynn's pastor, who eventually gravitated to lead this effort, would often say that they were "Reaching the forgotten and touching lives for Christ!"

After their first two weeks in the Mohave, Hannah approached Flynn as they got back to the small one room hut where they were staying. It was close to the chapel, but unlike the chapel, it had no air conditioning. There was running water, something they were extremely thankful for, and they did have electricity. It wasn't much though. There was one incandescent light bulb hanging from a wire in the center of the room and a flimsy ceiling fan that ran above it off the same line.

"Good thing it's cool at night here in the desert," Flynn said one night as they curled up together in their rickety single bed.

"Flynn," she said, "I don't know how to tell you this but I feel a tug on my heart for these people that I've never felt before in my life. It's like I know that I know that I am Christ's direct representative to these people. If they don't see Jesus in me, they may never see him. At least that's the way I feel."

"I know, I feel it too; knowing that I am using my aviation skills to help people like this … it's one of the things the Lord talked to me about that day on the grass."

They stopped talking about it at that point, but as they went to sleep that night, they both knew these feelings would grow and would soon become a vital, driving force in their lives.

## CHAPTER 9
## :CONFLICTING DREAMS

After they returned home from a month in the Mohave, Flynn and Hannah were tanned, exhausted ... and different. Something had ignited on the inside of them that was calling them to this type of ministry. They knew they would be back again and couldn't wait for that time to arrive. Yet, hardly a night had gone by when they were in the Mohave where Flynn did not go out to survey the desert night sky before he went to bed.

It was then that he could sense an inner conflict brewing. When he would look up at the stars, it was almost as if he could feel them calling him, beckoning him to come to them, somehow, someway. But at the same time, he could sense a drawing, an inner pulling that was seemingly leading him in another direction entirely. He felt the same tug that Hannah felt when it came to helping some of the forgotten tribes of those desert regions. He knew that what he was doing was exactly what he was supposed to be doing, but could not reconcile the new dream with the one that was always there when all was said and done: the quest for the stars.

It seemed he had two dreams now and he had no idea how to reconcile the two; they were similar in some respects but they were divergent in others. He thought about it and prayed about it often, struggling to come to terms with the dichotomy of two distinctly different visions. He finally settled on the only resolution that worked for him.

The Lord had said he would fly in space one day *but first*, he was to use his aviation and engineering skills to help people solve problems and to tell them about the saving faith that was in his name. The only way he knew to interpret that was to continue flying, finish his advanced degrees, and continue to apply for the astronaut program. He would do the things the Lord had mentioned until he got selected as an astronaut and then would turn his full energy and passion behind his lifelong dream of one day flying in space.

After beefing up and emphasizing the sections that Matt had suggested, Flynn polished off his second NASA application and sent it off to the Air Force astronaut board. This time though, he sent it with a prayer of consecration.

He and Hannah had prayed, and as hard as it was for him to pray this way, he had told the Lord, "I am sending this second application in to the astronaut program, but I submit it to your plans and purposes Lord and to your divine timing for my life."

A couple of months later, he was delighted when the commandant came to him and told him the good news.

"Flynn, you passed the Air Force screening. Your application has been sent to NASA for further consideration."

Flynn was elated and let out a loud and joyous "Thank you Jesus!" He got a little embarrassed when the commandant seemed to look at him funny.

He was relieved to hear him say, "Don't worry Flynn, you're not the only believer here at AFIT. Best wishes as you pursue the dreams that God has placed in your heart."

A few months later, Flynn heard through the grapevine that some of his references and former supervisors had been interviewed; definitely a good sign that they were giving him a closer look and that he might progress to the interview stage. The commandant stopped him in the hall a few weeks later and told him to expect an interview call.

## : CONFLICTING DREAMS

"I just got off the phone with NASA and you are *definitely* on the short list for this year's astronaut selection."

Flynn was flying high after that and found it difficult to apply himself to his studies. It was Hannah that reminded him that it would do him no good now to let down his guard just because he had been granted his first interview.

"You're right babe," he acknowledged, "you're absolutely right."

The next day after the mild scolding from his wife, he got a call from NASA telling him that he had been scheduled for the first round of interviews. He couldn't wait to get off the phone so he could at least get a message to Matt. Matt had started his mission training and as Flynn suspected would be the case, he had to settle for leaving a message at the astronaut office.

It was almost a week later before Matt called him back and they had a long, joyous conversation on the phone.

"Just let me know when you are going to be here and I'll see what I can do about hooking up with you. I've got a pretty tight training schedule, but I'll do the best I can. Flynn, this is great news! I will be praying for God's guidance, direction, and favor for you throughout the whole interview process."

"Thanks Matt. It means a lot to me to have a friend and a brother on the inside praying for me. Talk to you later, God Bless!"

When the first round of interviews began, Flynn travelled to Houston and was put through a rigorous set of physical and medical examinations that were more thorough than any military flight physical he had ever taken. He was in top shape and except for his stay in the hospital after the accident, had never been sick a day in his life. He breezed through all of the tests without a single hiccup.

He went back and forth a few times from Dayton to Houston for follow up evaluations, psychological assessments, and interviews with influential astronauts and mission support personnel. They were all friendly and Flynn came away from the whole process feeling like he was in good shape for selection to the program. Before he left, the selection manager told him he would be contacted by phone if he was selected and by letter if not. Flynn said thank you and headed back to Dayton.

When he got back home later that evening Hannah was waiting for him at the door, "Honey, Matt called me and told me things went well with the final round of interviews. He said we should hear something pretty soon now."

"Thanks babe. Now tell me what you've been doing with yourself while I've been gone?"

"Well, I have a bit of a surprise that I'm very excited about."

"Go ahead, tell me all about it?"

"Well, I know it doesn't sound like much, but while you were gone on this last trip, I signed up for Spanish classes. I really feel like I should bone up on my Spanish. I took it in high school and in college but I would like to be able to actually speak the language, especially when we go back to the Mohave. Not all the Indian tribes know Spanish in the region where we are working but many of them do. It seems to be the logical, common language to learn if you feel called to this type of ministry."

Flynn could not argue with the logic but was a bit taken aback that Hannah seemed to be on a different wavelength than him. He was focused on the stars and she was focused on the desert.

He didn't let on though, but simply replied, "That's great babe, maybe you can teach me once I get through my program here at AFIT."

"Would love to Flynn," she replied.

Flynn got the letter with the distinct NASA logo on it about a week later and knew when he saw it exactly what it meant. He had not been selected for the program and had to mentally prepare himself before he read the letter.

Hannah was there to console him as he read it and said, "God's timing is always different than ours, but it's always better too! Let's just trust him for the future and do what we know he has called us to do now."

"You're right as always, but it still causes me to ache on the inside, especially when I see some of the people that have gotten selected; people I know I'm ten times more qualified than!"

"Yes, I know Flynn, but it's a dangerous thing to be somewhere out of God's will and not in harmony with his timing, and I don't want that for you! Remember what happened to the Challenger crew a few years ago? Being an astronaut is still dangerous business. It's simply not the profession to be in if you are not perfectly in line with his will for your life. And I'm not passing judgment on any of Challenger's crew, God rest their souls, I'm just saying it's still a dangerous business and things can go wrong and people can get hurt."

"OK babe, I love you for always being straight with me, but I need to call Matt and get the lowdown from him."

When he was finally able to get through to Matt, Flynn fired off a series of rapid fire questions: "Was it anything medical, did they see the scar on my neck bone, was it my psych eval, was it 'cause I'm a Hog driver, was it anything you could put your finger on?"

"No Flynn, it was none of that. They were very impressed with you," Matt replied, "but I did get one board member to leak out something I think you should know about."

"What was that?" Matt asked hurriedly.

"Well, he said he would deny it if I quoted him, but they were concerned that you had been out of the cockpit for a while, military aircraft that is, so they were looking at you more as a mission specialist than a mission pilot. With that in mind, they thought you might be better qualified for future selection after you complete your PhD."

"Great," Flynn replied grumpily, "that means I'm two years away from being qualified in their eyes, and they want me to ride instead of fly!"

"It's just as well Flynn," Matt replied, "the rumor is there won't be another selection for at least two to three years anyway. Keep your chin up Flynn, you're gonna make it; just maybe not the way you envisioned it."

For the next year and a half, Flynn turned his attention to his graduate studies and on their increasing involvement in Operation Desert Reach. Hannah was going to the Mohave much more often now and soon abandoned her part time teaching job in Dayton. Flynn had to wait for the summers, but would horde his leave time so that he could spend at least a month at the mission chapel and distribution center. He acted as operations manager throughout the rest of the year, but would do so from his desk at the house and his telephone, recruiting and scheduling aircraft and pilot volunteers for the year round effort.

When he took his second trip during that second summer, he found that he had another set of talents that were coming into play in the desert outreach. His training in systems engineering helped to hone his natural ability to look at an engineering system from a top down, bird's eye point of view. He seemed to have a knack for the "big picture" on almost any system that he would analyze. Thus, with his inputs, the chapel and the distribution center were able to increase the efficiency of just about every system they were using.

## : CONFLICTING DREAMS

Electrical power, air conditioning, water filtration and irrigation, and other related systems were all maximized by replacing worn out components and by making system tweaks here and there as Flynn would direct. He even came up with a planning document which helped crews transport and assemble the prefab housing units more quickly and more efficiently.

When Flynn returned home from the Mohave, he was greeted with a telephone call from Matt who excitedly told him that a mission date had been finalized for him and his crew. It was a crew of five, Matt explained; all military, and all male. There was the mission commander, a shuttle veteran and Navy test pilot, then Matt, the mission pilot, and lastly three mission specialists.

"All of the mission specialists are PhDs," Matt told Flynn, "and only they are being trained for extra vehicular activity, EVA. Flynn, you might not like the prospect of being a mission specialist, but you will get to do something I'll never do. You will get to *walk* in space! Anyway, Emma has booked you guys into a hotel, and you will be our special guests for the launch. I know it will be tough for you Flynn, but *you have* to be there when I fly in space!"

"You know I'll be there Matt. There's absolutely no way I'm missing that!"

Flynn and Hannah travelled to Cape Canaveral that fall to watch Matt's launch at the Kennedy Space Center. It was an emotional time for Flynn but he made the best of it. He never actually saw Matt but was able to talk to him briefly on the phone. He and Hannah sat in the VIP bleachers that hot October day and waited for the launch of the shuttle mission that would carry his best friend into space. Emma was there, of course, with her parents and with Matt's, and he was surprised to see her as nervous as she was.

Hannah grabbed her at the T - 1 hour mark and said, "Come here Emma, we're going to pray."

So Flynn and Hannah prayed for Matt and his crew as privately as they could but not caring either if someone were to hear them. Emma remained quiet, sniffling slightly but nodding in agreement as Flynn and Hannah prayed. Hannah finished off by saying, "Thank you Lord for giving your angels charge over Matt and his crew and for taking care of them and keeping them safe from launch through recovery. In Jesus name we pray, Amen!"

"Thank you guys," Emma tearfully acknowledged.

Flynn looked her in the eye and said, "He's going to be all right Emma; just relax and enjoy the launch."

"I will," she said, "I will."

Hannah grabbed her hand and did not release it again until after the launch was over.

Flynn watched and listened intently as the shuttle main engines roared to life, followed shortly by the solid rocket boosters. They first saw the billowing smoke and flame erupting from the bottom of the craft which was followed shortly by the sound of the launch. They were several miles away so it took time for the sound waves to get to the bleachers where they were standing. When the sound finally did reach them, it was not just deafening it was earth moving.

Everything around them shook with the power of the sound vibrations, and Flynn could even feel the thumping vibrations in his chest cavity as the space vessel lifted off the pad. The power of the event was intoxicating, and Flynn soon found it to be the most emotionally wrenching event of his entire life. The majesty and the grandeur were overwhelming to him and the fact that his best friend was on board just plain made him cry. There was no stopping the flood of tears as he watched his best friend blast off into space, right before his very eyes.

Before he realized it, he found that he was reaching toward the craft as it lifted higher and higher, stretching his right hand toward it as if he could somehow possess it. Tears were still streaming down his face and he didn't care who saw him or what they thought. This was *his* destiny and there were few people here that he sensed could understand what that felt like. Hannah had been tightly clasping his left hand with her right, but had also held tightly to Emma's hand on her other side, all the way through the T + 1 minute mark of the launch.

She had glanced at Flynn every few moments and knew what he was going through. She wisely chose to leave him alone to his thoughts and concentrated on Emma who was also streaming tears from her eyes. Emma later confided that hers were more tears of relief than anything else.

Finally Hannah had burst into tears at the sight of Emma on her left and her husband on her right. Though it was an emotional event for all involved, Flynn would never be quite the same after that launch. It put everything into perspective for him. For Flynn, there was a visceral connection that went beyond the mere power of the launch event. This was what he was supposed to do with his life; he just knew it.

He came away from this event with only one prayer on his heart: "When Lord, when?" From that moment on, it would become a recurring prayer that he would pray for the rest of his life.

His last year at AFIT went quickly and he devoted most of that time to organizing data and preparing to write and defend his doctoral dissertation. He split his time that year almost evenly between this and his unofficial work for Operation Desert Reach. Things got a little busy at the end of the school year as he had to finish his dissertation, take his comprehensive exams, and defend his dissertation; all before he could take his months leave to go to the Mohave.

To add to the hectic nature of that year, there was the matter of orders. Where would they send Flynn for his payback tour? He now owed the Air Force a year of duty for every year of school, so he had a three year tour waiting for him somewhere. The original plan was to bring him back to Edwards and groom him for a command, and he was hoping that had not changed.

Hannah had become more or less fluent in Spanish from her many trips to the Mohave and was hoping along with Flynn for a return to Edwards. That way, they would be right next to the Mohave where they had become increasingly involved in Operation Desert Reach. Flynn saw it as a win, win. They would be closer to their base camp in the Mohave but he could get back into flying military jets as well. That way, he would be competitive for both mission pilot and mission specialist the next time there was an astronaut selection.

So when the news came that Flynn would be assigned to the Air Force Academy as an Assistant Professor of Mathematics and Engineering, they were flabbergasted.

"The Air Force Academy … how could that be the will of God?" they both wondered.

Hannah was the first to brighten up the day that they got the news. She said, "Well, it's still closer to the Mohave than Wright Patt, isn't it?"

"Yes, but it's a non-flying position! Just exactly what are they trying to do to my career?" Flynn retorted sharply.

"Not sure what's going on honey, but let's start praying about this and see if we can get the mind of the Lord on it."

"OK, you're right as always," Flynn replied, "let's start now."

After that, they began a time of praying and fasting that lasted for almost a week.

After the intense week of prayer, Flynn turned to Hannah and said, "I have to be honest. In my head I don't like this assignment, but in my heart, I have a peace about it. I can still put in for both the mission pilot and mission specialist, but this will probably pigeon hole me as a mission specialist. I've just been too long out of the cockpit babe ... too long."

Hannah chimed in as if on cue, "I get a peace about it too, and all I can say is, let's go with the peace and try not to figure it all out ourselves. Last time I checked, God was still a little smarter than the rest of us."

"You got that right!" Flynn agreed.

That last summer in Dayton was quite eventful. Flynn graduated with his PhD in Systems Engineering and a perfect 4.0 average. A few days later, he and Hannah took a month's leave and left Dayton for the Mohave en route to Colorado Springs. After a month with Desert Reach, they moved into Hannah's parent's house while they looked for a house of their own. Before long, they found a house a few miles from her parent's and got as settled as they could before Flynn had to begin his duties at the Academy.

The superintendent, a two star general, had greeted him a few days before he was to begin and gave him the not so happy news that he had to complete his senior PME to be ready for promotion to Lieutenant Colonel. So Flynn had to hit the ground running and accomplish that while gearing up to teach the classes that he was scheduled to teach that year. It made things busy for him, but in typical fashion, he completed his PME well ahead of schedule and taught his classes with the excellence that he expected of himself.

About midway through his first year as an academy professor, he got word from the superintendent that there was going to be another astronaut selection the following year. He put together his application, using much of the material from the last two.

Unfortunately, from his perspective, he had no new flight time to report, other than the civilian time he had accumulated. So there just wasn't much to add there.

However, he had completed his PhD, and that would surely place him squarely into the highly qualified category from which they chose their interviewees; this time most likely as a mission specialist. And he intended to make the interview round again, for sure. He got a boatload of top recommendations including his commanders at Edwards, his commandant at Wright Patterson, and the superintendent of the Academy who had let him know in no uncertain terms that he was in his corner when it came to helping him achieve his dream of becoming an astronaut.

Flynn got word fairly quickly through the supervisor that he once again had cleared the Air Force screening board, and that his application had been forwarded to NASA. The following spring, he got word again from former supervisors and commanders who had been contacted by NASA, so he knew he was probably headed for another round of interviews. A week or so later, he got the call from NASA and was asked again to come to Houston for the cycle of physicals, evaluations, and interviews. He went to Houston a few weeks later, convinced that this was his time. He had done the things the Lord had spoken to him about that day in the grass and now it was time for him to fly in space. He had been faithful, and now he would be rewarded.

Flynn left Houston after the last round of interviews with the feeling that he had this selection in the bag. It was only a matter of time, he thought. The interviews had gone well. He was in top shape as he had always kept his life's regimen of lifting and running. There was not a thing wrong with him medically; he was a top notch Air Force test pilot and had a PhD in Systems Engineering from the Air Force Institute of Technology. He had never finished anything other than first in every formal training program he had completed since he joined the Air Force. He could fly just about anything well, and he could speak engineer to anybody with an education and a modicum of common sense. He had met a lot of other talented and smart people during the interview phase, but he could honestly say there was not one he had met that was more qualified than him. Maybe there was one or two that were *as* qualified, but there was no one *more* qualified.

When he got back to Colorado Springs, Hannah met him at the door and said that Matt was on the phone. Flynn kissed Hannah and rushed in the room to talk to his friend.

"Flynn, I just wanted you to know how well I heard everything went. I can't tell you how I know, but you are the one to beat in this group for sure. Nobody can touch your qualifications; you seem like a lock for a mission specialist slot. That's what they are all saying unofficially!"

"Wow, Matt, I was kind of hoping that would be the case. In fact, if you won't call me cocky, I kind of thought that would be the case."

"You're not cocky Flynn, I know you too well. But you do need to pray. As great as everything sounds like it went, this one is still in the hands of the Lord."

Flynn said goodbye to his friend and turned to find Hannah who had been hovering over him a few feet behind and had been listening to every word.

With tears in her eyes, she said, "Babe, it looks like it's really going to happen this time, doesn't it?"

At the site of his wife, Flynn became emotional as well. Without saying a word he just stood up, grabbed her and hugged her as tightly as he ever had their whole life together. They stood there embracing and crying for several minutes before Flynn broke the silence.

"Lord, your will be done, not mine; your will be done!"

Then they both broke into tears again and continued embracing for a very long time.

Finally Flynn looked into Hannah's pretty blue eyes and asked with a sheepish grin, "Babe ... am I just getting more and more emotional as I get older?"

"Maybe, Flynn, but it's one of the things I love about you. You're a type A personality with a very tender heart. And it's growing more and more tender as the years go by."

And then they passionately kissed; a kiss of true love for one another.

About a week later, Flynn got a call from Matt. He sounded grim which put Flynn immediately on edge.

"Flynn, I have to tell you buddy, there is an issue with your flight physical that is being hotly debated right now.

I'm not sure how it's going to play out, but we have a new flight doc who has a reputation for being a hard nose when it comes to medical issues. It seems he has a problem with the hairline scar on the back of the neck bone that was broken in the accident. He says that it might increase your risk of injury during shuttle emergency egress, should it ever become necessary, or if you ever had to eject from one of the NASA T-38s that you're going to be training in if you are selected."

"That's bogus and they know it," Flynn retorted. "I got a clean bill of health from the flight doc at Edwards and flew the T-38 for another year and a half after the accident with no issues!"

"Yes, I know," said Matt, "but this is NASA, not the military, and their word is final on issues like this. All I can say is: you and Hannah need to pray. Emma and I have been praying and will continue to do so. Gotta go. God Bless!"

## : CONFLICTING DREAMS

After he heard the dial tone kick in, Flynn just sat there with the phone to his ear, in stunned silence for a few seconds.

He erupted in an angry outburst, "I work my whole life for a chance like this and some idiot flight doc is going to stop me now? Lord, you've got to tell me this is not you're doing! How can this be the will of God?"

Hannah had been in the kitchen and came running to the den when she heard Flynn hollering. This time there were no tears, only red faced anger. It took Hannah a few minutes to calm Flynn down and get him to tell her exactly what was going on.

When he finally explained it to her, she just looked at the floor and said, "We need to pray."

A week later, Flynn received a letter with the distinct NASA logo on it, and again knew exactly what that meant. The flight doc had won the internal battle that Matt had told him about, and he was out. He would not be selected, although most probably, the most highly qualified of all the applicants that were interviewed. It was the lowest point in his entire life and he slipped into a depression that was so deep Hannah wondered if he would ever come out of it.

She had prayed for him every day since he had read the letter but was concerned about how this might affect his relationship with the Lord. She noticed that Flynn kept most of his feelings to himself after that and rarely talked about his dream like he used to. His recovery, she thought, was going to be a long prayer journey, but she was determined not to abandon him in his darkest hour. She would be there for him until he could sort it out internally between him and the Lord.

She did not think it was a good time to tell him about her own internal struggle. Flynn and Hannah had agreed that it was time to start a family and she had stopped taking her pills over a year ago. Because of his recent ordeal with NASA, she knew he had not noticed how much time had gone by since that decision. But she had counted every month, and every month would wonder why she had not gotten pregnant. She now struggled with being there for Flynn *and* wondering why she couldn't seem to get pregnant. She would wait to tell him when the time was right.

Not one to shirk his official duties, Flynn continued to teach his classes at the academy with excellence. But it seemed as if the old Flynn was gone now; something had died inside him that day as he read that letter. Not only did Flynn realize how close he had come to being selected as an astronaut, but he seemed to sense that he would never come as close again. Time was now working against him and his age would increasingly become his enemy.

Although he was only 35, astronaut selections were being held more infrequently now and the next board was not scheduled for another four years. That would most likely put him out of the Air Force and around 40 by the time he reported for training, if selected. If not selected and the next board was another four years after that, he would be about 44 by the time he reported for training and would most likely be considered too old for the program. Without the driving force of his life there to propel him, he wondered if he could ever accomplish anything meaningful in life again.

At the end of his tour at the Air Force Academy, he was told by the supervisor about a new program that was offering early retirement for officers with 15 years of commissioned service. He had been promoted to Lieutenant Colonel the spring of that year and was told if he extended his tour for one more year, he could qualify for the program and retire with full benefits. He and Hannah prayed about it, but Flynn seemed resigned to it from the time he heard of the program.

"The chances of me getting another flying assignment after seven years out of the cockpit are slim to none, so I'm ready to leave." Flynn said to himself. "There's nothing to hold me in the Air Force any longer. We can work with Desert Reach as much as we feel led to, and I can still put in as a civilian applicant to the astronaut program whenever they hold a selection."

Flynn's attitude had now shifted to dutifully doing the thing that he knew the Lord had told him to do. The astronaut dream was now just an afterthought. He must have heard the Lord wrong that day on the grass. He wasn't quite ready to let the dream go entirely, but it no longer had the hold on him that it once had. He turned his attention to other things.

One day while they were talking about it, Hannah spoke to him with her trademark disarming boldness, "Flynn, are you willing to go a direction that God tells you to go, even it seems like it is causing the death of a dream that you know the Lord himself gave you?"

"What do you mean babe?"

"I mean, are you willing to lay your dream on the altar of God and let it die and trust him to resurrect it somehow, someway, just like Abraham had to do with Isaac?"

"I don't think I have a choice at this point. I know the Lord spoke specifically to me about using my aviation skills and my engineering education to help people solve problems and to help spread the word about the saving faith that is in his name. The only way I know to do that is to continue working with Desert Reach; to help make it a program that reaches multitudes for the gospel and changes their lives forever."

"Well then, let's throw our lives into that, spirit, soul, and body, until the Lord tells us to do something else," Hannah replied, "and when the time is right, the Lord will resurrect your dream, somehow, someway."

# :SUN SETTING DREAMS

CHAPTER 10

To their great delight, during their last year at the Academy, Hannah and Flynn found out that they were going to have a baby. It had been two years since she stopped taking her pills and they had just about given up on having children.

The day that she told him, Flynn replied with a repentant heart and with emotion evident in his voice, "God has been so good to us babe … so good. Will you forgive me for concentrating so much on my dream that I often failed to consider *your* dream. Will you forgive me for that babe?"

"Of course, my love … of course," she responded tenderly. Then, in typical Roberts' family tradition, they both embraced one another and burst into tears.

When Hannah had reached the 20 week mark, a sonogram had revealed that they would be having a baby boy. "Oh Flynn," Hannah had exclaimed joyfully, "you just don't know what this means to me, God has honored the desire of my heart and given me a boy."

Flynn retired from the Air Force after 15 years of service and he and Hannah felt like the Lord wanted them to settle in Colorado Springs. They would stay there to raise their newborn son and hopefully would have a few more children before they were too much older. By the end of his four years at the Academy, they had become so involved in Operation Desert Reach that the affiliated churches asked them to take over the reins of leadership. With their counsel and guidance, Flynn and Hannah formed a non-profit organization and called it the Desert Reach Foundation (DRF).

They had attached themselves to Hannah's home church during those years and had submitted to the pastoral leadership in both their personal lives and in their ministry. Eventually, that church too became one of the affiliated churches involved in DRF.

They rented a small office in a local shopping center and used it as a base of operations for the year-round efforts of Desert Reach. They started with one phone, one fax machine, and one computer. Flynn had adapted well to the PC revolution of the late eighties and early nineties and was on top of the latest upgrades in hardware and software; another asset he felt like he could leverage toward their new calling. Flynn and Hannah were licensed and ordained as ministers in the non-denominational organization that was the dominant influence in Desert Reach: Faith Churches of America (FCA).

Hannah took to it immediately, but being thought of as an ordained minister was something that Flynn would have to get used to. He still thought of himself as an Air Force officer and a military pilot, even though those days were now over for him. Still he was doing everything in his power, with his wife at his side, to do those things that the Lord had spoken to him about that day on the grass. He still flew, albeit in light civilian aircraft. He still used his engineering talents, and he used his leadership skills to manage the growing organization that DRF had become.

It became more and more fulfilling as the years went by and everything had been great on the home front except for one intensely personal issue with Hannah. She still pined about the fact that they had only been able to have one son, when she was in her late thirties. As she entered menopause, in her early fifties, it was especially painful for her, and she spent many an evening crying in Flynn's arms with her head on his chest.

"You're not the only one who had a dream," she would say, "It may sound funny to you but that dream burned in my heart the same way yours did."

Her dream had been to have a house full of kids and to teach them all to follow the dreams that God put in their hearts; to help them grow up knowing God the way that Flynn and Hannah did. She spent a lot of time in the Mohave ministering to the orphan children, loving them, caring for them, and mentoring them as much as she was able. It was her only outlet for the deep seated nurturing instincts that did not seem to wane as she grew older.

They had named their only son Sean Flynn Roberts, Junior, and he looked exactly like a perfect melt of the two of them. He had the facial structure and body build of his father, and the hair and eyes of his mother; a perfect mixture of Flynn's boyish good looks and Hannah's beauty. Just like Flynn's parents, they too had decided to call their son by his middle name and it seemed to fit him quite nicely. Flynn Jr. was a toddler the first time he went with his parents to the Mohave and before long, he became vitally involved in the ministry.

As Flynn's son grew up, serving at his side, he too had developed a fascination for the stars. It had not blossomed into the same kind of intensity that characterized his father's ambitions but there was always a deep appreciation for the stars and for flight. Flynn had spent many an evening telling his son about how God made the stars and about how unimaginably large the universe was. He had followed in his father's footsteps and had become a pilot, but only a civilian pilot, and only so he could use those skills for the work of the ministry. He had gone to Bible School instead of college and had developed into quite a powerful preacher.

After Bible School, Flynn Jr. met and married Wendy Moore, a young woman from Arizona who had caught the vision of Desert Reach while on a youth mission trip to the Mohave. By the time they were in their early twenties, Flynn and Wendy had become a tremendous asset to the DRF. A year so after they married, they gave birth to a red headed, spunky little girl who began to look and act very much like her grandfather as she grew up. They called her Mattie.

As he had determined he would do, Flynn applied dutifully for the astronaut program for two more selection cycles. And as he had predicted, he was in his mid-forties by the time he submitted his final application. He had listed his ministry activities on both applications in the faint hope that the folks at NASA might broaden their view of what an astronaut should look like. After all he thought, he had accumulated almost as much time in civilian aircraft as in military and was using his systems engineering skills to solve real world problems and to help real people.

But in the end he just didn't fit their mold any longer and neither of the two applications were successful. He was also getting a little long in the tooth, from their perspective, and that had definitely not helped. After submitting a total of five applications for the program, he never submitted another. If he was ever going into space, he thought, it was not going to be with NASA.

His friend Matt Parker had gone on to fly a total of three shuttle missions with NASA; the last two as mission commander, and Flynn and Hannah had been there for all of the launches. After his last launch, Matt had retired from the Air Force at the rank of Colonel and took a job as a consultant to a fledgling aerospace corporation called Space Reach International (SRI); one of the few that were involved in developing private-sector-based manned space flight programs. It was headquartered in nearby Denver, so Matt and Flynn saw each other often and kept each other posted on their respective organizations as the years went by.

Flynn and Hannah would spend six months out of the year in the Mohave and the rest of the time they would travel the country raising money for the DRF. Each year, Matt always saw to it that SRI made a significant contribution to DRF, which really helped it to grow and expand. Soon Flynn and Hannah's tiny start-up office had blossomed into a facility that housed 30 full time employees and a full complement of cubicles, each with its own phone and computer. Flynn and Hannah shared a small office with two desks at opposite ends of the room, each with their own phone line and computer. It was spartan by most company standards but functional enough for their needs.

As the years went by, Flynn had many opportunities to stand under the desert skies of the Mohave and stare at the beauty of a starlit night. He would spend many hours alone under those stars, praying and worshipping God, and thanking him for the life he had been given. The array of stars never ceased to be breathtaking to him and the sight of them always had the same effect. They seemed to be calling him, calling him by name sometimes, but always calling him to them. Though the dream had grown fainter, it was always there at some level, and there were many times that the tears would flow. But he had determined in his heart that he would not bring up the subject again to the Lord. It felt as if his dream of one day flying in space was slowly and agonizingly becoming a fading dream, a sun setting dream, and one that he would finally have to let go of, sooner or later.

During his fifties, Flynn had fought increasingly hard against the growing sensation that his dream was gradually slipping through his fingers. To his dismay, it would often manifest itself in the form of an uncharacteristic crankiness and an irritability that would come on him suddenly. He was alarmed to find himself snapping at his wife and son with a harshness and a bitterness that they had never seen in him before. It worried him a lot and he thought about it and prayed about it often.

There was the constant feeling that time had become his greatest enemy and each month and year that passed just added to the impatience of it all; the seeming impossibility of it all. He would often turn to the story of Abraham for consolation during these times. After all, Abraham didn't even *receive* his dream from the Lord until he was 75 and didn't see it begin to manifest for another 25 years.

Yet God managed to fulfill Abraham's dream; so why not his, Flynn often told himself. But then again, his circumstances seemed to be so different, and his dream very far removed from that of Abraham. It was an internal battle that he ended up fighting alone, for he had long ago stopped talking about his dream to anyone.

The years had drifted by as he faithfully followed the command of the Lord to use his talent, his education, and his experience to reach the unreached ... five years turned into 10 ... 10 years turned into 20 ... and 20 years turned into 40. Although there was a definite sense of fulfillment for all that had been accomplished through DRF over the years, the dream he had held for so long had become a nagging ache in his heart.

By the time he was in his seventies, Flynn had finally decided it was time to let go of his dream altogether. He was in the sunset of his life and it seemed fitting for him to do so. One day when they were in the Mohave, he and his son strolled out under the stars for a walk and a talk like they had done so many times before. Flynn Jr. was thinking about how much he missed his wife Wendy and their daughter Mattie. Not surprisingly, he thought, she too had inherited the family fascination for the stars and would have been there with the two of them if she could have been. He couldn't get over how brilliant she had become in such a short time in her life and was as proud as any father could be.

Mattie had developed a particularly strong aptitude in mathematics and science and had qualified for a special scholarship to the Massachusetts Institute of Technology (MIT). She had finished high school at age 14 and by the time she was 20 had earned her PhD in Physics from MIT. Mattie had concentrated her research in astrophysics and space science and had been invited to start a Post-Doctoral fellowship at the Keck Observatory. Wendy had stayed behind to help her pack and prepare for the move from Boston to Hawaii. Flynn, Hannah, and Flynn Jr. would be leaving the Mohave soon to help her with that move.

Flynn was in a reflective mood and for the first time in his life had mentally added up the years he had dedicated to the ministry since he had left the Air Force. By his count, he had spent the last 40 plus years of his life dedicated to the vision of Operation Desert Reach. With the stars as a backdrop, he finally decided it was time to tell his son about his childhood dream of one day flying in space. And even though the dream seemed lost to him now, he felt compelled for some reason to share his heart with his son like never before.

Perhaps, he thought, it was his way of symbolically laying his dream on the altar of sacrifice, like his wife had advised him to do so many years ago. It would be his way of finally letting go; of plunging the knife into the heart of his dream, once and for all.

Flynn Jr. listened intently as his father finally told him that he had always wanted to fly in space but never got the chance. Although it took him a while, and he became very emotional at times, he was able to tell his story between occasional bouts of weeping and wiping away of tears. When it dawned on Flynn Jr. that this was a special time of release for his father, he began to tear up also.

He reached out to his dad and they embraced one another tightly, weeping together for quite a long while. When the emotion had finally subsided somewhat, they stepped back from their embrace and Flynn Jr. took a good long look at his father. To him, he looked as if he had finally exhaled a breath that he had been holding for his entire life.

Though he was still very emotional and his words were slow and halting, Flynn Jr. felt it was time to speak, "Dad ... I know all about it ... and I know it's a sensitive subject with you ... and that you have never, ever talked about it with me. But mom and I have talked about it ... and prayed about it a lot over the years. Dad ... all I know to tell you is this: I don't believe any of the energy you expended chasing that dream was wasted. One day God will use it for his purposes, for his glory; maybe not in this life, but in the next."

"Maybe so son ... maybe so," Flynn replied.

He felt a gentle hand slip into his own and turned to see that his beloved Hannah had walked out under the stars to be with them. The gray streaks in her hair seemed to shimmer in the starlight as she kissed him softly. Over the years, those streaks had become quite beautiful to him, but he knew she did not feel the same way about them as he did.

"Thought I'd find you two out here," she said.

The three of them just stood there for a few moments, staring at the stars and not uttering a word. Together they breathed in the beauty of the great canvas that had been stretched out before them by the Creator; the same God that all of them had served with all of their hearts. It was as if, for a moment, the stars were theirs to possess. As they gazed into the heavens, Flynn was the first to raise his right hand and reach out toward the brilliant display. He was followed shortly by Hannah and then by Flynn Jr. Tears gently flowed down their cheeks as they stood there together, quietly reaching toward the great canvas of the stars.

# SECTION TWO

# :NEXT LIFE

# :PROLOGUE

After the Transformation, Flynn had finally gotten to visit another world, only not in the way he had always imagined. Although he knew that the distance traveled was unimaginable, his trip to the Sides of the North was over in an instant. There was no sensation of space travel or of the billions of light years that were traversed in just a moment of time, at least not for him. One second he was on the Earth and the next second he was on the Sides of the North, and all he knew about the Sides was that it was a planet in another dimensional realm, in the Second Sphere, located some unfathomable distance due north of Earth.

He suddenly found himself on the Sides and in the midst of the Great City of the First Born. He was surrounded by multitudes of the Many Brethren, all of them transformed together in an instant.

The first thing he noticed was he seemed to be younger, about 33 he thought, though he knew that just a moment ago, he was in his seventies. The next thing he noticed, with great delight, was that his gray hair was gone and the loose skin under his neck, his "turkey neck," as he often called it, had firmed up or disappeared. He felt a strength in his body that was clearly supernatural and was aware that his new body possessed amazing capabilities. His eyesight was keen, his hearing was acute, and his mental faculties were amazingly enhanced.

His youthful appearance would take some getting used to, he had noted, especially when he was reunited with his parents. They had died some 20 years before the Transformation and he had buried them next to one another in Bedford, barely a year apart. And yet now, here they all were, looking as young and as vigorous as they did in their thirties. When Hannah, Flynn Jr., Wendy, and Mattie had joined them a short while later, it was a sight to see; four generations of the Roberts family standing together, and except for Mattie who looked a bit younger, they all looked essentially the same age.

And then there were the new found powers that would also take some getting used to. He was in some sort of immortal and indestructible body and he had the sense that he had barely tapped into its full potential. It could do some of the same things his other body could do yet this new body had profound capabilities that far exceeded the capabilities of the previous one.

He could eat food for example, but only if he wanted to. It was not necessary because the source of his nutrition and energy was his ever present connection to the First Born. When he did eat, he was delighted to discover that the food was completely energized by his body systems with no need to void any waste matter whatsoever. Now that was something he could definitely live without, he chuckled to himself.

As it turned out, there would be a time of intensive training dedicated to getting to know his new body and to developing and growing in these new found powers before the coming invasion.

Before the training began, everyone had to stand before the Bema Evaluation which was conducted by the First Born himself. Your assignments in the Next Life, to a great extent, were determined by how things went during that evaluation. Everything you had accomplished in the First Life was evaluated whether good or bad. For some it was a time of great loss but for others it was a time of great reward.

Most individuals received their assignments immediately but many had to wait until after the invasion to receive theirs. Flynn was in the latter category, but he took it in stride. Things had gone well for him at the Bema Evaluation. He was told by the First Born that he would receive a series of assignments. He would exercise authority throughout the Middle East region and then beyond. Two initial assignments would segue into one that was extremely important to the Kingdom and very near to the heart of the First Born. He would be given the details immediately after the invasion, and for Flynn that was good enough. He concentrated on his training and prepared himself mentally, physically, and spiritually for the coming invasion.

Near the end of this training there was the Great Feast of the First Born which was followed quickly by preparation and planning for the great invasion; the invasion of Earth by the First Born and the armies of the Many Brethren.

Wonderful and indescribable as it was, his time in the Great City seemed to fly by and Flynn soon found himself back on the Earth with a new mission and a newly transformed body. The invasion had been swift and although resistance had been massive by Earthly standards, it was over in a matter of hours.

Although seen as excessively violent by some on the Earth, the necessity of a swift and decisive invasion was beyond question from the unique vantage point of the Many Brethren. They had watched from the Sides as the culmination of rebellion on Earth had coincided with the imminent destruction of the planet. And this destruction was not confined to Earth alone. Indeed the fabric of space-time itself had begun to violently unravel. Had the First Born not intervened when he did, every star in the universe would have been extinguished, every habitable planet would have been destroyed, and not a single human being would be left alive in the First Dimensional Sphere.

Soon there would be the gruesome task of finding and burying the hundreds of millions that had fallen opposing the invasion. After that, there would be the enormous task of cleaning up, containing the radioactive contamination, and rebuilding the cities of the world that had been ravaged during the Time of Jacob's Trouble.

Though their tasks were varied and their titles were different, the Many Brethren had one overriding charge that they all shared. They were to assist the First Born in his benevolent reign over Jacob's Children, the ones who had survived the Time of Jacob's Trouble. They were to help them rebuild their world and render assistance as the Knowledge Seas were loosed for the benefit of all of mankind. The promotion of the Children's welfare, peace, and prosperity was the Brethren's highest priority.

There were now two classes of human beings that occupied planet Earth, the Brethren and the Children. The Brethren would never face death again because of the Transformation, but the Children owed their continued longevity to right choices and chief among them was their allegiance to and their love for the First Born.

The antediluvian moisture shield in the upper atmosphere of the Earth had been restored and thus, the remnant of harmful ultraviolet rays that could not be filtered by the Earth's ozone layer alone had been effectively neutralized. Excessive exposure to ultraviolet radiation had long been suspected by some to be a prime reason that human cells ceased to reproduce themselves after a person reached a certain age. They were correct, for the most part, and this enemy of life that had plagued mankind for thousands of years had steadily abated during the first hundred years of the Millennium. Thus, for the faithful Children, the aging process beyond what was required for full maturity had been stopped.

The world system that had wielded such influence over mankind was now completely under the control of the Kingdom of the First Born, and the Dark One had been confined to the Second Sphere, imprisoned in the Endless Void for the duration of the Millennium. Thus, two out of the three evil influences that had plagued mankind since the beginning of recorded history had now been removed. The only thing left to affect mankind now was the desires of the flesh: the individual passions and lusts that still reared their ugly influence from time to time, given the wrong kind of encouragement or the wrong set of circumstances. Every other vestige of the curse had been removed.

As a result, sickness, disease, and death were rare, but were not unheard of. Yes, even in a near perfect world of peace and prosperity, there were those who stubbornly refused to bow to the Kingdom of the First Born. On rare occasions, these individuals would incite violence and rebellion which would result in sickness, accidents, injuries or death. Consequently, in addition to their many other duties, the Many Brethren were to assist the First Born in enforcing the peace throughout the Kingdom. Anywhere in the world where violence or rebellion was found, it was to be put down by the Brethren. Even if you were not a member of the Kingdom Peace Enforcers (KPE), whether Local, National, or International, all the Brethren had an ancillary duty to support this mission. There would be no wars during this period because the KPE and the Brethren would be there to neutralize any discord or rebellion before it escalated out of control. The protection and safety of the peoples of the world were first and foremost.

Since the Knowledge Seas had been released, many of the scientific puzzles that had stymied mankind before the Millennium had now been solved. It was as if the lights had been turned on in a room where everyone thought the lights were already on. There was an explosion of revelation that spawned the greatest expansion of applied knowledge, technology and creativity that the world had ever seen. Even if you combined the waves of knowledge released in the Renaissance of the fourteenth through the seventeenth century with the Industrial and Information Revolutions of the nineteenth through the twenty first, there was no comparison with the tsunami of synergistic knowledge and creativity that characterized the release of the Knowledge Seas.

Within the first 100 years of the Millennium, there were quantum leaps in the arts, literature, agriculture, transportation, infrastructure, architecture, and especially in power production. Irrigation techniques and new methods of enhancing crop yields were introduced that soon rendered world hunger a thing of the past. Only able bodied individuals who refused to work suffered hunger and then not for long. Hunger turned out to be a powerful incentive that worked against laziness wherever it was found.

In addition to these major breakthroughs, medical technology had advanced to the point that all of the world's dreaded diseases had been eliminated. Hospitals and emergency rooms existed but were there for the occasional accidents that still occurred in a modern society and for the few that did get sick from time to time.

The Knowledge Seas also birthed a new era of innovation and entrepreneurship that boosted worldwide commerce and resulted in a booming global economy. Millions of businesses, ranging in size from small businesses to large industrial conglomerates were birthed as a result, bringing worldwide unemployment to around 1%. Only nations and individuals who actively rebelled against the authority of the First Born or the Many Brethren suffered in any meaningful way. Most of the pain or suffering experienced in this new world of the Millennium could ultimately be traced back to self-inflicted causes.

Even our basic scientific understanding of the universe, how it was made, and how it existed, was greatly enhanced. With a little help from the First Born, even the vaunted and much sought after *Theory of Everything* had been developed into a cohesive mathematical and physical description of the laws of the universe. The four fundamental forces of the universe, electromagnetism, weak nuclear force, strong nuclear force, and gravity had been pulled together into one surprisingly simple explanation of how everything worked. Though not completely validated, elements of string theory had been found to be an accurate explanation of how the laws that governed quantum mechanics and the laws that governed general relativity co-existed together in perfect harmony. But there were twists. As it turned out the universe was not as complicated as it had been made out to be by some. There were no multiple universes, for example, just one expanse of created existence that manifested itself in three distinct dimensional spheres.

The First Sphere was the realm of the known physical universe and the one that mankind was most familiar with. The Second Sphere was the realm of the Celestial, the Angelics, the Sides of the North, and the Great City of the First Born. Mankind had had some dealings with this realm throughout history, but it was not nearly as familiar to them as the First. Finally, the Third Sphere was the realm in which the Creator shared his existence with the other two.

Each of these spheres of existence manifested itself in three spatial dimensions, although they were not exactly the same as one another in all respects. With this is mind, there was a total of nine distinctly different dimensions within the universe that we shared with the Creator. Time was the tenth dimension that governed all cause and effect relationships and linked together all three spheres.

But beyond the Third Sphere, the realm of shared existence, there was a realm that was exclusive to the Creator, where only he could dwell. Others could visit this realm on rare occasions, but only by permission. It was referred to in the Sacred Text as the Third Heaven, but to the scientific world, it was the so-called eleventh dimension that had been theorized by many before the Millennium.

# :RECONSTRUCTION

After the invasion was over and resistance had been neutralized, Flynn was instructed by the First Born to find a place to live in the Old City of Jerusalem. He quickly found a modest two bedroom townhouse in the heart of the Old City and spent the first few nights in his new home. He wasn't sure how long he would be living there, but he definitely liked the fact that he would be living, at least temporarily, where all the action originated, close to the Royal Palace, and close to the First Born.

The first night that he spent in the townhouse, he was sitting alone on his couch wondering what his first assignment would be. So far, all he had been told was that he would be staying here in the Old City and that he would exercise authority of some kind in the Middle East region. Beyond that, he had no idea what he would be doing.

He was startled by the sudden appearance of a man that looked almost identical to him. He stood facing Flynn in the living room, directly across from the coffee table where he had just propped up his feet. The stranger was dressed in a white suit and looked to be about the same height, weight and build as Flynn. He had the same hair and eye color and except for his skin tone, looked very much like a carbon copy of him. The one distinguishing difference was the burned brass tan that covered him from head to toe. He had not come through the door but had just materialized in front of Flynn's coffee table. Flynn pulled his feet off of the coffee table and sat there for a moment wondering who he was and how he should address him.

But the stranger spoke before he could think of something to say, "Greetings Dr. Roberts, my name is Magan Flynn, which means 'shield or protector of Flynn'. You have not always known me, but I have always known you. I am your Guardian and was assigned to you the moment you were conceived in your mother's womb. I can now reveal myself to you and render to you whatever assistance may be necessary to carry out your Next Life assignments from the First Born."

"Was that you at my side during the Transformation?" Flynn asked with the faintest of recognition. "Your voice certainly sounds familiar. I know I've heard it somewhere before."

"Yes that was me at your side during the Transformation and yes, you have heard my voice before. I stand ready now to serve you further. What are your instructions for me?"

Before responding to Magan, Flynn wanted to take the opportunity to get to know him a little better. He wasn't sure how frequent these visits would be so he started with a few basic questions.

"As you have said, you know me much better than I know you. And I am sensing on the inside that you have been there many times to help me, to keep me safe, sometimes even to keep me alive, and most of the time I was barely aware of it. Am I correct?"

"Yes, Dr. Roberts, you are correct," Magan responded. "In your First Life, it was my pleasure to serve you in this capacity. I served as your protector and your shield. There were many times that I kept you from harm and one time in particular where I saved you from an untimely death."

"I assume you are referring to the accident I had at Edwards," Flynn replied with an emotional tremble in his voice.

"Yes, Flynn, I helped to save you that day and was glad that you were able to complete the assignments given to you later as you stood on the grass," Magan responded.

"That is the essence of my mission," Magan continued, "that for which I was created; to assist you in completing the assignments given to you by the Creator. The only thing that has changed in this Next Life is the nature of my service. You no longer need me as a protector, but I will continue to serve you as a messenger. The First Born will speak to you on the inside, sometimes through dreams and visions, and sometimes in person, concerning major assignments, but I will be there to help you, to give you amplifying instructions, and to provide details of how you will carry out those assignments."

Flynn was tempted to ask Magan for more details of the times that he had kept him from harm, especially the day of the accident, but sensed a deep humility in him and a modesty that would make it uncomfortable for him to talk too much about himself. He settled for one request and asked Magan with a smile on his face, "Would it be all right if I gave you a hug?"

"It would be my pleasure, Dr. Roberts," Magan replied. Flynn stood up, walked around the coffee table and embraced Magan. To his surprise, Magan hugged him back, firmly and emotionally. And in that one embrace, Magan was able to convey the full extent of how he felt about his charge. Flynn felt a deep and abiding love that emanated from within Magan and flowed powerfully into his own heart. He recognized it immediately as the same Spirit that connected them both to the Creator and to the First Born.

Still reeling from the depth of love that he felt in that embrace, Flynn released Magan. He stood back and said, "Magan, thank you for all the times you have been there for me and I didn't even know it."

Magan smiled and said, "You are welcome Dr. Roberts. Now if you have any more questions or instructions for me, I am at your service."

Flynn replied, "Do you know what my new assignment will be here in the Old City?"

Magan replied, "I do not know at this time but I have been instructed to tell you that you are to reunite with your wife Hannah. After some well-deserved time off, you are to bring her back here to the Old City. Your son Flynn Jr. and his wife Wendy are already here and have been charged with caring for and teaching the refugees and orphans that were left here during the Time of Jacob's Trouble. When Hannah gets here, she is to join them in their important work helping the little ones who have been so devastated over the last seven years of conflict. After this, you will be given your first assignment by the First Born."

"Wow, how awesome is that! I'll be right here with my wife, my son, and my daughter in law doing the work of the First Born in the heart of the Kingdom?" Flynn exclaimed excitedly.

With a bit of a smile on his face, he continued. "As far as instructions are concerned, I want you to know that giving you instructions is going to take some getting used to. Nevertheless, could you help me coordinate a simultaneous teleportation so that Hannah and I can reunite in Colorado Springs?"

"Of course I can, and by the way, whether you realized it or not, I was always there to assist you in the First Life. You needed only to speak words that aligned with the Sacred Text and the will of the Creator for me to carry out your wishes. The same is true in the Next Life which you have just begun."

Flynn thought about that and realized he had missed a lot in the First Life. How much more had he missed because of simple ignorance, he wondered?

"Well, OK then, get to it Magan. Report to me when you are done!"

"Very well Dr. Roberts," Magan replied.

And with those words he disappeared upward in a flash of light that Flynn thought resembled something like a controlled lightning bolt.

"I think I'm going to like this arrangement," Flynn said aloud.

"Yep, I am definitely going to like this!"

After settling in to his new surroundings, Flynn was given three months leave and was given permission from the First Born to execute a simultaneous *jump* with Hannah. They would reunite at their old home in Colorado Springs.

The men of the Brethren were required to train and to fight in the invasion but women only did so if they wanted to. Hannah had chosen, as had most of the women, to teach and to help nurture The Discarded Ones, the vast multitude of children that were being raised in the nurseries, playgrounds, and schools of the Great City. Thus, Flynn had been in the Old City in Jerusalem since the invasion but Hannah was still on the Sides in the Great City.

At the agreed upon time, they executed their *jump*. Flynn *jumped* from the Old City in Jerusalem on the Earth, and Hannah *jumped* from the Great City on the Sides.

They both arrived within a fraction of a second apart, Hannah first, then Flynn, and were close enough to immediately join hands when they saw one another in the backyard of their old home.

"How did you beat me here Hannah?" Flynn cocked his head and continued, "You came all the way from the Sides, and I just came from the other side of the Earth."

"Well, remember, Flynn, we have new bodies and new abilities, but we're still not perfect, nor will we ever be. We still can't do this as precisely as the First Born."

"Yea, I guess you're right," Flynn said as he embraced her and hugged her tightly.

"So good to see you babe, I missed you, especially during the fighting. Not that the outcome was ever in doubt but I'm so glad that part is over … all those people … it was so sad … so sad," he said with a tremble in his voice.

"I know honey, but now we get to do the exciting part; we have a world to rebuild. We get to prepare the way for the Knowledge Seas to be loosed on the Earth. But first let's start with getting this house in shape, what do you think?"

"Yea, let's do it!" exclaimed Flynn. He grabbed Hannah's hand and they headed for the back door. They had materialized in the backyard where their privacy fence had allowed them to do so discreetly, without anyone knowing about it but them, and of course the First Born.

When they had completed three months' worth of clean up, remodeling, and restoration, it was time for Flynn to meet with the First Born in Jerusalem to receive his first assignment. As instructed, Flynn took Hannah with him and they traveled together to Jerusalem via conventional means.

It had taken a while to get the world's airline industry up and running again but things were returning to normal quickly. Those first few months after the invasion were dedicated to clean up; to making way for the coming reconstruction and modernization, and one of the first things that had to be revived was the world's transportation infrastructure.

"This is so much slower," Flynn whispered as they rode on one of their airliners, "but I guess we need to learn to travel this way unless there is a good reason to do otherwise."

"It's OK babe, it'll give us time to talk some more. I've been meaning to ask you if you've heard any news about Flynn Jr. and Wendy. We haven't seen them since we were together on the Sides and I was wondering if there was any news about their assignments. And also, when were you going to tell me why *I'm* going to Jerusalem with you? Don't get me wrong, I'm thrilled to be with you, but I'd like to know what I'm going to be doing. All Magen Hannah told me was that I would be working with children and you would fill me in on the details at the appropriate time."

"So you met your Guardian too?" Flynn whispered inquisitively.

"Yes, I met him while I was on the Sides in the Great City, and by the way, he told me that Guardians with female charges use the feminine form of the Hebrew, for them Magen is spelled with an e."

With a sense of wonder in his voice and a smile on his face, Flynn continued. "Well now that our secret is out on that, let me tell you what Magan Flynn told me right before I left to meet you at our house. I wanted it to be a surprise and was going to wait till I received my own assignment, but since you asked, here is what I know so far. Flynn Jr. has been charged with teaching the refugees and the orphaned children in the Old City, the ones who survived the Time of Jacob's Trouble. He and Wendy are already in Jerusalem and you'll be working with them both; nurturing and caring for the little ones that need so much love at this time."

Tears welled up in Hannah's eyes as she spoke with a palpable anticipation, "Thanks be to the Creator for the wisdom of the First Born! I can't think of anything I'd rather be doing during this time! And I get to work with my son and daughter in law too!

Flynn, I just know your assignment will be as fulfilling as mine, I just know it!"

Shortly after they arrived in Jerusalem, Flynn was summoned to the Royal Palace and received his first assignment from the First Born himself. He was to be at the forefront of reconstruction and modernization efforts as the Chief Technology Advisor for the Middle East region. Rebuilding aviation and associated infrastructure were to be his special emphasis. His familiarity with desert topography and ecology would be especially helpful in the region and would complement his experience in aviation and systems engineering.

As Hannah had predicted, his new assignment was right down his alley and very exciting to boot. Flynn was thrilled that he would get to use many of the skills he had learned in his First Life in an aviation related, high technology based endeavor. And it was an important assignment; important enough that it had been given to him personally by the First Born.

He was to set up a small headquarters in Jerusalem and was assigned a staff of 15 leaders and 400 workers, all of them from among Jacob's Children. They were all to be housed in Jerusalem but were advised to be ready for travel at any moment. The jobs would come swiftly and sometimes sporadically, so they needed to be ready to go at a moment's notice.

Their efforts would be funded by the taxes that were paid to the Kingdom of the First Born. Every working individual in the world, regardless of what nation they belonged to, paid the same tax rate to the Kingdom, regardless of their income. This was in addition to the tithe that was given to their local place of worship. Ten percent for the spiritual Kingdom and ten percent for the physical Kingdom eventually spawned the mantra of *10/10 for the Kingdom* and was freely and willingly given by the faithful Children of the world.

The tax rate was modest compared to the rates in the industrialized nations of the world before the coming of the First Born. But the people of the world soon realized that if every working individual paid the same modest rate of ten percent, huge amounts of revenue could be collected while leaving plenty of individual wages left over to stimulate the world's economy. This in turn would broaden the tax base by creating millions of new jobs, and would increase revenues to the Kingdom by even greater amounts. Upon implementation of this simple tax, the First Born ensured a booming world economy which would be necessary to fund the worldwide reconstruction efforts.

They only had 50 years to complete their assignment as it had been given to Flynn, and he was determined to make the deadline that had been given to him by the First Born: MA 51. The new time took a little getting used to, as well as all the other things, but after a while it was as natural as AD and BC had been in the First Life. MA was an acronym for the Latin phrase, *Millenial Annus*, which means Millennial Year. Thus MA 51 was Millennial Year 51.

Their charge was to rebuild and modernize the aviation infrastructure that had been destroyed or damaged in the Middle East region during the time of Jacob's Trouble, a monumental task to say the least. It would involve rebuilding runways, towers, hangar facilities, power plants, radar systems, aircraft manufacturing plants, and the necessary modernization of these facilities to help build or to accommodate the new space planes that were being manufactured by Space Reach International of Denver, Colorado.

SRI's Starliner had been chosen in a space plane fly-off competition at the end of MA 1. And although prototype testing was almost complete, it would take the better part of the 50 years they had to produce the craft in the numbers required to meet the demands of the burgeoning air-space transportation sector. Not only would intercontinental travel be revolutionized with these craft, but flying into low Earth orbit would finally be the relatively routine exercise that had been envisioned for decades but never achieved.

Matt Parker, Flynn's best friend from the First Life, had been CEO of the massive company that SRI had become before the Transformation, and their connection would be a tremendous asset in the rebuilding efforts. Matt was now one of the Many Brethren and was Flynn's counterpart on the aviation asset side of the reconstruction equation. Flynn would prepare the facilities and Matt would supply the Starliners.

In some cases it would involve supplying a preassembled fleet of the new craft to a modernized air-space port, and other times it would involve supplying the engineering and technical support that would allow a particular plant to manufacture key components or in some cases, to completely assemble the craft. In either case, it would present many opportunities for Flynn and Matt to work together and to reestablish their friendship. Flynn looked forward to their first meeting with great anticipation.

His first meeting with Matt was in Jerusalem and it was truly a joyous occasion. He had last seen him about a year before the Transformation and had gotten a tour of the SRI main manufacturing plant in Denver. They had talked at length about their plans to field a space plane capable of flying from an airport runway all the way into low Earth orbit and back again. It would be a craft that was also capable of intercontinental travel at unheard of speeds by skimming the edge of space at hypersonic speeds during its flight profile.

Attempts had been made before to produce such a space plane but funding had always fallen short, usually because it was attached to some government program and was subject to the whims of politicians who always seemed to be short sighted when it came to a vision for space. Through Matt's leadership and vision, SRI was able to assemble a solid coalition of companies with the strong backing of investors who had very deep pockets. They had developed a prototype design that had been tested with a few trips to low Earth orbit and only needed to work through a few technical glitches before full scale production could begin.

After the Transformation and the Great Vanishing, there was widespread chaotic disruption of world commerce and the company had to temporarily suspend operations. After the invasion, Matt had been charged again with overseeing company operations and was instrumental in restoring order and productivity at SRI. Within a year they had successfully test flown their prototypes, the Starliner XP, passenger liner, and the Starliner XC, cargo vessel. This had clearly demonstrated the feasibility of space plane operations of this kind.

Their design was deemed the best available technology in a very competitive fly-off competition, and soon they were given the monumental task of providing these platforms for the emerging air-space ports of the world. The other two companies that had invested billions of dollars on their own alternatives were awarded support contracts to keep them viable and to provide parts and expertise from more than one manufacturer. It was a fair competition, yet the First Born did not want to encourage the possible development of any new technology into a monopoly. As it turned out, there would be plenty of opportunities for high tech companies to ride the wave of the Knowledge Seas and develop new and exciting technological breakthroughs for the benefit of the world.

Flynn and Matt embraced one another warmly, and there were a few tears as well.

"I haven't seen you since the Transformation, and for some reason we never ran into each other on the Sides," Flynn said with a big grin on his face.

"Sorry about that," replied Matt. "I had several private meetings with the First Born on a confidential project."

"Well, as usual, I feel like I'm the last to know about some things, but I'm not about to question the wisdom of the First Born," Flynn declared.

Matt then picked up the conversation on space plane operations exactly where he had left off the last time they were together. He quickly got Flynn up to speed on the progress that had been made with the Starliner XP and the Starliner XC. The XP was about the size of the old Concorde Jet and was equally sleek and beautiful. The XC was a little more bulky in the center to make room for medium to large size cargo containers but still managed to take on a kind of pregnant sleekness, like a beautiful woman who was nevertheless great with child. Both variants would be used not only for intercontinental transport but also to fly personnel and cargo back and forth from a planned orbiting space station.

After several hours of planning and negotiations, Matt said goodbye and left Flynn's office. They had both agreed; SRI would meet the required production schedule and Flynn's Reconstruction/Modernization (RM) teams would have the designated airports and aircraft manufacturing facilities ready in time to accommodate *both* versions of the Starliner within the specified timeframe. They covenanted together that day to do whatever was necessary to assist one another in the process. Together, they would work to meet or beat the deadline of MA 51.

After the meeting, Flynn left his office in a reflective mood. As he walked home to his small but cozy two bedroom townhouse, he thought about how miniscule it was compared to the palatial home he had left in the Great City. But he didn't mind. It was only a few blocks from the high rise office complex where his temporary headquarters were located. It was in the heart of the Old City of Jerusalem and as he walked, he thought about the dramatic turnaround of events that had demonstrated to the world how ludicrous it was to consider Jerusalem to be anything other than the capital of Israel, a land that had been given to the descendants of Abraham by the Creator himself. In the midst of reconstruction efforts, there were still signs of the destruction and devastation that reminded the city's occupants of the historical and prophetic significance of these events.

Furthermore, Jerusalem was now the capital of the world, and the First Born himself was there to make sure everyone in the world recognized that fact.

"The human death toll was staggering," he thought, "so many had lost their lives because of unwillingness to acknowledge what was plainly true."

And after the Transformation, the conflict over the status of Israel had escalated to truly horrific proportions. He still felt deep pangs of sorrow as he realized that two thirds of the world's population, over five billion people, had been slaughtered during The Time of Jacob's Trouble.

He tried not to think about it anymore and chose to think about the solace of his townhouse and the company that was waiting for him there. As he opened the door to his home, Hannah was there to greet him. She was absolutely stunning, especially since the Transformation. She looked to be in her early thirties with jet black hair, shimmering blue eyes, a perfect figure, and smooth wrinkle-free skin. He never said it, but he often thought how much he missed those silver streaks that appeared in her hair as they grew older and grayer together in the First Life. He kissed her and hugged her and then they sat on the couch in their small den to share the latest with each other.

There was still that romantic feeling between them despite what they had been led to believe would be the case in the Next Life. The only thing that was missing from their former life together was their physical intimacy. That type of union was no longer possible or necessary with the Many Brethren, which, in spite of the traditional name, included all the females who had also experienced the Transformation. Strange as it may have seemed, neither of them missed that part of their former life for they knew that they had access to a unity that was far deeper and superior.

This was especially true for those who were still married to one another at the time of the Transformation. They were still husband and wife in the Next Life; they just didn't sleep together, in the intimate sense that is. They could still curl up together under the covers if they wanted to, but sleep was simply not as necessary as it was before the Transformation.

Sleep for the Brethren was only necessary to provide a platform for dreams to be communicated from the First Born. During those times of intimacy with him, dreams and assignments would be planted in their hearts that would help chart the course of their Next Life.

As they sat there on the couch enjoying one another's company, Flynn turned to Hannah and excitedly told her, "Flynn Jr. and Wendy will be coming to see us later this evening. They're wrapping up their teaching for the day and will be here soon. I thought we could all have dinner together."

That evening during dinner, Flynn Jr. and Wendy talked about their daughter Mattie and about the assignment she had been given back in Colorado Springs. She, of course, was one of the women who had chosen to fight in the invasion so it was a bit of a letdown afterwards when she was assigned as the STEM Curriculum Director for that region of the country. She was asked to work with the school boards to bolster their academic programs in mathematics and the sciences. It was an important assignment because the Knowledge Seas were just beginning to be loosed, and the Kingdom was interested in preparing the coming generations for the high tech world that was to come.

She had been hoping for a space related assignment as well so they were concerned about what that would do to her internal motivation. The study of the stars was the passion of her First

Life, and she hadn't even made it to her Post-Doctoral assignment at the Keck Observatory when the Transformation happened.

"But she's a good trooper," Flynn Jr. remarked. "I know she will serve faithfully in her new role. And I am convinced that, ultimately, the First Born will not forget the desire of her heart."

"Well I suppose we'll just have to wait and see how that all works out," Flynn added resolutely. "One good thing, babe, Mattie has been an excellent tenant and has taken real good care of our house in Colorado Springs. In the meantime, we have our own assignments to keep us busy, eh?"

As they thoroughly enjoyed each other's company that evening, the four finally turned their attention to finishing the sumptuous dinner that Hannah had prepared. They were together once again, if only for a little while; each with their own new assignment and the anticipation of something truly exciting about to unfold.

# :TECHNOLOGY ADVISOR

During the time of reconstruction and modernization, Flynn had to do a lot of traveling with his teams throughout the Middle East. He kept busy, but so did Hannah. She would spend the bulk of her days with Flynn Jr. and Wendy in the Old City, teaching and caring for the young orphaned Children. The months went by quickly and soon turned into years and then … decades.

By the time that Flynn had completed his initial assignment, MA 49 had rolled around and Flynn Jr., Wendy, and Hannah were teaching the grandchildren of those original orphans. The school they had built had started out ad hoc in hastily prepared shelters and rented buildings but had grown into a full scale education facility now called the Kingdom Education Institute (KEI).

KEI was dedicated to teaching the Children of the region basic academics such as reading, writing, science and mathematics. In addition to these basics, the Children were taught from the Sacred Text, about the First Born and the glories of his Kingdom. In the course of their studies, each of the students would eventually be given the opportunity to give their love and their allegiance to the First Born, their King and their Lord. With KEI as a model, similar centers of education sprang up all over the world. Soon there was no place on Earth where they had no knowledge of the First Born or his Kingdom.

Flynn had finished his assignment two years early, and the Starliners had become as ubiquitous as regular jet airliners. They were becoming extremely popular as well, affording travel all over the world, at unheard of speeds, and at reasonable prices.

In the spring of that year, Flynn was called again to meet with the First Born and was given another assignment. He was to shift his duties as the Chief Technology Advisor for the Middle East Region and would concentrate on the proliferation of new technology power production.

Commercially viable, sustainable fusion power was among the long sought after but never achieved dreams of the late twentieth and early twenty first centuries. It was like lighting your own sun on the Earth and safely containing the hydrogen plasma that burned at about 100 million degrees centigrade was an enormous technological challenge. Tokomak reactors had been successfully developed that used toroidal shaped chambers to magnetically confine and squeeze the hot plasma to produce the fusion reactions.

Problems with plasma turbulence and other magnetic containment issues caused frequent disruptions that would shut down the prototype reactors and prevent the long term sustained operations necessary for practical use in power production. Then there was the fact that you had to put in just about as much energy to produce the fusion reaction as you got out of it, thus rendering it not ready for prime time, commercially.

The target of $Q = 10$, where you produced ten times more power than you introduced to the system, was a target that always seemed to be about 50 years in the future. Yet when the Knowledge Seas were loosed, it only took 25 years to produce fusion reactors with thermal outputs that approached that goal. By MA 49, the technology had advanced to the point that thermal outputs of $Q = 50$ were not uncommon. Thus, fusion power was proven to be a safe, clean, practical, and economic means of electrical power production and began to proliferate all over the world. Flynn's job was to manage that proliferation in his region.

During the first 25 years of his new assignment, Flynn operated out of his home offices in Jerusalem while Hannah, Flynn Jr., and Wendy continued to work with KEI. He first worked with the lead scientists and engineers that were developing commercially available fusion power until he had a complete understanding of how the technology worked and was knowledgeable in all the nuances of how it could be applied for power production at various levels. During this time, the concept had been thoroughly vetted, and Flynn had become an expert in fusion technology.

During the next 25 years, all Flynn had to do was educate the citizens, government officials and business owners of his region as to the viability of fusion power and its emerging spin-off technologies and applications. He would then work with the companies that manufactured the reactors to sell them and integrate them into the region's local economy and infrastructure. Compared to his first assignment, this was a piece of cake, he thought, with the added benefit that he could spend more time with his beloved Hannah, and with Flynn Jr. and Wendy.

The only member of his family that he had not seen in a long, long time was his granddaughter Mattie. He longed for the time that he would see her again. She had visited them pretty regularly during those first 50 years after they had all gotten their initial assignments but had not been to see them since he had gotten his latest assignment.

By the fall of MA 99 Flynn had completed his second assignment and was thankful for the coming break. He was to take the rest of the year off and help the First Born with preparations for the coming Millennial Centennial Celebration. Hannah, Flynn Jr., and Wendy had also been given time off and were assigned to work at his side. All of Jerusalem was buzzing with excitement and there were smaller festivals and celebrations already underway throughout the city. These smaller events would culminate with the Festival in the Great Hall on the last day of the Centennial, celebrating the first 100 years of the Millennium.

The whole family had fun as they helped to plan the festivities and they thoroughly enjoyed the last three months of that year. They were able to spend a lot of time together and looked forward to the Festival with wonder and excitement. No one had ever seen a party like this one, Flynn thought, and it was all being done above board and without the usual trappings of such events in the past. There would be no drunkenness, reveling, carousing or any other unsavory activities. It would still be great fun though; a simple celebration yet certainly not lacking in extravagance. It would simply be a joyous gathering of Brethren and Children from all over the world to celebrate the great strides that mankind had made under the benevolent rule of the First Born.

To Flynn's great delight, it ended up being everything that they had expected it to be and much, much more. To top it off, Mattie had contacted them a week before to tell them she was coming to be with the rest of the family during the Festival and as far as Flynn was concerned, that had made it all the more enjoyable. When he was finally able to hug her in person, Flynn's heart was bursting with joy.

At the end of all the celebrations, they all sat together in his townhouse and talked for hours about the magnificence of the Centennial Festival.

At one point, Flynn Jr. piped up and said, "There's just one thing dad. Am I supposed to feel guilty for all the wonderful different kinds of food that I ate? Even though I ate a lot of stuff tonight, I don't even feel full. And the amazing thing is: I know the great quantities of food I ingested will be energized by this amazing new body before the night is over, and I still won't gain any weight!"

Everyone laughed at the thought of it until Flynn finally responded and said, "As long as we don't make a habit of it, I think it will be OK. We just have to be careful around the Children. We need to set the right example. It's still possible for them to overeat you know."

With a smile still on his face, Flynn turned to Mattie and said, "Mattie, other than the occasional message telling us that the house is doing fine, we haven't heard from you in a long, long time. What have you been doing with yourself lately? Are you still working as the STEM Curriculum Director in your region?"

Mattie looked back at him with a smile that looked remarkably similar to his own and said, "G-daddy, I have been working on a confidential project for the last 50 years. All I can say to you at this point is this; when you find out about it, you are going to love it. In fact, you're going to be blown away!

The whole family looked intently at Mattie with puzzled looks on their faces. No one, including Flynn, had any idea what she meant by that last statement but he was intrigued nevertheless.

Flynn's response was calm but matter of fact, "OK Mattie, I guess we'll all have to wait for the appropriate time; when you've been released to tell us all about it, huh?"

"That's right g-daddy, she responded, "but I still can't wait to tell you!"

# :SOME DREAMS FOLLOW

A few days after the Centennial Festival had concluded Flynn was relaxing in his townhouse watching a rugby match that was being played in Australia on his HD TV. It was a Saturday and Hannah had gone to visit Flynn Jr. and Wendy at their apartment. The picture quality was insane, he thought, almost as if the rugby players could, at any moment, literally jump out of the thin flat sheet that was on the wall in his den. Suddenly, as he was watching a particularly good run by his favorite team, Magan appeared before him with an excited look on his face.

"Dr. Roberts, you have an important appointment with the First Born. We are to report to the Bethel Space Station immediately. I'm sorry, but you don't even have time to say goodbye to Hannah. Just send her a message and then we must be going.

"We have a Starliner to catch at the Ben Gurion Airport in Tel Aviv and we're going to have to jump to the airport or we'll miss our flight."

"OK Magan," Flynn consented.

He was a little frustrated at the frantic nature of the request and asked only two short questions, "What is the Bethel Space Station, and why do we have to meet the First Born there?"

"I'm sorry Dr. Roberts, I have been sworn to secrecy, and I cannot give you any details. Just come with me as the First Born has asked," Magan replied.

With those words, Flynn snapped out of his resistant mood and said, "Very well, since you put it that way, let's be on our way."

Flynn spoke a quick message to Hannah into his wrist phone, told the TV to shutoff, and jumped with Magan to the airport terminal. They were careful to materialize in a secluded hallway, and then merged with the flow of people in the busy airport terminal.

*"I am sorry about the way we had to scurry you out of your townhouse earlier this morning but for reasons that will become clear shortly, I had to get you out of there quickly,"* said the First Born.

Flynn suddenly realized that he had come out of the trance-like state in which he had relived all of the key events of his life up to that point. And though many years were covered in that experience, he was shocked to find that only a few minutes had passed since he had drifted into that trance.

"My Lord," he said, "that was probably the most unusual thing I have ever experienced."

*"Yes,"* said the First Born, *"I have used this method with others to prepare them for important assignments, and they almost always react the same way that you have. Now, let's get to the point. Are you ready to receive your new assignment Flynn?"*

"Yes Lord, you know that I am," Flynn replied.

*"OK then let me begin by giving you some context and some background from some of the lives recorded in the Sacred Text. The prophet Elijah was a man that served the Creator well during his generation. He was known for his ability to wield the gifts and powers of the world to come; the world in which we now live. He operated in supernatural knowledge and wisdom and*

*performed many acts of power to help turn the hearts of his people toward the Creator.*

*"His understudy and faithful servant Elisha asked before his master departed if he could be granted those same abilities, but at twice the level. After recovering his master's mantle which was a symbol of those supernatural abilities, Elisha began to walk in those same abilities but at a much higher level.*

*"Now you can check this out later Flynn but trust me when I say that there were exactly 14 instances recorded in the Sacred Text where Elijah operated in these supernatural abilities before his departure. However, if you count the number of times that his protégé Elisha operated in those same abilities before his death, you will find that number to be exactly 27.*

*"Is the Sacred Text in error or is there something that most people have missed when they read this story?"*

"I know the Sacred Text is not in error, my Lord, for it is the foundation of everything. But I can honestly say I have read that story hundreds of times and have never noticed this," Flynn replied curiously.

The First Born continued, *"Well, as it turns out, many years after the death of Elisha, the people of the Creator were once again under the dominion of oppressors, so much so that they had to secretly bury their dead for fear that the enemy would catch them out in the open and slay them without mercy. During these times there was a group of men who came to bury their friend in the same cemetery where Elisha had been buried many years before. When they spotted a band of the enemy headed in their direction, they decided their best course of action was to place the body of their friend in the same tomb that contained the bones of Elisha.*

*"As I am sure you are aware, the young man sprang to life again when his body touched those bones. You see Flynn, many*

*people have misunderstood this story, but it is really quite simple. Those powers of the world to come, that just a few men walked in during those days, are so potent that they linger many times on the clothes and even on the body of the person who operates powerfully in them. But there is something else going on here and this is the point I really wanted to emphasize.*

*"If you add this instance to the total number of times recorded in the Sacred Text where Elisha operated in these powers, you will find that it now comes to exactly 28, or exactly twice the number of times as his predecessor Elijah."*

Flynn was *stunned* to find such a simple yet profound mathematical puzzle contained in the Sacred Text, especially since it was one that he never even knew was in there.

"That is amazing, my Lord! Once again this proves that the Sacred Text is indeed precise and without error."

The First Born replied with emotion evident in his voice, *"Yes Flynn, but as I said earlier, it only provides context for the thing that you need to know; the thing that I have longed to tell you but am only now able to."*

"What is that my Lord?" Flynn replied.

*"Listen to me carefully Flynn, you need to understand this,"* replied the First Born.

*"Above all else, this story illustrates the absolute faithfulness of the Creator. You see Flynn ... <u>some dreams</u> follow you into the Next Life."*

When Flynn heard this, he suddenly started to tremble. He was not sure why but he knew that something was about to happen that would change everything. He just didn't know what it was.

The First Born continued, *"Elisha had a dream that he would operate in the powers of the world to come, but at twice the level of his predecessor Elijah. But when he died, it seemed that his dream had died with him. Just like many others spoken of in the Sacred Text, Elisha essentially died in faith, and took his promise to the grave. He had performed many more acts of power than that of his master, Elijah, but was still one act shy of the number required to make that dream a reality in his life. But today <u>he knows</u>, and now <u>you know</u>, that <u>that one act of power</u>, performed by <u>his body</u>, after he had moved on to his Next Life, demonstrated the faithfulness of the Creator to the promises and to the dreams that he places in the heart of his believers.*

*"Flynn, I know that you assumed that your dream of one day flying in space was lost to you as you came to the end of your First Life. In your case, you were alive at the time of the Transformation and so you passed from the First Life into the Next Life without ever tasting death.*

*"And when you made that transition, you felt you had left that dream behind in your former life. Yet here you are, having flown a space plane to a space station in low Earth orbit, sitting with me in the commander's quarters no less."*

"Yes, my Lord, and I am grateful for that," Flynn replied, still trembling. Inwardly, he was hoping that the First Born would not notice just how anticlimactic those events had seemed to him.

Yet, the First Born seemed unfazed and continued speaking. *"Flynn, I know that we just watched this a few moments ago but I want to take you back there one more time so you can hear a portion of the important things that we discussed that day on the grass."*

He once again drifted and found himself in the trance like state from which he had just emerged. He watched the replay of this key event again and heard and saw everything the exact way that it happened that day on the grass.

He saw and heard the Lord speaking to him and saying ... "Flynn, you <u>will</u> fly in space one day, just as you dreamed you would, and it will be more glorious than you can ask, think, or imagine. But before that, I want you to use your education to help people solve problems, to make life better for them, and I want you to use your flying abilities to help feed and care for the people of the world and tell them about the saving power that is in my name. Will you do that for me Flynn?"

"Yes Lord, you know that I will," Flynn replied with tears streaming from his eyes.

"Very well then, when you recover from your injuries, I want you to use the educational opportunities that will come your way, together with your aviation skills in the way that I have asked you. If you are faithful to carry out your assignment, you will be rewarded."

Then as quickly as he had emerged from the first trance, Flynn came out of the second. He was still sitting in front of the First Born and was dismayed to find that he was still trembling.

"Flynn, you accepted the assignments that I gave you that day and were faithful to carry them out, right up until the time of the transformation, the last day of your First Life. Because of your leadership and your involvement in the Desert Reach Foundation, that organization touched the lives of thousands among the desert Indian tribes that otherwise would have been unreached and untouched.

"Generations of these Indian tribes were introduced to the Creator and to the saving power that is in his son. You used your aviation skills and your engineering education to help improve their lives just as I had asked you to. Because you have been faithful to carry out your assignments, even those that I have asked you to carry out in the Next Life, you will now be rewarded. As I said earlier, some dreams that are planted in your heart are for another time ... some dreams follow you into the Next Life."

Flynn just sat there listening to the First Born, still trembling, and still wondering what this was all about.

*"Flynn, what did you think of the Providence, is she not magnificent? ... Would you like to know why you felt such a powerful connection to her the first time you laid eyes on her ... and why you still feel that way now?"*

As he listened, Flynn felt the trembling give way to shaking and his eyes began to flood with emotion.

*"The reason that you feel so passionately about her is because the Providence was made for you Flynn. You are to be her captain, and you are to take her to the stars just as you imagined you would one day!"*

Flynn broke down before the First Born. He just couldn't help it. His lifelong dream becoming a reality…not only was he going into space but he was going to the stars, and as the captain of his own starship! And it had all come about at the hands of the First Born, his Lord and his King! He was overcome by the magnitude of the moment and by the greatness and faithfulness of the Creator.

He dropped his head on the desk between them and began to sob, shaking uncontrollably. The First Born put his hand on his shoulder and let him vent his emotions for a good long while. He knew that Flynn's dreams were deep seated and still very much alive in his heart. And although they had been suppressed through many years of disappointment, those dreams were now erupting anew from inside of Flynn, and he was wise enough and patient enough to give him space for that to happen.

"… Words cannot express … Lord … I don't know what to say …," Flynn finally muttered between sobs.

*"Remember, I told you if you carried out the assignments that were given to you that you would be rewarded,"* the First Born quietly replied. *"This is your reward, Flynn. And you can thank*

me by carrying out this new assignment with the same faithfulness and excellence that you have always exhibited. It is a very important assignment and we are counting on you to rise to the inevitable challenges that you will face as you take the Providence on her maiden voyage. "

When Flynn was finally able to compose himself, he asked, "why has this project been kept a secret from me, my Lord? In my work with the Starliner space planes, I had heard about the construction of a new space station, but never imagined something as spectacular, as massive, and as advanced as this. And I *certainly* knew nothing about the Providence."

The First Born responded, *"One of the assignments that I gave your friend Matt Parker was to work with the design teams at SRI to develop a vessel capable of both interplanetary and interstellar travel. They had to work with a number of other firms who were building the Bethel Space Station, but the Providence was their baby.*

*"Matt and Nadia Habibi, the Chief Architect at SRI, worked together to build a vessel that was based on one of her original designs. They have been working together on this highly confidential project for 50 years and now the Providence is just about ready for her space trials. It was a bit tricky at first because they had to build portions of the Bethel first before they could begin construction on the Providence.*

*"And whether you realized it or not, your work on the Starliner fleet was crucial to this whole process. We could not have built Bethel or the Providence without them. The reason why we kept it from you Flynn was because <u>I wanted it to be a surprise</u>. And if you are wondering why the Providence looks the way she does, I can answer that too. You see, I was able to provide my own input to the design team ... she was made to look as you had imagined her when you were a young boy. It is no more complex than that, Flynn. I just wanted you to captain a ship that looked the way*

*you thought it would when those dreams were first placed into your heart."*

"I don't know what to say, my Lord, this is such a shock. I thought I had let that dream go long ago, but the moment I saw the Providence, everything came rushing to the surface. I do not have the words to describe how I am feeling at this moment. All I can say is, how great is the faithfulness of our Creator! How great ... how great!" he said still wiping tears away from his eyes.

He looked up and was surprised to see the First Born grinning from ear to ear and wiping tears from his eyes as well.

*"What a wonderful day this has been Flynn! You have no idea how long I have been waiting to tell you about all of this, you have no idea!"*

Flynn jumped from the chair he was in and rounded the table as the First Born moved to meet him. They embraced each other tightly for several minutes, and the tears again flowed freely.

When the first lull in their emotions finally came, the First Born suddenly whispered into his ear, *"And there's more Flynn. Much, much more."*

Flynn released his grip on the First Born and stepped back with an incredulous look on his face.

"More?" he asked.

*"Yes, much more Flynn. But first I need to tell you how we are going to prepare you for a very important mission ... I want you to take the next year to become familiar with your crew and with your ship. Then you will take the Providence out for her space trials. Are you ready for that Flynn?"*

Flynn gushed. "My Lord, I've been ready for that practically my whole life!"

With a smile on his face, the First Born looked at him and said, *"Yes, Flynn, I know that you have. And now ... at last you get to do what you have always dreamed you would do. Now let's go aboard the Providence!*

*"I want you to meet your crew. They are eager to meet you and tell you all about your new ship."*

# :THE CREW

## CHAPTER 14

The First Born led Flynn out of the commander's quarters, through the command deck and out into a corridor that led to a small elevator. Together they stepped into the elevator that was clearly designed to move between the various decks of the space station.

Before he could ask any questions, the First Born spoke up and said, *"There are four of them Flynn, and they're evenly spaced around the cylinder. And if you are wondering which way we consider to be "up" when we use these elevators, we use the gravity field lines as a reference. The field generators energize a gravity field with 'down' lines that run through the cylinder from the designated 'north' side to the 'south' side. Up is north and down is south. The decks are numbered so that they increase in the 'up' direction; opposite to the 'down' field lines."*

After the elevator door swished closed, the First Born selected Deck Ten on a small touch screen display on the left side of the elevator. Within seconds, they were moving rapidly "up" toward their destination. During the short elevator ride, questions began to form in Flynn's mind. Although the thrill and the exhilaration of captaining his own starship were still very much at the forefront of his mind and emotions, there were questions that were forming that he knew he would have to ask sooner or later: "Why are we doing this ... what will we find out there ... what comes after the space trials ... what about returning to the moon and what about mars ... what kind of propulsion will take us to the stars ... and who's paying for all this?"

When they reached Deck Ten, the door opened and they stepped into a corridor that led directly to an airlock. Once inside the airlock, there was an enclosed circular tunnel attached to the opposite end that looked similar to the walkways that were used for final boarding on conventional jetliners. Only this one was a bit more robust, and Flynn could tell it was pressurized to match Bethel's 14.7 pounds per square inch of oxygen.

The First Born turned to Flynn and said, *"This is the entry tunnel that will take us aboard the Providence. Follow me and keep in mind that we will be leaving the gravity field of Bethel while in the tunnel. You won't sense gravity again until we get aboard the ship."*

At that point the First Born reached up and grabbed a small handle that was connected to some sort of conveyor line that appeared to run the length of the corridor. Flynn followed suit and grabbed the one that was about ten feet behind but connected to the same line. As soon as he grabbed his handle, the conveyor system began to pull them gently as they walked the first few steps into the tunnel. Flynn noticed that they passed a series of red and yellow striped warning lines with signs marked in bold letters with the words "Leaving Gravity Field Now".

As they moved past those warning lines he felt his feet and body rise from the tunnel floor and trail behind him as they were pulled toward the ship. After about a three minute ride, he saw what he surmised to be the airlock leading into the main deck structure of the Providence. As they passed another set of gravity field warning lines he could feel the force of gravity pulling his feet toward the open airlock and could see that both he and the First Born were being aligned with the new "up" that corresponded with the ship's gravity field lines. As this began to happen, they both let go of the handles so that they ended up standing upright in the upper deck of the Providence.

There was a service elevator in the center of the airlock that jutted out from the floor of the deck without connecting to the top. Probably, Flynn reasoned, so it could be properly isolated from the pressurization chamber that essentially took up the entire deck. As he looked up, he realized he was right when he saw a nautilus-like hatch in the expanded, open position. It connected with the boundaries of the entry tunnel they had just come through to form a pressure seal.

As the First Born headed for the elevator, he shot back to Flynn who was right behind him, *"There is a safety mechanism that will not allow the service elevator to open on the top deck unless the pressures are equal. No matter how many times you push the button, it will not open until they are within a certain tolerance of one another. Not a factor for you and me Flynn, but as you will soon find out, only a handful of your crew are Brethren; the rest were chosen from among Jacob's Children."*

"Add that to the growing list of questions that I have," Flynn thought. "What was the purpose of a crew that was predominantly from the Children? Wouldn't that expose them to risk, indeed outright danger, on a ship like this?"

"This is going to be amazing!" Flynn quietly surmised as his excitement level once again ramped up from within.

As they entered the elevator and the door swished closed, he saw the First Born push a touch screen control that corresponded with Deck Seven. There was a diagram on the elevator control panel, and he could see that the top deck was Deck Eight and Deck Seven was the Main Bridge.

"Wow!" he thought again with a slight chuckle of excitement "this is just going to be amazing!"

He felt like a kid who kept running out of adjectives. How many times was he going to think of how *amazing* this was going to be? How about *awesome*?" he thought.

A few seconds later they arrived at Deck Seven and the door swished open.

As they stepped out of the elevator, Flynn saw a group of people that were evidently waiting for them on the Main Bridge. Upon seeing the First Born, he noticed that all but one of them rendered the traditional greeting which identified them as Brethren. The only thing that was omitted was the verbal response which was not normally delivered in a group setting.

The only exception was a female dressed in a burnt orange uniform that resembled some sort of flight suit. It had insignia on it that he did not recognize. She gave the traditional bow customary for members of Jacob's Children. He recognized her immediately as Nadia Habibi, the designer of the Providence that he had met earlier that day on the command deck. He quickly noted that all but three members of that group were dressed in the same type of uniform that Nadia was now wearing.

As they drew nearer to the group, the First Born said, *"Rise, my friends, it is good to see you again."*

As they got closer to the group, he immediately recognized Matt Parker. His tall, lanky frame was hard to miss. He too wore the same burnt orange uniform. Then he spotted Hannah, Flynn Jr., Wendy, and noted that they were the only ones who were not in that uniform. And standing with them in the middle of the group was Mattie. She was wearing the same burnt orange uniform.

"What was going on?" he thought. "Why is my whole family here for this and what's the meaning of these uniforms? Even Mattie's wearing one!"

A huge grin grew on Flynn's face as he made his way to Hannah first. He had just seen her that morning but it seemed like so much time had passed since then.

"You guys knew about this?" He asked.

"Yes honey. Magen Hannah told me it was a surprise arranged by the First Born and told me to meet at Flynn Jr.'s this morning. When I got there, Flynn Jr., Wendy and Mattie were all waiting for me and filled me in on the details."

Flynn turned quickly to embrace his son, then Wendy, and finally his granddaughter Mattie. She was grinning ear to ear and her red hair was as brilliant as he had ever remembered it.

"What in the world are you doing here Mattie?" He asked with a delighted yet puzzled look on his face.

"I will let the First Born tell you all about that g-daddy," she replied. He embraced her again as they both wiped tears from their eyes. It was then that he noticed that Matt had been hovering over them, waiting for his turn to embrace his best friend.

Flynn turned and embraced him firmly before stepping back and saying, "Matt, you've got some explaining to do!" he said with a small smile, "What's this all about?"

"Well, I think it would be best to let the First Born take the lead with introductions and explanations, so I'll turn it over to him."

The First Born had been standing there watching their reunions with a satisfied smile on his face. He then turned to Flynn and said, *"OK, I think I've been quiet long enough. It's time to put all of this into perspective for you Flynn. Let's start with Mattie, and then we'll work our way out from there."*

*"After serving faithfully as a STEM Curriculum Director in Colorado for 50 years, Mattie was selected to help us establish a new academy which is only now being made known to the public. We call it the Royal Space Flight Academy, RSFA for short. It was established on the campus of the old Air Force Academy in Colorado Springs. Because of her expertise in astrophysics and space science, she was selected as one or the initial cadre at RSFA*

and helped to build their astronomy curriculum from the ground up.

*"After 45 years as one of our eminent professors, she was the first of a special group that was handpicked for a five year training program in star mapping and space navigation. At the end of that program she received a direct commission as a Lieutenant Commander in the recently formed Royal Space Exploration Corps (RSEC). The RSEC Headquarters is collocated with, and they get all their future leaders from, the RSFA.*

*"I have left out a lot of the details for the sake of time but she is to be the Chief Navigator on your ship, formally referred to as His Majesty's Space Ship, HMSS Providence."*

When he heard the story of his granddaughter Mattie, he was overjoyed to know that he had been right about Mattie's future. The First Born had not forgotten the desire of her heart and had given her an assignment that was far beyond anything she could have imagined. He not only loved the fact that Mattie was involved; he loved the fact that she would be a key member of his command staff. And he absolutely loved the whole concept of both an academy and an organization that were dedicated to star flight, navigation, and exploration.

It was an overwhelming feeling and Flynn struggled to quantify his thoughts before he spoke another word. In the end, the only thing he could think of to say was, "This is going to be amazing!" Immediately he thought; "I can't believe I just said that again! Adjectives, Flynn … adjectives!"

The First Born continued, *"Next, I would like you to meet Mtafiti Kasomo. Because of his skill in path finding, his people called him Anayejua. It is Swahili for searcher. We call him AJ."*

AJ stepped forward from the group and Flynn got a good look at him for the first time. He was about the same height and build as he was and although he was definitely black, he had a hue that resembled that of the First Born. It was the first time he consciously realized that this was true of all the Brethren. No matter what nation or race that they came from, no matter what the skin color, male or female, they all had a curious resemblance to the First Born.

"I am very pleased to meet you sir. I have heard much about you. It will be my pleasure to serve you," he said with a polished yet distinctly African accent.

"Pleased to meet you as well AJ," Flynn replied as he grabbed his hand and shook it firmly.

The First Born politely interjected, *"AJ was one of the trackers for the great missionary explorer Dr. David Livingstone. Because of his reputation, Dr. Livingstone had employed him for his last expedition that originated in Tanzania. He was known in the region for his skill in tracking and path finding. Ever since he was a young man he had longed to explore new and different lands so he jumped at the chance to join the Tanzanian expedition.*

*"At the beginning of their journey together, one starry night on the shores of Lake Tanganyika, he was asked by Dr. Livingstone if he wanted to meet the one who made the stars, the one who held his destiny in his hand. He gave his life to the Lord that night, and after the expedition answered the call to build a mission and a school for his people.*

*"He had to lay down his dream of exploration to follow that call and spent the last 35 years of his life dedicated to serving his people and introducing them to the Creator and to his Son. But as you are now aware Flynn, some dreams follow, and this was the case also with AJ. After a five year helmsman training program, he graduated from RSFA and received a Direct Commission to the rank of Lieutenant Commander. He is to be your Chief Helmsman."*

The First Born continued, *"Next I would like you to meet Hans Jurgens."*

Hans was taller than Flynn and had a lanky build similar to his friend Matt. He was blond haired, blue eyed and had an amiable looking smile. He stepped forward and took the initiative with a firm handshake before Flynn had the chance to initiate one of his own.

"I like that," Flynn thought, "a kind of controlled aggressiveness that will be necessary from time to time on a ship like this."

In perfect English Hans said, "Very pleased to meet you sir. I look forward to working at your side on this wonderful ship."

"Pleased to meet you as well Hans; it's going to be amazing," Flynn replied.

"There I go again," he thought. "Adjectives, Flynn. Adjectives!"

*"Hans was the ship's engineer on a German U-Boat during World War I,"* said the First Born. *"But after the U-20 crew sank a hospital ship and then the Lusitania, he became disillusioned with the war and with the conduct of the German U-Boat fleet.*

*"One night he was alone on the ship's bridge gazing at the beautiful stars in the clear and crisp skies of the North Atlantic. In his search for meaning in life, he reached out to the Creator and gave his life to the Lord. He became a Moravian minister after the war and answered the call to become a missionary to the Inuit people of Labrador. He worked side by side with British missionaries and faithfully carried out his calling for the last 30 years of his life.*

*"He loved being a ship's engineer and longed to once again sail the high seas, to explore unknown lands, and to have another*

ship that was his to care for. Once again, Flynn, some dreams follow, and such was the case with Hans. After completing a five year ship's engineer program at RSFA, Hans received a Direct Commission to the rank of Lieutenant Commander. He is to be your Chief Engineer.

*"Next, I want you to meet someone that is very near and dear to your family, although you have not met her until today. Her name is Nadia Habibi."*

She stepped forward immediately and said, "Very pleased to meet you sir. I have heard so much about you over the years. I look forward to serving at your side during this great adventure we are about to embark upon."

"Finally," Flynn thought, "somebody is as excited as I am about the sheer adventure."

Nadia was about five foot two and petite with dark hair and eyes that gave her a somewhat mysterious look. She was a thinker he surmised; someone who was always reasoning about why things were happening and why they were significant to those that were experiencing them.

"It is a pleasure to meet you as well, Nadia. I look forward to hearing the connection with my family that the First Born mentioned."

*"She was a Palestinian refugee and an orphan in the Old City during the Time of Jacob's Trouble,"* interjected the First Born. *"Her parents were killed in the great earthquake just prior to the invasion. A few days after beginning his assignment in the Old City, Flynn Jr. found her living in the rubble next to her old house. It was only a block or so away from the school he had founded which eventually became the Kingdom Education Institute.*

"He took her under his care along with the others that he had found, and he, Hannah, and Wendy helped to raise her and educate her during those years of transition. After giving her life to the Lord, she began to display an unusual combination of artistic flair and pragmatic ingenuity which was encouraged by Flynn Jr. and Wendy. After graduating from the charter class at KEI, she attended Tel Aviv University and received dual degrees, a Bachelor of Architecture and a Bachelor of Science in Electrical Engineering.

"Unbeknownst to you, Flynn Jr. contacted Matt Parker and asked him if they would consider taking her on as an intern at Space Research International. Over the span of 50 years she rose through the ranks at SRI to become their Chief Architect and Design Engineer. She had a vision for the Providence which she submitted to Matt and to the company leadership. Based on her original design, along with my input, they designed and built your ship, the HMSS Providence."

"Wait," Flynn said as his eyes turned toward Hannah. "Is this the girl you used to talk about at the apartment in the Old City? I didn't remember her name but I do recall that you would often talk about her, how special she was and what a blessing and an inspiration she had been in your life."

"Yes," Hannah replied, "and although you never got a chance to meet her, I prayed many times that one day she would be a blessing to you as well."

At this point the First Born adroitly picked up the conversation saying, *"The Creator is good, is he not? After completing a two year leadership course at RSFA, Nadia received a Direct Commission to the rank of Commander. She is to be your First Officer."*

Even though it was not specifically mentioned by the First Born, Flynn made a mental note of the fact that Nadia would be the only non-Brethren member of his command staff. Important leadership positions in the Kingdom were normally reserved for the Brethren. He thought back to earlier that day when he had met Dan Steele, Bethel's commander, and Mike Johnson, her chief engineer. They too were from among Jacob's Children. They must be stellar individuals, like Nadia, he thought.

The First Born then looked at Flynn Jr. and said, *"Flynn, there are a few more surprises left and one of them concerns your son. He is not in uniform yet, but he will be soon. He leaves tomorrow for Colorado Springs where he will begin a one year Chaplains course at RSFA. After that, he will receive a Direct Commission to Lieutenant Commander and will report back to the Providence. He is to be your Ship's Chaplain."*

Before Flynn had time to react to that bit of news, the First Born continued, *"Finally Flynn, we are all gathering now at the Captain's Station near the forefront of the bridge for a short ceremony. Before we begin, there is an attendant waiting there to escort you to the captain's lounge on the starboard side of the bridge. There, you will find a uniform without rank insignia. Please change into that uniform and meet us back at the Captain's Station."*

At this point Flynn felt absolutely numb. Even in his new body he found that such physiological reactions were possible at times like this. He felt joy, excitement, wonder, exhilaration, and anticipation all at the same time. It was almost overwhelming. He was experiencing so many different emotions that he was having a difficult time sorting them all out. He finally resigned himself to just go with the flow and let things happen the way that the First Born had obviously planned for them to happen. He would save the questions that had formed in his mind for a later, quieter and less eventful time.

He moved with the group to the Captain's Station and was met immediately by an attendant named Ensign Munn.

"Sir, I am here to escort you to the captain's lounge, please come with me," he said nervously.

Flynn left the group and followed him toward the lounge which was on the far side of the starboard side of the bridge. He noticed that there was another door to the left of the lounge that was marked "Captain's Quarters" and realized that he was the only member of the crew that had quarters on the same deck as the bridge. The lounge door swished open and Ensign Munn waited outside as he entered the room.

As the door closed behind him, he took two steps inside and saw the uniform hanging in a coat closet just to the left of the door. He took off his suit and changed into the uniform. It was the same burnt orange color as the others he had seen with the same insignia, only without rank. As he pulled it on, he realized that it fit him perfectly and was as comfortable as any uniform he had ever worn in his life.

He noticed that the uniform had boots that were built into the lower portion of the trouser legs. As his feet slipped into the boots, he felt the inner liners shrink and conform to his ankles and feet. It was almost as if his feet were being shrink-wrapped in a way that made the boots conform to the natural movements of his feet whether standing, walking, running, or jumping. And they still managed to look sharp, he thought, as he looked at himself in the mirror.

He left the room and headed for the Captain's Station with the young ensign in tow behind. As he got closer, he noticed there were two more people that had joined the group he had left. Tears welled up in his eyes as he immediately recognized his father and his mother. He had not seen them since just prior to the invasion and was simply overjoyed at the sight of them. He rushed to hug his mother first, and then his father and they all had a good cry as the rest of the group stood all around them.

He could tell by looking at their faces that he was the only one who did not see this coming. It was the final surprise in a day of surprises, and it was a fitting end to an emotional day.

"I wasn't going to miss this for the world!" said his father, wiping the tears from his eyes.

"We're so proud of you Flynn, you have waited so long for this," his mother said, also wiping tears from her eyes.

Before Flynn could ask them anything about how they had been doing or about their millennial assignments, the First Born spoke out loudly and formally, *"Sean Flynn Roberts, stand at attention!"*

Flynn faced the First Born and snapped to attention.

*"By the authority given to me by the Creator and with the full consent of the Royal Space Exploration Corps, I now promote you to the rank of Captain with all the responsibilities and privileges that accompany that rank."*

His father then emerged from the crowd with Captain's shoulder boards and fastened them onto his uniform epaulets. When his father had shaken his hand and stepped out of the way, Flynn fell to his left knee and stretched out his arms toward the floor with his palms facing forward. With his head and shoulders bowed in reverence, he said, "My Lord and my King! I am honored to once again be in your presence! As always, I am at your service!"

*"Rise, Captain Roberts, and receive your orders,"* replied the First Born. After Flynn stood back to attention, he continued, *"You will remain aboard the HMSS Providence for the next year and get to know your crew and your ship. During this time, we will bring mentors and instructors from RSEC Headquarters to the Providence who will administer a one year Captain's Course that has been tailor made for you.*

"Your ship and your mission are the first of their kind and you have much to learn. As you know Captain Roberts, you have been preparing for this your entire life, and you are ready for the challenges that lay ahead. After the year is over, HMSS Providence will be ready for her space trials. You will be briefed in due time as to the nature of the space trials and the important mission that will follow afterwards. God bless and God speed, Captain Roberts."

After concluding the short commissioning ceremony, the First Born turned to the group and said, *"Please enjoy yourselves at the reception we have scheduled on the Mess Deck. Ensign Munn will escort you there after I leave. Captain Roberts, I apologize for not being able to be there but I have other matters I must attend to at this time."*

As he turned and headed for the Main Bridge elevator, he looked over his shoulder and said, *"We will talk again soon, goodbye."*

Still overcome with emotion, Flynn beckoned back to him, "Goodbye Your Majesty ... and thank you ... this is going to be awesome!"

As he entered the elevator, he turned and spoke to Flynn with a mischievous looking smile, *"Now there's that new adjective you were searching for ... and there will be more my friend ... see you soon."*

He pressed the elevator touch screen, and the elevator door closed in front of him.

Ensign Munn waited a moment and then marshaled the group toward the same elevator. As he opened the door for them to enter, they all realized that the elevator had not even left the Bridge, yet it was empty. They glanced at one another with quizzical expressions.

As they entered the elevator, Munn whispered, "He does that all the time ... you get used to it."

Flynn was the last one to enter as he attempted to take a quick look around before they left. He had been so distracted by the surprise reunion and promotion ceremony that he hadn't had a chance to really look around the Main Bridge. He wasn't concerned though. Over the next year, he knew that he would be spending the majority of his time here, and there would be plenty of time to take it all in.

His first impression from what he *did* see was that the layout, with its various control suites and functional stations, was streamlined in a perfect merger of form and function, much like the command deck of the Bethel. He was definitely looking forward to checking it out more thoroughly in the very near future. As the elevator door closed, Ensign Munn pressed the touch screen button that would take them to Deck Four, the Mess Deck.

When they got to Deck Four a few seconds later, the elevator did something he was not expecting. He had not noticed, but there were doors on each of the four sides of the elevator. Unlike the Main Bridge which was one large open room, the Mess Deck had four corridors running fore, aft, starboard, and port of the elevator. All the doors opened up at the same time, allowing access to whichever corridor you needed to follow.

Ensign Munn led them through the starboard running corridor till they came to a door on the left with a sign that said "Officer's Wardroom." As they entered the room, Flynn thought, "Now this looks more like some of the conventional sea vessels I am familiar with. A lot of this is really old school, right down to the Navy ranks. It's going to take some getting used to, but it's all still so cool."

When they entered the room, there was a large ornate table at the center with stylish looking tables and chairs all around it. It was beautifully decorated and decked out with a buffet style menu of hors d'oeuvres and entrees.

After Ensign Munn said grace, Flynn passed on the food, grabbed Hannah and made a beeline for his parents. Flynn Jr., Wendy and Mattie joined them at their table. It had been a hundred years since he had seen them. He embraced them once again and immediately engaged them in conversation while the rest of the family listened intently.

They shared with him how they both had received assignments in Indiana near Bedford. Flynn's dad had become a comptroller and supervised Kingdom tax receipts from businesses and organizations in the Midwest region, and his mom was administrator over a network of hospitals in the same area. They loved being able to help the Children live prosperous and healthy lives and delighted in the fact that they had gotten to know so many of them and had developed wonderful relationships as a result, some of which had spanned several generations. They explained that they had been contacted a few weeks ago and were told about the building of the Providence and the fact that their son would be her Captain.

"I have to tell you Flynn, it was probably the most wonderful surprise that your mother and I could have ever been a part of," said his dad. "Your mother and I have been sailing high ever since. After all, we raised you, and we know how much this means to you."

"Mom ... dad," Flynn replied, "there are simply no words to describe what I'm feeling right now. The goodness and the faithfulness of the Creator are beyond anything I could have imagined."

His father looked him square in the eyes and said, "Son, you have always made us proud and I know you will continue to do so. We love you and will follow your adventure as closely as we can."

He looked behind Flynn to see that Matt Parker had strolled over to their table. Matt put his hand on Flynn's shoulder just as he was turning to see who it was that walked up behind him.

"Flynn, I wanted to speak with you alone for a moment if you don't mind," he said. "Mr. and Mrs. Roberts, if you'll let me borrow him for just a few minutes, I promise I'll send him back to you when I'm done."

"Of course Matt," his mother replied, "we're just thankful that you and the First Born wanted to include us in this joyous occasion."

Flynn turned to Hannah and said, "I'll be back shortly after I talk with Matt." She nodded her approval with a hint of a smile, and he left to follow Matt.

Matt escorted Flynn to a table that was sufficiently removed from the rest so they could have a private conversation. After they sat down, Matt engaged him immediately.

"Flynn, you are the first to Captain a ship like the Providence but you won't be the last. That's why your mission is so vital and so important. You are paving the way for the rest of us. You are our pathfinder, our forerunner."

"Yeah," said Flynn. "I've been meaning to ask you ever since I saw you in that uniform. I noticed that you have the same Captain's boards that I do."

"Yes Flynn," he replied. "I received a direct commission from the First Born in a joint ceremony with Nadia. Both of us have left SRI for good and will remain aboard the Providence with you. Just so you know; you and I will complete the Captain's Course together."

"That's awesome," replied Flynn, "does that mean we will rotate as commanders on various missions?"

"No Flynn, it's much better than that ... after you take the Providence out for her space trials, SRI will begin construction of a new ship ... it is to be my ship ... the Heritage. We are going to learn as much as we can from the design and testing of the Providence and will modify the design of the Heritage based on the results of your space trials.

"Flynn, you are leading the way, but I wanted you to be the first to know, I won't be too far behind. I'm next in line to follow you to the stars!"

"Awesome!" Flynn shouted, "Simply awesome!"

"Awesome indeed!" shouted Matt in reply. They both jumped up from the table and embraced one another tightly. Then they started walking around the tables, pumping their fists up and down like two adolescent football players about to play the game of their lives. At that point, the atmosphere became charged with excitement and the rest of the crew jumped to their feet to join them.

The civilians watched with joy and laughter as the crew danced around the tables, fist pumping, high fiving, and shouting at one another, "We're going to the stars! ... Man, can you believe it? ... We're actually going to the stars!"

It was only a matter of time before the sheer exhilaration of the coming adventure had risen to the surface in all of them. It could be suppressed no longer. Mattie was the last to join the throng. She leaped from her table and ran to her g-daddy. They immediately locked arms and starting spinning in circles like old fashioned square dancers. The raucous celebration continued unabated for several minutes until Nadia made her way for her chair, exhausted. The rest of the crew simmered down shortly afterwards out of respect for her.

It was a subtle reminder to the Brethren that the majority of their crewmembers were like Nadia, from Jacob's Children. Their physical limitations were the reason that such a ship as the Providence had been built in the first place, and it was something they would have to keep in mind at all times. As Flynn made his way back to his chair and his curiously on-looking family, he cruised by the table with the food and noticed that no one had eaten a bite.

"What a shame," he thought, "such a nice spread."

Hans Jurgens came over to where he was sitting with a big smile on his face, "Sir, in all the excitement, I almost forgot to tell you. I am to give you your first tour of the Providence. We can begin any time you are ready."

Flynn looked toward his family, and they all gave him a unified look of approval, including Hannah who nodded approvingly and blew him a kiss.

"How about right now?" he shot back. He turned to the rest of the group and said, "Is it OK if I leave you guys for a couple of hours?"

Nadia answered, "Of course Captain Roberts and you needn't worry about saying goodbye to everyone just yet. All your family will be staying with us till tomorrow. Enjoy your tour sir."

# :THE PROVIDENCE

CHAPTER 15

Hans began the tour by taking Flynn on the elevator down to Deck One. He would begin there and give a deck by deck overview of the main living and functional areas contained within the crew compartment of the ship. After that he would sit down with Captain Roberts and cover the basics of the ship's power, life support, and propulsion systems.

Deck One was at the bottom and housed the Lower Airlock and the Falcon, the Planetary Landing Vehicle (PLV). Hans explained that it was very similar in design to the Starliners he was so familiar with. Certain modifications had to be made, Hans explained. They had to develop a V/STOL version which was augmented with pure rocket thrusters to accommodate the different type atmospheres they might encounter.

Deck Two was the Engineering Deck, and it housed the command and control computer systems for all the ship's power, propulsion and life support systems. It was one large open room with cubicles and work stations appropriately distributed around a central control desk adjacent to the elevator. From this desk, the Duty Engineer would command all engineering personnel and monitor all systems which were organized into three functional sub-stations: Ship's Power, Ship's Propulsion, and Ship's Pressurization and Life Support. There was a direct connection from the Ship's Propulsion sub-station to the Helmsman Station on the Main Bridge so that the Duty Helmsman could control the ship's power and set the ship's course from there.

Deck Three was the Refrigeration Deck where most of the perishable food stocks were kept. It was one large room with an organized array of 100 large refrigeration units. They could store enough supplies to last up to 15 years with a crew of 300 Children. They were manned by a cadre of attendants who did nothing but monitor the environment and the state of these refrigeration units. There was a central control desk adjacent to the elevator which was manned 24/7 by a Duty Fridge Engineer.

Deck Four was the Mess and Fellowship Deck which housed several small and large dining facilities. These facilities included the Officer's Wardroom, the Crew Cafeteria, several snack bars and beverage stations. The Mess Deck also housed several large storage units where all the non-perishable food stocks were kept. The Ship's Chaplain lived in the aft portion of the deck right next door to the Chapel and the Fellowship Hall.

Deck Five was the Gymnasium and Medical Deck. It contained several work out facilities and a track that ran around the outer rim of the deck. The work out facilities contained treadmills and exercise machines of all types. But just like the rest of the ship, everything was bolted down in some fashion just in case the ship experienced unexpected and uncontrolled accelerations. The Ship's Flight Surgeon and his medical staff operated a small medical facility near the center of the Gym Deck with an infirmary, an operating table, and a few beds.

Deck Six was the Crew Quarters Deck. The Quarters Deck was unique in that it contained a labyrinth of corridors that maximized access to the individual living quarters. The Officer's Quarters were in the forward portion, and the Non-Officer Quarters were in the aft portion of the deck. Hans noted that the crew quarters were comfortable and quite roomy compared to the cramped and almost unbearable accommodations he was familiar with during his U-Boats days. He went on to explain that the Captain was the only member of the crew who did not have quarters on this deck. He would live in the quarters on the starboard side of the bridge that Flynn had already seen.

Deck Seven was the Main Bridge Deck which housed all the command and control stations for the entire ship. It was split in half and there was a bulkhead that ran port to starboard which separated the Bridge into two main compartments: the Main Bridge which was forward, and the Command, Control and Data Center (CCDC) which was aft.

Deck Eight was the Upper Airlock that he had seen when he entered the ship with the First Born. It was too small to house another PLV like the Lower Airlock but served as a launch point for individual and small group EVAs when they were necessary. As Flynn had also observed first hand, the Upper Airlock served as the primary docking interface for the ship.

After touring each of the decks, one by one, Hans and Flynn returned to the Engineering Deck and sat down at the central control desk. As they sat together in the captain style chairs that were mounted under the main desk, Flynn spoke up first. "Hans, I can read up on the ship's systems in more detail later. What I really want to talk about now is power and propulsion. Can we cut to the chase at this point?

"Of course Captain, of course," he replied. If truth be told, those were his favorite topics as well so he eagerly complied with Flynn's request.

Hans explained that the ship's electrical power was supplied by two hydrogen powered Tokomak style fusion reactors, a primary and a backup. These reactors were recognizable as the first two ring-like structures attached to the aft portion of the ship's boom. The reactors were highly efficient versions of the type that Flynn was familiar with, and the power produced was used to drive the ships electrical power generators.

Sensing an eagerness in his captain to get to the topic of ship's propulsion, he shifted the subject immediately and started with an explanation of the fusion boosters.

Attached to the aft portion of the outer hull assembly were two hydrogen powered, direct conversion, fusion boosters. The fuel for the boosters was stored in the booster assemblies as well as the four fuel tanks that ran the length of the ship above and below the boosters. These boosters would provide the initial thrust that would take them out of Earth orbit. They could accelerate the Providence, fully loaded, up to .1c or 10% of the speed of light.

Flynn interupted him, "Let me stop you right there and ask you some questions that relate to the state of the space program before the invasion, specifically on the topic of propulsion."

"OK," Hans replied.

"Well, as I recall there was some pretty poor leadership at the presidential level that caused the U.S. to more or less surrender its position as the international space leader to the Russians and the Chinese. The U.S. was stuck having to *pay* the Russians an exorbitant amount of money to get *our* astronauts to the "International" Space Station that everybody knows we paid for. It was absolutely humiliating.

"And although the Chinese failed in their quest to land on the moon just prior to the invasion, at least they failed trying to push the boundaries of their own program. They at least tried.

"Now I know we made some real progress in space, despite having only a few presidents with real vision, but I don't recall any nation that had come close to developing a propulsion system that could take us to the stars. And even though I'm guessing that the fusion boosters you mentioned are extremely fuel efficient and offer the highest specific impulse currently available, you know as well as I do that .1c isn't going to cut it. At that rate it would take us around 100 years or more to get to our nearest neighboring stars and back, assuming we didn't run out of fuel first, which we most certainly would.

"I know that time is not as great a factor now that the longevity of man has been restored, but something tells me that the First Born has a quicker timetable in mind. Unless we can accelerate to at least 50 to 70 percent of light speed and can carry the necessary fuel, which is just about impossible I might add, we can't make roundtrip visits to any of them in less than 20 years or so. Am I missing something or are you about to tell me that the other engine, the one with the scoop, can get us up to those kinds of speeds?"

"Well sir, here is where it gets very interesting!" Hans exclaimed very excitedly, "It will take a good bit of explaining."

"Let me first begin by borrowing from an old American advertising slogan. These are not your father's fusion thrusters. Over the last 100 years since the Knowledge Seas were loosed, we have made tremendous strides in fusion propulsion.

"The Providence is 1200 feet long, just a hair longer than a Reagan Class nuclear carrier from the days before the Millennium. With a ship that size, you can carry the fuel necessary to feed the fusion boosters to get us up to around .1c. After that, we need help to get in the range of .5 - .7 c. With that kind of speed, and with a little help from the Lorentz contraction of the distances involved, we can approach what we call "equivalent light speed" and get to some of our nearest neighbors in less than 20 years.

"Before I can tell you about the other engine, we have to talk about the latest discoveries in the field of astrophysics and subatomic particle physics. As I am sure you are aware by now, the Sacred Text makes mention of natural bodies versus celestial bodies. And we are only just now beginning to better understand that the differences described actually refer to two different forms of matter, one that exists in the natural or physical realm of the First Sphere and another that exists primarily in the celestial realm of the Second Sphere.

"Physicists just prior to the Millennium were struggling to get their arms around the concept of what they called 'dark matter' and 'dark energy'. Their existence had been hotly debated, but has now been confirmed. Interestingly, because of the negative connotations of the term dark, the First Born has directed all research scientists and engineers who are engaged in this type of research to refer to these phenomena as 'celestial matter' and 'celestial energy'.

"Furthermore, he relayed to the scientific community that the Creator had designed celestial matter and energy to work in concert with the ordinary matter of this dimensional realm to precisely control the expansion of the universe.

"The exact nature of celestial matter is still a matter of intense research but we now know that it is comprised of subatomic particles called neutralinos. Neutralinos have tremendous mass and just happen to be their own antiparticle. This means if you could devise a scheme by which large numbers of neutralinos were collected and forced to collide at high energies, they would annihilate one another converting 100% of their mass into energy. This enormous source of energy could be harnessed into a thruster powerful enough to propel a ship to near light speeds.

"The problem is that celestial matter is known to be weakly interactive with ordinary matter meaning you would have to build a device that could collect and compress the neutralinos without allowing them to simply pass through the walls of the collector or the compressor. So when the RSEC starting working with Nadia and SRI to build the Providence, the method of propulsion was the first thing that needed to be addressed.

"Everything about the ship was to be built around the main propulsion system. Nadia's idea was to take the concept of the Bussard Ramjet and apply it toward building a celestial matter drive; ideas that were first advanced by physicist Robert Bussard in 1960 and then modified by Jia Liu fifty years later. Liu's idea was to use Bussard's basic concept but to collect dark or celestial matter instead of hydrogen.

"She believed she had a workable design for the collection and compression of celestial matter, but knew that it could not be constructed of ordinary matter. She also knew that if they could build such a drive, it would eliminate the need to carry the massive amounts of fuel required to get to our nearest neighboring stars. Since celestial matter is abundantly available throughout the known universe, albeit at different concentrations, fuel could be collected and burned continually throughout any journey that was planned.

"During this time, the First Born came to SRI and said he had a critical design input that he wished to discuss with Nadia and the design team. He told them if they could design a drive with an appropriate collector and compressor, he would help them with the right kind of material to provide celestial matter containment.

"A couple of months later, hundreds of crates arrived in the main warehouse at SRI in Denver, which he said were filled with special alloy plates. These plates were an alloy of conventional composite materials but were doped with a high concentration of celestial matter. With this configuration, He explained, the ordinary matter in the plates would contain the celestial matter without leakage and provide the means to collect, contain, and compress the fuel necessary to make the celestial matter drive operate as envisioned. The plates could be molded and shaped as required to accommodate the drive as designed by Nadia and her team."

"But how was such an alloy constructed?" asked Flynn. "I know of no process that could forge such an alloy. Other than the Brethren, who are composed of a mix of ordinary and celestial matter, celestial matter still cannot be seen or detected in this realm apart from its gravitational effects on ordinary matter. That's why they used to call it dark matter."

"That's exactly the point I think," replied Hans. "The first Born explained that we, as Brethren, share the same trans-dimensional characteristics as these alloys in that they leverage the relative strengths of both ordinary and celestial matter together. Very similar to the way that we were formed, these special materials were constructed via celestial processes only available in the environment of the Great City on the Sides of the North. They had been forged there and personally transported to this dimensional realm by the First Born himself.

A prime example of such materials, he said, was the transparent gold that was abundantly available in the Great City. There, impurities in ordinary gold can be completely removed by doping it with celestial matter via processes that cannot be duplicated in this dimensional realm.

After mulling all this over Flynn could no longer remain silent and burst forth with an incredulous question, "Are you saying that the First Born has deliberately helped us tap into the celestial matter that is used to precisely maintain the controlled expansion of the universe in order to propel us to the stars at unheard of velocities in this ship?"

"That is exactly what I am saying," Hans replied. "Furthermore, without his help, there is no way we could do any of this. The Knowledge Seas, which he personally loosed, have taken us further technologically in a hundred years than we could have gone in a thousand years on our own. It suggests to me that this is much more than the fulfillment of *your* dream and *my* dream; this is much bigger than that.

"Surely this has to do with the destiny of all mankind and the plans and purposes of the Creator since the beginning of time!"

"I'm inclined to agree with you Hans and all I can say is, wow! This is going to be an *extraordinary* adventure and I can't wait to get started!"

"Neither can I," said Hans. "Neither can I."

Flynn was quietly pleased that he had managed to conjure up another adjective. He had graduated from amazing, to awesome, to *extraordinary*. "One more thing Hans," Flynn blurted out. "You've got to tell me a little more about these gravity field generators. Just exactly how do they work?"

Hans explained the concept of these devices as succinctly as he could. The gravity field generator that gave the crew compartment of the ship its artificial gravity operated on an advanced concept which involved the use of super computers that manipulated extremely powerful electromagnetic fields in such a way that two virtual masses could be constructed. Each virtual mass would exhibit its own artificial gravity field. One virtual mass was given an opposite polarity so that the diallel gravity field lines between the two masses would behave more like magnetic field lines. The virtual masses were configured so that the "down" lines of gravitational force ran from "north" to "south" and worked to pull one toward the bottom of the ship's functional decks at exactly one g.

There was a secondary gravity field generator that was used to counteract the ship's acceleration and could be configured so that the "up" lines ran counter to the g-force generated by the ship's direction of motion. That way, the only g-force you would sense would be the down lines coming from the top or north side of the ship.

In other words you could stand up "normally" on the deck structures during the sustained periods of one g acceleration and deceleration that would be encountered during their mission profile. The secondary system was not used for the shorter and sometimes more intense periods of acceleration and deceleration that would sometimes be necessary.

"Thank you Hans," Flynn declared. "I'm sure I'll have lots more questions as the year goes by, but for now, I think I've got a good feel for the Providence and her systems. "I'm really looking forward to working with you."

"Very well Captain," Hans replied. "I'll escort you back to the Wardroom at this time."

As they rode the elevator back to the Mess Deck, Flynn's imagination was ablaze with activity. It had been a day like no other in his entire existence, overwhelming yet invigorating at the same time. The ship's tour had only served to stoke the fires to an even greater degree. He could not stop thinking of what it would be like to light the burners on those engines and streak through space toward destinations unknown.

*Readers interested in more details of the ship's systems can find them in the Technology Appendix at the back of the book. Others not so inclined can skip this section and go directly to Chapter Sixteen. However, keep in mind that the Particle Beam Emitter (PBE) described in this appendix will play a major role in the events of book three in the trilogy,* **Millennial Conflict.**

# CHAPTER 16
# :SPACE TRIALS

Flynn and Matt threw themselves into the Captain's Course with the zeal and discipline that was common to them both. They became completely absorbed in the process of learning the ship and of engaging in the leadership discussions, the training scenarios, and the simulation runs that were integral parts of their training. They would spend many an hour together afterhours quizzing one another continually on various aspects of crew leadership, ship systems and operations. As a result, the year passed quickly.

There were several visits by Hannah and Ellen who would come together to visit them on the ship, much like the old days in the First Life when they would come to visit Flynn and Matt at Edwards AFB. Flynn was thankful for these times and was grateful that his family had become such an important part of this fantastic dream. One of the most enjoyable things that came at the end of the year's training was the fact that Flynn Jr. had completed his Chaplain's Course, and Flynn had been privileged to place the Lieutenant Commander shoulder boards onto Flynn Jr.'s epaulets during the commissioning ceremony that was held on the ship.

Of course, he knew that he would miss Hannah and Wendy during the space trials, but was comforted by the knowledge that they would continue to be engaged in important Kingdom business at KEI.

Flynn would miss Matt too, but knew he would see him as soon as the trials were over. The two would spend a great deal of time together debriefing afterward.

## : SOME DREAMS FOLLOW

The day after the completion of his training, the First Born arrived on the ship to personally brief Flynn and his command staff. Flynn had gotten to know them extremely well as they had all participated in his training over the last year. Every time he had sat at the Captain's Station during emergency drills, scenario training, and simulated mission profiles, they had manned their respective stations while training their cohorts in ship systems and operations.

In all there were a total of 100 crewmembers that would man the ship during the space trials. During that year, all of them had spent as many or more hours as Flynn, training at their respective stations or duty assignments.

As they had expected, the space trials would involve a gravity assist around the Sun that would propel them out of the Solar System. Before leaving, they would remain in orbit around Earth for a planned test landing of the Planetary Landing Vehicle, the Falcon. If everything went well with the PLV landing, they would rendezvous and recapture the PLV, and then light the fusion boosters to accelerate out of Earth orbit.

After leaving Earth orbit they would intercept a transfer orbit which would eventually place them in orbit around Venus, moving one planet closer to the Sun. They would orbit Venus enough times to test all their planetary sensors and then boost out to another transfer orbit which would take them around the Sun. They would slingshot around the Sun and accelerate past the orbits of Mars, Jupiter, Saturn, Uranus, and Neptune on a planned trajectory toward the Alpha Centauri AB system.

After passing the Kuiper Belt and reaching .1c, they would engage the CM drive and accelerate to .7c. Once they reached .7c, they would shut down the CM drive and remain in collect mode only. They would continue to collect and store celestial matter in the CM collection tank right up to the deceleration phase of their journey.

At this time they would turn the ship to align and fire the CM drive for deceleration. After deceleration, they would arrive in an orbit around Alpha Centauri B roughly 100 million miles out. If they found no habitable planets orbiting Alpha Centauri B, they would proceed to Alpha Centauri A. They would investigate any promising planets and set up orbits around them for a closer look and for further study. They would deploy a landing party only if it had been determined that a planet was habitable. Since they only had one PLV and therefore no margin for error, they would keep these excursions to a minimum.

After spending no more than a year investigating the Alpha Centauri system, they would employ a similar profile for the return trip to Earth. The Alpha Centauri system was 4.4 light years from the Earth and contained our nearest neighboring stars. Factoring in about eight months to accelerate at one g to .7c, and another eight months to decelerate at one g from .7c, the mission profile would average roughly .64c. Thus the roundtrip journey with the one year tour of Alpha Centauri would take them about ten of their years to complete. Because of the relativistic time dilation, about 13 years will have passed on planet Earth when they finally returned home.

When the First Born had finished laying out the planned space trials, Flynn sensed it was finally time to ask him some of the nagging questions that had formed in his mind over the past year.

He looked directly at the First Born and said, "My Lord, I beg your indulgence and ask that you entertain a few basic questions."

*"Of course Flynn"*, he replied. *"I'm sure you are not the only one with questions, so go ahead."*

"My Lord, I have a string of them and thought it best if I voiced them all at once, and let you answer them as you deem appropriate. To begin with, Lord, why are we doing this? What will we find out there? What about the Moon and Mars? And who's paying for all of this?"

## : SOME DREAMS FOLLOW

The First Born smiled as he looked approvingly at Flynn, *"Well Flynn, the answer to the first question is related to the second and will probably take the most time, so I will begin by answering you're last two questions about the Moon and Mars and the funding of this monumental project. By the way, the name of this project has been withheld till now; we call it Project Star Bound.*

*"I will start with the funding question. Star Bound has been deemed by me as one of the most important projects we will embark upon during the Millennium. Therefore no expense has been spared or will be spared when it comes to the Royal Space Exploration Corps, to the training facilities at RSFA, or to the future ships that we will be building here at Bethel and at other places. Some aspects of the project will be cost shared by the Kingdom together with small and large business entities. However, other portions will be funded exclusively by the Kingdom through worldwide tax revenues. The bottom line is this: we are <u>going</u> to do this, and Star Bound will be fully funded. It's that important.*

*"Oh, and the reason we are bypassing the Moon and Mars for now is because they are not habitable. We are looking for habitable planets that can support human life without extraordinary technological intervention. And for that, we must go to the stars. There are plans for the Moon, and Mars, and the other planets in this Solar System which we will discuss at a later time.*

*"As to your first two questions; let me begin by saying that the quest for exploration and to search out new lands is something that the Creator firmly placed within the heart of man from the very beginning. Man <u>must</u> explore because it is in his heart to do so. He <u>must</u> reach out toward the unknown and make it known; it is a powerful drive that simply has to be fulfilled."*

He looked around the table at the rest of Flynn's command staff and continued, *"Some, like you and the members of your staff, have this quest more deeply imprinted into their hearts. Indeed, it burns within you like a bright and enduring flame. This* is why you have been chosen to be leaders in this vital project. Simply put: mankind must explore, it is in his heart to do so, and you have been called to lead them in this quest.

"But there is an equally important reason why you must go to the stars. To provide context, let me say that it has always been the plan of the Creator to have a people that would grow <u>without bounds</u>. It is an important part of the promise he made to Abraham; that out of him he would bring forth a people who would be as innumerable as the stars themselves. Just because the Dark One was able to corrupt mankind does not mean that the Creator has changed his mind concerning his original plan.

"As you are about to find out, the original plans of the Creator <u>will be</u> fulfilled, no matter what, and the wise man will do well to follow his plans, not his own, and not another's. With this in mind and with the knowledge that the longevity of man has been restored, it will not be long before the Earth will not be able to contain the people that will come forth.

"With the intrinsic growth rate we are currently experiencing, the population of the Earth will grow to 34 billion within the next 900 years. That's about one acre of land mass per person. Not a whole lot of room and definitely not what the Creator had in mind for his people. You must pave the way for mankind to go to the stars because we will soon run out of room here on the Earth. It has always been their destiny. It is where they <u>must</u> go and you have been called to take them there!

"As to what you will find out there, that is for you to answer, not me. I may know, but it is not in your best interest that I tell you everything I know. Let me quote from the Sacred Text: 'It is the glory of God to conceal a thing: but the honor of kings is to search out a matter.' You are my chosen kings, and so it is your honor to search out these matters for yourselves.

"To tell you ahead of time what you will find out there would quench your thirst for knowledge, and douse your inner longing *to probe the unknown and find your own answers. The one thing I can tell you for sure is this: there will be surprises."*

There weren't that many tearful goodbyes on the Bethel the day that the Providence was scheduled to leave and embark upon her maiden journey. Except for Flynn and his son, the remaining crewmembers chosen for the space trials were all handpicked single individuals who would leave no wife or children behind. There were goodbyes said to mothers, fathers, brothers and sisters but that had been accomplished during the shore leave that was granted to the crew the week before their scheduled launch. Most of the tears from those goodbyes had long since dried and had been replaced with the excitement and anticipation of a journey that was the first of its kind in the history of mankind.

"Where are Flynn Jr. and Wendy?" Flynn asked as his small group assembled on the Main Bridge to say their farewells.

"They said their goodbyes about an hour ago, one on one, and Wendy is already aboard the Starliner. Flynn Jr. has returned to the Chapel to offer last minute prayers for our safe journey."

"Oh, OK, really glad he's praying for us," he acknowledged as he hugged Hannah one more time. He kissed her softly and whispered, "You're coming with me one of these days."

"Maybe sooner than you think, my love, maybe sooner than you think," she replied.

Matt and Emma had escorted her there for the final farewell, and when Flynn finally released his wife, Matt grabbed him by the shoulders and shook him, "Remember buddy, I'm right on your heels! Oh, and just so you know; I'll be in the control tower for the PLV landing and turnaround at Edwards. Kind of like the old days but way cooler, huh?"

"That's good to know Matt; good to know," Flynn replied. He turned to Emma and said, "Take care of the big guy while I'm gone, will ya?"

"Of course," she answered. "Be careful out there Flynn, and remember that your crew are almost entirely Children and are not indestructible. Not sure why I said that but felt like I needed to."

"Thank you for that Emma," he replied, "I covet your prayers for our safe journey."

"You got it. I'll double up with Hannah on that score as well."

Hannah managed to squeeze in one more hug before the group entered the elevator for the ride to the docking interface. She blew him a kiss as the door to the elevator closed. As he watched the door close, Flynn thought, "Man, I'm gonna miss that girl!"

Four hours later, all the pre-separation checklists had been run, and it was time for undock and launch of the Providence. Flynn assumed his position at the Captain's Station and remained standing while the Providence undocked from Bethel and the final pressurization and major systems checks were run. The whole process took about an hour and it seemed like to Flynn that they would never get out of there and out into open space.

He was relieved when he finally heard Captain Steele relay over the radio, "Providence, you are go for Space Station exit."

"Go for Space Station exit," Flynn responded.

"Engineer, confirm release of all tethers, power connections and docking interface," he ordered.

"All tethers, connections and docking interface released," Hans replied from the Engineer's station.

"Navigator, maintain this orbit till we reach safe separation, downrange 500 meters," he barked.

Mattie answered cheerfully from the Navigator station, "Maintain orbit till safe separation, downrange 500 meters."

"Helmsman, fire verniers in two three burst sequences with preset intervals, one second between," Flynn commanded with suppressed excitement in his voice.

AJ replied, "Aye, Captain. Two three burst sequences; preset intervals; one second between."

He fired the verniers a second later and they popped into action with their distinctive sounding: "chee, chee, chee … chee, chee, chee," until the Providence began to lurch forward ever so slightly. She lumbered toward the downrange end of the Bethel at what seemed like a snail's pace.

But as they had learned in numerous simulations, the separation maneuver was designed to be very slow and deliberate. The last thing they needed was a collision with the inner walls of the Space Station. Flynn peered out the front window panels on the bridge so he could keep his visual scan going during the maneuver. He knew that the ship's wrap around radar would sound a warning the moment that the Providence moved an inch too close to the walls, but it comforted him to be able to see what was going on from the bridge.

He tried to make the time pass quicker by counting bulkheads and panels with his peripheral vision as they moved through the Bethel, but soon the crew compartment was about to exit into open space. At that point he directed all his attention to the magnificent view available through the forward bridge windows.

He could see the curvature of the Earth with the stars in the background and the sun in the distance.

"What a view," he thought, as the crew compartment exited the Bethel. Then his mind shifted to the rest of the ship behind him.

"OK, the front end is out, but this is a big ship. There's a lot of tail behind us and I can't see what's going on from up here."

Finally, he calmed himself by recalling how many times he had simulated this maneuver, and how amazingly accurate those simulations had been. Though it seemed like an eternity to Flynn, it had only taken two minutes for the entire length of the ship to exit the Space Station after the first round of verniers had been fired.

"You are clear of the Bethel," relayed Captain Steele. "God's speed on your journey."

"Copy; clear of the Bethel, thanks Dan," Flynn replied with evident relief in his voice. "Helmsman, fire one burst of six with preset interval."

"Aye, Captain," replied AJ, also sounding relieved. "One burst of six with preset interval."

"Chee chee chee chee chee chee" popped the verniers and the ship accelerated downrange.

When they reached the safe separation point Flynn issued the next order, "Helmsman, inflate 10 kilometers."

"Aye Captain," replied AJ, "inflating 10 kilometers."

A few minutes later they reached their desired altitude, and Flynn issued orders for the Navigator and the Helmsman to lay in the automated sequence for maintaining a station-keeping orbit. Once this was done, Flynn shifted his thinking to preparations for the upcoming PLV test.

The Providence was scheduled to complete two full orbits around the Earth before the PLV test began. At their orbital velocity of 17,500 miles per hour, that would take them a little less than three hours. As they locked into automated station-keeping, Flynn told the bridge crew, "OK, everyone, separation maneuver complete; station-keeping established. Let's relax for a while but don't stray too far from your stations. Please be ready to go 30 minutes prior to PLV prelaunch checklists."

The Providence had three two man PLV crews that had undergone a rigorous training regimen at the Edwards RSEC support base. During that last year before launch, they had undergone hours and hours of simulator training and had accomplished numerous live launches and rendezvous with the Bethel. But this would be the first time that the PLV would be launched and recovered from the Providence. It was a critical test of system integration and crew coordination and involved an extensive ground control network that would track the ship during its orbit and during the launch and recovery of the PLV.

The U.S. space program was the only one of the national space programs that had not fallen into complete disarray after the invasion. Although the program had declined significantly, it was reconstituted rapidly under Kingdom leadership. The combination of a booming global economy, private sector and government investment, along with real leadership at the top, had helped to turn the program around. Eventually NASA and the remaining elements of other national programs were absorbed into the new Royal Space Exploration Corps.

After 100 years of Kingdom support, the RSEC had become a truly international space program with a highly sophisticated network of launch facilities, support bases, and tracking stations that spanned every continent. This network would monitor the Providence as it maintained its orbit and would follow every step of the planned deployment and recovery of the PLV.

One week later, Flynn was standing at the Captain's Station looking through the forward bridge windows staring out into open space. Everything had gone pretty much as planned on the PLV launch and recovery. The flight crews had performed in stellar fashion, he thought, with some really great flying done during the tests.

Crew One had performed a successful launch from the Lower Airlock, followed by a textbook reentry profile. The planned profile ended in a final approach and conventional landing on the long runway at Edwards. There was a one day break while the ground crews inspected the lander and serviced it for another launch.

Crew Two swapped seats with Crew One and flew a profile which took the lander to 360,000 feet and then back to a simulated thin atmosphere descent and transition to hover landing at a pad just a few miles south of Edwards.

The following day, Crew Three took over and performed a hover launch with a vertical transition and ascent to orbit, followed by the final rendezvous with the Providence. Everything went without a hitch and Flynn was reveling in that fact. The fourth generation SCRAM jet engines and auxiliary rocket thrusters had performed even better than expected, especially during the V/STOL phase of the testing. Even so, he remembered well the collective sigh that everyone had breathed once the Falcon was safely aboard, the Lower Airlock door had closed and the pressurization sequence had begun. And now, he was thinking, it was time for the really big show. It was time for the Providence to leave Earth and head to another star.

Flynn turned to the bridge crew and announced, "OK folks, all checklists have been complete; prepare to light the fusion boosters."

Unlike all the previous orders he had issued up to that point, this one was broadcast over the ship's intercom. Every crewmember on the ship was required to strap into their designated acceleration racks during phases of flight where acceleration was going to be a factor.

These racks were built into bulkheads, or walls, or on support struts near every crew station and in every one of the crew quarters. Because of the orientation of the ship's artificial gravity, they were already experiencing one g vertically, but when accelerating, the occupants would experience g forces perpendicular to their bodies and opposite to the ship's direction of motion. Thus, the accel racks were oriented vertically such that the individual would stand and strap himself into the rack during times of ship's acceleration. All the critical crew stations like Helmsman and Navigator could access all the required controls from their accel racks through easily accessible remote control stations.

Once the fusion thrusters were lit, there would be one g of acceleration that would last until they had attained escape velocity of 25,000 miles per hour, about 11 minutes in duration. That speed would allow them to leave Earth orbit and transition to an orbit that would take them to Venus. Once they departed Earth orbit, the secondary artificial gravity would be ramped up to counteract the one g of acceleration. At this point the crew would be allowed to leave their accel racks and return to their work or leisure stations.

After leaving Venus, they would head for the Sun. Once they got close enough, they would take advantage of its enormous gravitational field and perform a sling shot maneuver to whip them around the Sun and give them an extra boost of acceleration. This boost of acceleration together with the powerful fusion boosters would allow them to depart their Solar orbit and assume a trajectory that would take them beyond the Solar System toward Alpha Centauri AB. At .1c they would shut down the fusion boosters and engage the CM Drive. After reaching .7c, they would shut down the CM drive and coast for three and half years to the deceleration point in their profile.

Flynn was ready to go and turned and spoke to Flynn Jr. at the Chaplain's Station, "Lieutenant Commander Roberts, please do us the honor of praying for the Lord's guidance and for a safe and productive journey for Providence and her crew."

"Aye Captain," Flynn Jr. replied.

He waited a moment and continued over the ship's intercom, "All crewmembers please bow your heads in prayer.

"Dearest Heavenly Father, we thank you for your abiding love and for blessing this crew with the honor of doing something that no one has ever done before in the history of mankind. We beseech you for your continual guidance and protection and ask that you give us the courage we need to fulfill our duties as crewmembers to ensure a safe and productive journey. Lord, bless this ship and bless this crew. With your help we will fulfill our mission and pave the way for all mankind to reach their destiny in the stars, for your glory! We pray it in the name of our High Priest, Jesus! Amen!"

"Amen," Flynn said emphatically. "I had a wonderful speech prepared but that prayer says everything that needed to be said. I don't know about you, but I'm ready to get this mission started. Helmsman, light the fusion boosters in five!"

AJ responded enthusiastically, "Lighting the fusion boosters in five, aye … five … four … three … two … one …"

The trip to Venus was relatively uneventful. All the sensors and telemetry equipment were checked out and operated the way they were supposed to. The sling shot around the Sun was a little anticlimactic in that no one actually felt like they had been shot through a slingshot during the maneuver. There were a few tricky moments on the backside of the maneuver where the Helmsman had to coordinate the settings on the fusion boosters, and the Navigator had to align the trajectory precisely so that the ship could maximize the resulting boost of acceleration. The crew only had to get into the accel racks for a short period of time, and the most pressure anyone felt was about three g's of acceleration. Other than that it was not the big event that many had built it up to be.

Eight months later, the Providence had long since left the Solar System and was approaching the point where the Celestial Matter (CM) Drive would be lit. The biggest question in everyone's mind after they reached .1c was whether the CM Drive would work as advertised. The fusion boosters represented known technology so everybody pretty much expected them to work. Not that anyone doubted the wisdom of the First Born, but the whole concept of the CM Drive was largely theoretical; there was no known way to simulate ramming celestial matter particles at speeds of up to .1c into a smaller scale model or prototype engine. They wouldn't know for sure if it really worked until they lit the CM Drive for the first time. Consequently, everyone on the ship, including Flynn, was just a little bit nervous as the CM Drive pre-light checklists began.

After about an hour or so, the fusion boosters had been shut down and it was time to light the CM Drive. At .1c, the collection of celestial matter had been underway for some time. Some initial compression was accomplished through the ram effect of the high energy particles as they entered the scoop and into the central collection tank. But the compression necessary for ignition would not occur until the CM Compressor itself was engaged.

"Helmsman, light the CM Drive in five," Flynn barked.

This was one critical phase of flight he wanted to get through as quickly as possible, he thought. They were used to quick countdowns but the standard five seconds wouldn't pass fast enough to suit him.

"Lighting the CM drive in five, aye," AJ replied tersely, "five … four … three … two … one …"

AJ moved the knob forward on his control panel that engaged the CM Compressor and the CM Drive pulsed into life. AJ then engaged the automatic thrust controller which would ramp up the thrust level and slowly bring them up to one g of acceleration. After that it would synchronize its increase in thrust so that the ship continued to accelerate but never beyond one g. It was programmed to do this until the ship reached .7c, eight months later, after which the CM Drive would be disengaged.

Everyone was in their accel racks just in case, but there was only a small jolt of acceleration before the secondary artificial gravity was engaged to counter it. There was, however, a noticeable increase in the noise level. The white noise generators placed throughout the ship had done an excellent job of lowering the ambient noise level of the fusion boosters over the last eight months. In fact, they were barely audible as a high frequency background hum that you eventually drowned out of your mental processes.

The increase in noise level was expected but was more noticeable than the crew had anticipated and it was accompanied by an increase in vibration that was a little unsettling. After the vibration dampers kicked in, the vibration was reduced to a lower level and the noise seemed to fade a bit. Before long the CM Drive manifested itself as a slightly more noticeable vibration with a little bit louder background hum. It would take some getting used to but the ship's Flight Surgeon had assured the crew that it would not cause permanent damage to their hearing.

As Flynn and the rest of the Bridge Crew unstrapped from their accel racks, there was evident relief on everyone's face. The CM Drive appeared to be working as advertised. Good thing, Flynn thought, without it they were not going to get anywhere very fast and would have been forced to return to Earth using the fusion boosters only.

## :HIDDEN PLANET

## CHAPTER 17

The first three and a half years of their journey passed much quicker than Flynn had imagined. It wasn't like they didn't stay busy; there was always plenty to do on the ship. There were continual drills and regularly scheduled training sessions to prepare for the next major phase of flight on their profile. Training sessions and drills usually lasted for half a day, each day, during a five day workweek. The other half of the day was typically spent studying technical manuals for your respective crew position and attending regularly scheduled functional group meetings.

Crewmembers were required to maintain excellent physical conditioning and spent much of their free time on the Gym Deck working out. There was a digital library that could be accessed in all the quarters on the ship, and the crew had access to a huge data base of films and books. Regular socials were held in the Chaplain's Fellowship Hall so that everyone could get to know one another better. As a result, by the time they approached their destination, everyone on the crew was on a first name basis with one another.

Flynn had emphasized that military style protocol was expected while in uniform and on duty, but it was OK to be more familiar with one another in a social setting or outside of duty hours. Chapel services were mandatory for everyone unless you were on duty and were held twice a week on Sunday mornings and Wednesday evenings. It was kind of old school, Flynn thought, but comforting in its familiarity as well. Many of the crewmembers became involved with the Chaplain's ministry and helped Chaplain

Roberts and his small staff to organize and conduct regular church services, special worship services, and group prayer meetings.

95 of the 100 crewmembers on the Providence were Jacob's Children and of those, 32 were female, so the inevitable attraction between the sexes was something that had been anticipated. Dating was allowed but was subject to strict rules and guidelines. Any relationships that formed had to be conducted with the dignity, honor and purity expected of RSEC members. No male crewmembers were allowed in female quarters at any time and vice versa, and all crewmembers were subject to a midnight curfew which was strictly enforced by the ship's security detail.

If a couple's relationship developed to the point that marriage was being discussed, they were required to interview with Captain Roberts and could not get engaged without his permission. If permission was granted, they had to agree to regularly scheduled courtship, dating, and marriage counseling with Chaplain Roberts for the duration of the journey. These guidelines had been established as expected RSEC protocol for long range missions of this kind and had been made clear to prospective crew members before they signed on with the Providence. All crewmembers understood and appreciated these guidelines. Intimate interpersonal relationships that could disrupt their mission in any possible way could simply not be condoned.

Furthermore, they could not get married until their journey was complete and they had returned to Earth. The mission was going to last ten years, at least, and the ship was not equipped with a nursery. Although they hoped to avoid danger on their voyage, it was by no means guaranteed. Bottom line, the Providence was an experimental starship, the first of its kind, and was no place for children.

Flynn convened his weekly command staff meeting an hour earlier than normal because he had an interview scheduled afterward with Ensign Zachary Munn and Ensign Laurie Giddens. He had come a few minutes early as was his custom and had brewed up some fresh coffee. He poured himself a cup and sat there at the conference table wondering what he might say to them. It was the first time he would conduct a relationship interview and he wasn't quite sure what to expect. He thought about how unlikely it seemed to him that his shy and sometimes awkward captain's aide had managed to attract the attention of the pretty young nurse that was the Flight Surgeon's right hand man, so to speak.

He had discussed it with Commander Dave Ivey on a few occasions, and all he could say was that many times, opposites attract. He looked up as he saw that AJ was the first to come through the open door.

"Shikamoo, Captain Roberts," he said with a respectful nod of his head.

With his hands in the air, Flynn replied with the traditional Swahili response, "Marahaba my friend, Marahaba. I'm the Captain of the first starship in the history of mankind and only ten months away from our nearest star system. How much better could it be for a guy like me?"

"For me as well, as you know Captain," AJ replied.

Flynn rose from his chair and embraced him with an affectionate hug. He had developed a strong rapport with AJ and had taken the time to read up on Swahili and East African culture. Of all of the members of his command staff, aside from Mattie, he had become closest to AJ and enjoyed the playful banter that often accompanied their greetings.

After that, Nadia came in, followed by Hans, then Mattie.

"Good morning everyone," Flynn said, "Let's get started right away. I have an interview in an hour and I don't want to be late. The coffee's fresh or you can get some other beverage from the wall fridge if you like. I want to brief everyone on the upcoming deceleration phase of our profile."

He waited until everyone had the beverage of their choice and was seated at their customary place around the conference table.

He continued, "First of all, Nadia, I want to apologize for the fact that you have not had a lot to do thus far on this journey, other than watch everything I have been doing that is. I know we have not discussed this but I feel like a change to the task order is justified and I want you to take the Captain's Station for the ship's repositioning maneuver and the lighting of the CM Drive for the deceleration phase of our profile. From now on, you will run all drills and will report to me anything that you feel is a matter of concern. If I don't hear from you, I will assume that everything is as it should be. You've got about two months to get ready so I thought for starters I would turn the staff meetings over to you.

"I will continue to attend the meetings and will be on the bridge for most all of the drills, but you'll be running the show until we arrive at the Alpha Centauri AB system. Once we establish an orbit around AC Bravo, I will resume command duties. Understood?"

"Understood Captain," Nadia replied with a surprised look on her face.

"OK then Nadia, you got the rest of the staff meeting, I'm going back to my quarters to pray and ask the Lord for guidance concerning my upcoming interview, good day everyone."

"Aye Captain, I'll take the meeting from here," she said.

Flynn picked up his coffee cup then stood up and walked over to where she was sitting. He smiled at her and squeezed her shoulder firmly then walked briskly out the door headed toward his quarters.

As he passed through the bridge, he acknowledged the duty crew and then went forward to look out one of the Main Bridge windows. It was his custom to spend at least an hour or more a day, peering out at the amazing display of stars that were visible in deep space. Far from civilization, there was no light pollution to deal with and the view was always spectacular, especially now that AC Alpha and Bravo were becoming more and more prominent. Each day that they got closer, the two stars became more clearly visible as a two star system and grew larger and larger to the naked eye. They could even see the small red dwarf, Proxima Centauri, technically considered a part of the AC system, and the closest of the three to Earth at 4.22 light years.

He would use these times to meditate on the events of the day and prepare himself mentally for the events of the following day. He would often offer up quiet prayers so as not to disturb the duty crew and would spend the time communing with the Creator. Thanksgiving always flowed abundantly from his heart and many times there would be tears of gratefulness.

This particular morning, however, he only had a few minutes to spare and spent the time pondering the sheer wonder of the fact that they were almost four light years from Earth and were traveling at 70% the speed of light. Of course, you couldn't tell by looking out the window. Except for the fact that AC Alpha and Bravo grew noticeably larger by the day, there was absolutely no sensation of motion. There was no sound or vibration from either the fusion boosters or the CM Drive. They had been silent for just over three years. There was nothing to indicate that you were moving through space at such an incredible speed. Often times he would walk over to the Navigators Station and ask for their current position. If Mattie happened to be the duty Navigator, she always seemed to know what he was up to.

After giving the official answer according to military protocol, she would wink at him and whisper something like, "G-daddy, we have moved 210,000 kilometers since the last time you asked."

Although he knew internally exactly how far they were from Earth at any given moment, it was reassuring to Flynn to have an independent confirmation. Once Alpha and Bravo became more prominent, he did this less frequently than he had done during the first part of their journey.

When the time arrived for the deceleration phase Nadia performed as brilliantly as Flynn had expected she would. She commanded, and the crew performed, a flawless reposition and relight of the CM Drive. And now that the background noise and vibration was back, it felt to Flynn as if they were once again moving. Never mind the fact that the ship was now pointed away from their destination and that they were actually slowing down; there was just something comforting about that.

After almost eight months of deceleration, navigation sensors had confirmed that they were close enough and slow enough to reposition the ship for a tour of the Alpha Centauri system. The CM Drive had been shut down, and the day had arrived to turn the ship around and light the fusion boosters. Nadia was at the Captain's Station and Flynn was seated in the chair next to hers.

The pre-maneuver checklists had been run and Nadia began the maneuver with the first command in the sequence, "Helmsman, prepare to bring the ship about."

AJ responded with "Prepare to bring the ship about, aye."

She continued, "Fire forward port and aft starboard yaw verniers; five second burst; in five."

AJ responded swiftly with, "Fire forward port and aft starboard yaw verniers; five second burst; in five, aye ... five ... four ... three ... two ... one."

The verniers hissed into action with an uncharacteristically long burst, and the ship started a slow turn toward the starboard side of the ship. About half way through the turn there was a noticeable increase in brightness, and it increased rapidly as they rounded the turn. Just before the first star came into view, the auto polarization of the bridge windows kicked in and the brightness dimmed to the point that you could look directly at the star without using your hand to shield your eyes.

As the bright orange star came into view, Mattie blurted out excitedly, "That's AC Bravo! Alpha will be to the right and further out. We should see it any moment now."

A few seconds later, AC Alpha sprang into view. Because Bravo was the closer of the two, it dominated the view with a blazing intensity. Although Alpha appeared smaller, it shone with a yellow brilliance that rivaled its sister star, making it clear that it was actually the larger and brighter of the two.

It had been eight months since they were able to look at the two stars, and they were much larger and brighter than the last time that they saw them. A hush came upon all who were on the bridge as everyone took a moment to take in the magnitude of what they were observing.

They were the first human beings in history to visit another star system and now the two stars in the Alpha Centauri system were right in front of their eyes. In fact, at just over 100 million miles out, Bravo was about as close to their eyes as their home Sun was to Earth on a clear summer day in July.

Nadia had kept her focus throughout the maneuver however, though equally taken by the moment.

"Helmsman, reverse vernier sequence to complete the yaw maneuver in five."

"Reverse vernier sequence to complete the yaw maneuver in five, aye ... five ... four ... three ... two ... one."

AJ fired the verniers to arrest the ship as she completed her turn, but his eyes never left the two stars that were in their direct field of view. It was a sight to behold, he thought, and an awesome answer to prayer as well.

"Bwana asifiwe," he whispered softly as he stared intently at the two stars. "Bwana asifiwe!"

He looked over at Flynn and they both rose to their feet at the same time. With his eyes transfixed on the two stars, Flynn echoed the quiet exclamation of wonder, "Bwana asifiwe, bwana asifiwe, praise the Lord!"

Without taking his eyes off of the two stars, Flynn turned toward the intercom transmitter at the Captain's station and made the following announcement: "This is the Captain speaking, all crewmembers report to the bridge. Let's do it by decks, starting with Deck One to keep the crowds down. You gotta see this for yourselves. If you're on duty, rotate with someone who's already been up here but get up here and take a look as soon as you can."

It wasn't long before the bridge became a conduit flowing with a steady stream of crewmembers, all taking their turns and staring with wonder at the sight before them. The momentous nature of what they saw was not lost to a single soul. The two stars clearly visible in their field of view represented the greatest technological achievement in the history of mankind.

Flynn turned to his son who had joined them late and was arm in arm with his father.

"Chaplain Roberts, please lead us in a prayer of consecration and dedication; consecration to the purposes of God, and dedication to our God-given mission."

"My pleasure Captain, my pleasure," Flynn Jr. replied. He cleared his throat briefly and moved to the ship's intercom.

"Let us pray dear brothers and sisters. Dear Heavenly Father, we ask for your help and your guidance as we seek to do your will. Lead us by your Spirit to the place that you have for us on this mission. We know you did not bring us here just to say we saw Alpha Centauri up close and personal. We are convinced there is a place for us here.

"We consecrate our lives to you and trust that as we dedicate ourselves to this mission, we will fulfill your plan for us as individuals and as crewmembers aboard this great ship, His Majesty's Space Ship Providence. We pray it in the name of our High Priest, Jesus."

There was a collective *amen* breathed by everyone on the bridge and throughout the ship and then things began to return to normal, at least as normal as they could with the kind of excitement in the air that was generated by the sight of these two stars.

About an hour later when most of the crowds had dissipated, the sensor operator suddenly blurted out, "Captain, multiple sensor inputs point to significant gravity perturbations in Bravo's orbit around Alpha. It would seem to indicate the presence of one or more planet sized objects. The closest one looks to be on the other side of Bravo about 80 million miles out. It might be a planet but we're not in position to know for sure."

"Thank you for the information Ensign Nelson. Perhaps our prayers have been answered," Flynn said resolutely.

He turned to Mattie and continued, "Navigator, compute a trajectory that will get us to the other side and intercept that object. And let me know how long it will take us to get there."

"Trajectory computed Captain. Our speed is just right to intercept an orbit 80 million miles out from Bravo. Once we do that it will take us about 3 months to arc around Bravo and take a closer look."

The entire duty crew turned and looked at Mattie, amazed at how fast she had completed the task. Flynn realized then that she had seen the same data the sensor operator had seen and had already done the calculations in anticipation of his command.

Nadia turned to Flynn and murmured, "Captain, you have the bridge and you have command."

"Sorry about that Commander Habibi, I got caught up in the excitement and forgot about protocol," Flynn replied sheepishly. "I resume command and will try not to let that happen again."

He turned again to Mattie, "Navigator, lay in that trajectory. We'll coast around Bravo to take a look. If it's a planet that looks promising, we'll establish an orbit.

"Helmsman, maneuver the ship onto that trajectory."

Mattie and AJ replied in sequence, "Aye Captain," and then immediately got busy.

The dinner chatter in the Officer's Wardroom was unusually high on that particular evening. The last three months had gone by quickly and everyone had been abuzz over the view that was now available from their 300 mile orbit over the planet. The Main Bridge windows were now facing the planet and offered a spectacular panorama. It looked very similar to Earth except there was not near as much water covering the planet. There were large bodies of water that seemed randomly distributed across the globe, but nothing large enough to be considered an ocean, at least not by Earth standards. All totaled, these sea-like bodies of water covered about one fifth of the planet.

The other thing they noticed was that there were no polar regions at all. This was visual confirmation of what ship's sensor data had indicated; the planet rotated exactly 90 degrees perpendicular to its plane of rotation around AC Bravo. Its estimated size was just a bit larger than Earth with a diameter of

9,000 miles and a circumference of just over 28,000 miles. The planet rotated about its axis at the equator at about 1200 miles per hour which amazingly yielded a day night cycle of just under 24 hours. Gravity there would be about 1.1 times that of Earth according to science staff calculations. There was a similar atmosphere to that of Earth with a mix of about 30% oxygen and 70% nitrogen.

What had everyone buzzing was that the planet seemed to be predominantly green indicating that plant life was already thriving there. There had also been signs of animal life as long range optical sensors had picked up what looked like large migratory herds moving across some of the vast grassy plains that seemed to be everywhere. In short, if plant and animal life were already thriving there, the planet appeared perfectly suited to support human life.

Furthermore, the science crowd had been convinced that AC Alpha, a G2 yellow star almost exactly like our Sun, would be the one most likely to host a habitable planet. They had been puzzled at the choice of AC Bravo, a K2 orange star with less than half the brightness of the Sun, as their primary target.

"What do you think about all this Hans?" Flynn asked as he passed him a dinner roll. "You've spent most of your time on the Engineering Deck during this trip."

"Captain, I cannot tell you how excited I am! I have been sneaking up to the bridge on a regular basis to take a look at the planet. And since you asked the question, I've been meaning to ask you something.

"I am requesting permission to be on the first landing party. I simply cannot miss it sir, I just cannot."

"Well Hans," Flynn replied with a smile on this face, "you will be pleased to know that the first landing party will consist of all Brethren for safety's sake. You and I, Mattie, AJ, and Flynn Jr.

will be on that first landing party. The only Children that will be on that trip will be the two pilots."

"That is very good news indeed, Captain, very good news. I cannot wait to see this new world that awaits us," Hans replied excitedly.

"Keep this to yourself for now Hans," Flynn said, "practically everyone on this ship wants to be on that first landing party, and I don't blame them."

"Absolutely, Captain," Hans replied, "I will tell no one."

Lieutenant Commander Brian Salley was the aircraft commander of the PLV, the Falcon, and he was busy conferring with his copilot, Lieutenant Cory Brown. They were both standing outside the Falcon on the Lower Airlock Deck looking at their e-pads, checking their profile one last time before the scheduled launch.

The plan was to fly a conventional atmosphere approach profile with a V/STOL landing at the end. There would be no prepared strip for them to land on, so they had coordinated with the science staff and had picked a large grassy plain near the equator for their primary landing spot. All indications were that the vegetation would be light and there would be no problems with a vertical landing. As they heard the elevator door open, they turned to see the landing party exiting and heading their way.

"Good morning Captain," Brian said as they approached the Falcon.

"Good morning Lieutenant Commander Salley," Flynn shouted. "Let's get this show on the road!"

"Absolutely sir," he replied, "but first, let's gather round the Falcon for our crew/passenger preflight briefing."

"Of course Commander, don't let my zeal knock you out of rhythm. Let's do everything by the book," Flynn responded.

The briefing was standard and took about 15 minutes to complete. After Flynn Jr. prayed a short prayer thanking God for divine protection, they were ready to board the Falcon. Since everyone was suited up as a precaution, it took a while to load up and strap in the entire landing party. Flynn was thankful that the space suits they wore were lightweight and much less bulky than their predecessors. Otherwise, it would have taken much longer to load up and strap in.

There were two rows of passenger seats directly behind the pilots' seats and each row had five seats. Flynn, AJ, Mattie, Flynn Jr., and Hans all sat together in the row immediately behind the pilots. It offered the best view possible, other than the pilot seats, and nobody wanted to miss a thing visually if they could help it.

The depressurization went without a hitch, and before long the airlock doors were opened and they were on their way. Commander Salley maneuvered the aircraft manually to intercept the reentry profile and the protective heat shields moved out of their slots and covered the front and side windows of the Falcon. Once they reached the entry point, he engaged the automatic approach system and radioed to the Providence that the reentry profile had commenced.

Soon after, they would lose radio contact and would not regain it completely until they had penetrated the upper atmosphere and they had cooled down a bit. Flynn was watching everything he could from the back seat and was definitely in his element. These guys are good, he thought, no wonder they got selected as Crew One.

After a pretty bumpy ride of about 10 minutes, they had cooled to the point in their descent where the window shields could be retracted. As they did, he could see that they were clear of clouds and were low enough that they could soon convert from glide to fly mode and engage the scramjets. A second or two afterwards, he saw Brian and Cory flip some switches and the scramjets roared to life. He could see by the central multifunction display that they were right on profile and were just about to complete the spiral portion of their descent. He watched as they completed their last spiral and lined up for their final approach to the grassy plain that had been selected.

Once they had started down their final glide path and had descended into the thick of the atmosphere he noticed that there was a blue sky which had just a hint of green mixed in, probably because of the higher oxygen content, he reasoned. It was then that he noticed that he could clearly make out the two suns that hung quite beautifully together in the sky.

Alpha was much smaller, down and to his right, definitely yellow but contributing significantly to the brightness of the day. Bravo was up and to his left, larger by far, but clearly orange in color. That was going to take some getting used to he thought, but what a beautiful looking world.

He could see majestic mountains in the distance to his right and vast grassy plains with patches of jungle to his left. It looked like the Serengeti of Africa, but so far there were no signs of life of any kind. There was a river that ran from the mountains down toward the jungle patches. It stretched from north to south as far as the eye could see. It was not until they sighted the grassy plain that had been selected as a landing site and started the conversion to V/STOL mode that he realized how quiet everyone had been.

Except for the checklist chatter between the pilots, everyone else had been glued to the windows and was taking it in just like Flynn. As they descended through the last few hundred feet and started the landing transition, he scanned the designated landing area in all directions. It was a large grassy meadow, surrounded by low brush and hedge-like shrubs. The brush was thicker in some places than others and he noticed that the entire area seemed to be devoid of any signs of animal life. Just then, he saw what appeared to be movement in some bushes to his left, the south side of the grassy plain. He looked again and saw nothing, convinced that he was just seeing things.

Wishful thinking, he thought. Maybe the sensor operators had been wrong about the signs of migratory animal herds. They should just be thankful that there was an abundance of plant life and that fresh water looked to be plentiful in this portion of their new world. While he pondered that, he was startled by a sudden increase in thrust that meant they were about to touch down. Thirty seconds later, the throttle was reduced just as the four landing pads touched the grass of the plain. They settled into the shocks as the engines wound down quickly to idle.

Commander Salley was well aware of the historic nature of the moment and made a familiar sounding report over the radio, "Providence, the Falcon has landed!"

There was no small stir on the Main Bridge of the Providence and everyone cheered the momentous event. Nadia made an announcement over the ship's intercom and soon the whole ship was buzzing with excitement.

On board the Falcon, the excitement had built rapidly as well, especially since the final descent had offered such spectacular views of the new world they were about to visit.

As briefed, they sat at idle until Flynn was ready to disembark. He would be the first to step foot on the new planet and the others would follow. Flynn had put this decision to his command staff and they had voted unanimously that the honor would be his. He was deeply moved by that and spent a week or so trying to come up with appropriate words to mark the occasion.

As he exited the left side hatch and stepped off the ladder, his feet sank into a foot of soft, yellow-green grass. Underneath the cushion of grass, the ground felt firm and warm under his boots. With a surge of emotion and with his voice trembling slightly, he made the following proclamation over the open comm frequency: "I claim this planet in the name of His Majesty, King Joshua the Only, First Born from the Dead! May his reign extend to the farthest corners of the universe and his people and Kingdom spread throughout the heavens!"

The Main Bridge of the Providence erupted again in cheers, only much more intensely than before. And again, Nadia made an announcement over the ship's intercom. There was an air of jubilation and wonder that spread throughout the ship. The fact that they were on the cusp of mankind's eternal destiny and were privileged to be a part of it was not lost to a single soul.

A few minutes later, the rest of the landing party followed Flynn out of the hatch and formed a circle about 50 feet from the Falcon. Flynn was first to take off his helmet to test the air. He took a deep breath and knew immediately that the air would be breathable for the pilots. They were Children after all, and there was no need risking their lives if the Brethren could check things out first with no possibility of harm.

He could tell that there was just a hair over one g of gravity; the temperature was about 85 degrees Fahrenheit, and the humidity was about 20%. The weather was beautiful, not a cloud in the sky, and there was a slight breeze blowing from the north. Flynn took it all in for a moment, then turned to his fellow Brethren with a big grin on his face. Flynn Jr. and Mattie looked at each other intently, also smiling. Hans and AJ looked at Flynn expectedly to see what he would say or do next.

Still smiling, Flynn turned toward the Falcon, locked eyes with Brian in the commander's seat, and gave him a big thumbs-up. With that signal, the rest of the landing party took off their helmets and all eyes turned toward the Falcon. A second later, the engines began to wind down from idle and shut down completely within about 10 seconds. A few minutes later, Brian and Cory unstrapped and bounded out of the vehicle. They joined the circle and took their helmets off immediately. All the Brethren watched them for a few moments to make sure that they could indeed breathe the air, and then the celebration began.

AJ started and Flynn followed with, "Bwana asifiwe, Bwana asifiwe!" The circle spread out as they all started yelling, "Bwana asifiwe, Praise the Lord! Bwana asifiwe, Praise the Lord!"

Before they had gotten too far into the celebrations, Flynn was suddenly overtaken with a sense of imminent danger. "Hush everybody, hush!" he shouted. Just as the group had quieted down a bit, he heard the bushes rustle behind them and caught a sudden burst of motion out of the corner of his eye. As he turned to see what it was, he saw a large tan colored creature, about the size of a lion that had leaped out of the bushes and was headed right for Cory.

Flynn couldn't believe how fast this creature was. It had covered a distance of 100 yards in a matter of seconds from the time he first saw it. It had a large dark brown mane like a lion, but the mane was draped around its shoulders instead of its head. The head of the beast looked more like that of an extremely large pointy eared dog. Whatever it was, he knew he only had a second or two to act.

Cory had turned just in time to see the creature bounding toward him but had little time to react. He just stood there for a second like he had resigned himself to certain death. Flynn extended his right hand and sent an energy pulse toward the creature as it was making its final leap towards Cory. The pulse of energy hit the creature at exactly the same time as AJ's did. They had both acted at precisely the same moment and the dual blast of energy hit the creature in mid leap and knocked it off its intended flight path. The entire landing party, now transfixed by the sight of this ferocious looking creature, watched as it landed in an unconscious heap just to the right of Cory. He had just enough time to brace himself for impact and was visibly shaken by the unexpected turn of events.

Flynn shouted, "Everyone back to the Falcon ... Now! Brian, you and Cory first, hustle!"

Nadia inquired excitedly over the radio, "Is everything OK Falcon ... what's going on down there? We're picking up heart rates of 180 plus on Cory and Brian's sub-q biosensors!" But Flynn was more concerned with getting everyone back onboard than answering her call.

Within seconds, the entire landing party was back in the craft with all the hatches closed. It was a good thing too because the creature that had almost killed Cory was regaining consciousness and looked like it was very angry. They watched it as it got back to its feet and began to circle the Falcon. As it did so they got their first really good look at the creature.

It was heavily muscled with a huge chest that tapered rapidly to a slender waist. Its hind legs and its fore legs were thick and powerful, clearly made for sprint-like speed. Its paws were fully twice the size of a man's outstretched hand with an array of long curved claws on the ends. It growled at them repeatedly, revealing large, razor sharp teeth. It was truly an enormous beast as its head was a good five feet off the ground.

Flynn estimated the creature to be about eight feet long and reckoned it weighed about 400 pounds. Its deep yellow eyes were fixed on the occupants of the Falcon as if it could not wait to stalk them again. Just then, they heard something in the distance that sounded like a baritone version of a coyote howl. The creature looked in the direction of the howl, looked back at them briefly, and then bounded off into the bushes and out of sight.

Flynn thought, if there was a more fearsome creature that existed somewhere else on this planet, he wasn't sure he wanted to see it.

"What the heck was that thing?" Brian exclaimed.

But Cory clearly had something else on his mind, "How did you guys do that? I mean I knew you guys were different from us but ... Wow! ... That was really something! ... And uh ... how come it didn't kill the thing ... anyway, whatever it was ... thanks for saving my life!"

Flynn did not respond at first. He and AJ had reacted instinctively with the energy beams, but he knew for a fact that it was the first time either of them had used them since the invasion.

"I'll explain later as best I can, but for now, we have to get back to the ship. It's too risky to stay here overnight. Who knows how many more of those dog-lion things are lurking in the bushes of these plains. The good news is; we have established the fact that there is abundant plant life and evidently abundant animal life on this planet.

"If a predator like that exists then there must be prey. That means there's a food chain of some kind which means there have to be other animals on this planet. The air is breathable, the climate is near perfect and humans can definitely live here. The bad news is we have to come up with a plan to deal with the dangers of this world before we return. Let's strap in and return to the Providence."

Once they were safely airborne, Brian reported to the ship that there had been an incident with the landing party but that everyone was safe and unharmed. They would make a full report after returning to the ship.

Flynn spent the entire rendezvous reflecting on the near brush with death that they had just encountered. How could he have been so careless, he wondered? Did it not stand to reason that if they had spotted evidence of large migratory herds of animals that there might be predators on this planet as well? His first obligation to the Children was to protect them from harm and he had almost failed to do that, right out of the chute, on their first visit to another world.

He thought back to the farewell words of Matt's wife Emma who evidently felt compelled by the Spirit to remind him to be especially mindful of the vulnerabilities of the Children. They could be hurt and they could be killed. While it was rare on Earth, it was not something that was impossible. In fact, it seemed eminently possible now, especially on what appeared to be a hostile world; at least the very small part of it that they had just visited.

Lots of questions swirled in his mind, not the least of which was why an obviously carnivorous predator had attempted to kill one of his crewmembers. He could not reconcile how the cycle of life and death for predator and prey had been peacefully resolved back on Earth, yet not on this world. Back there, lions and other land predators had undergone a transformation after the invasion and could now subsist on a vegetarian diet. The animal kingdom there had finally found peace in that no creature had to die so some other creature could live. Why was it not so on this planet?

Wasn't the First Born Lord of the Earth and of the whole universe? And along those lines, why did this planet seem so perfectly suited for life, almost tailor made for Earthlings to inhabit? What other kinds of animal species would they find, and why did the creature they saw seem so similar to Earth animals. For that matter, why were there animals at all on this planet? Were there other planets like this, he wondered? Surely there were.

After wrestling with these questions for quite some time he shifted his thinking back to the task at hand. The questions would have to wait. There was one thing he knew for sure. They would have to come up with a comprehensive plan which addressed physical security in an airtight fashion before he would let anyone else return to the surface of this planet.

He turned to his son and said, "I would like to schedule an impromptu prayer meeting for tonight if it's OK with you. Right now I feel pretty clueless about what to do next. We need to get the mind of the Lord on this."

"I was hoping you would ask me to do that," Flynn Jr. replied, "I feel the same way ... Wow, the First Born wasn't kidding when he said there would be surprises ... and I have a feeling there are a few more of them in store for us before we head back home."

As soon as they had returned to the ship and had had time to get out of their suits, Flynn announced over the intercom that he was holding a meeting in the Officer's Wardroom. He wanted the command staff there, the medical staff, the science staff, and the security detail. He gave them 15 minutes to get there and made sure everyone knew it was mandatory. Only those who were on duty were exempt.

Once they had assembled, Flynn relayed the details of their encounter to an audience that was clearly shocked, both by his demeanor and by the tale itself. He was visibly upset and was looking for answers as quickly as he could find them. No one said a word, they just sat and listened.

Flynn concluded by saying, "I'm giving you all one week to come up with a plan to establish a base camp on this planet. Safety and security are first priority so keep that in mind as you prepare your plan. We need to pick a place that has a representative sample of the terrain, topography, and geography found all over the planet. Also keep in mind that we've only got one PLV so we need to minimize our trips to the surface as much as possible.

"Once we establish a base camp, we will use it to study the planet as best we can. We'll stay here no more than six months and then we'll pack up and move on to AC Alpha to check for habitable planets there.

"We're going to start things off with a special prayer meeting tonight at 1900 in the Fellowship Hall. After that, I will commit myself to prayer for the next week and will continue to seek the guidance of the Lord on these matters. I expect all of you to do the same.

"Command staff: let's meet in the Main Bridge conference room exactly one week from today at 1300. If I think the plan you present is sound and can be executed without undue risk, we will proceed with it immediately. Are there any questions?"

# :TERRA PRIME

*CHAPTER 18*

They had decided to name the planet Terra Prime because of the abundance of landmass available on its surface. From their 300 mile orbit, it appeared that there were no discernible continents, just one continuous land mass with several large bodies of water randomly distributed over the globe, more like seas than oceans.

The plan that was adopted by Captain Roberts involved establishing a base camp near the shores of one of the seas that was close to the equator. The sea was surrounded by an abundance of the grassy plains that seemed to characterize much of the planet's geography. In addition, it was relatively close to a small mountain range to the west. The base camp would be established halfway between the mountains and the sea in the midst of one of the grassy plains. That way, small teams could fan out and explore the most common geographic features found throughout the planet. It was felt that this plan would yield a reasonable snapshot of the ecology, geology, climate, and zoology of the planet.

All landing parties would include at least one of the Brethren and weapons would be carried by everyone. As a precaution prior to launch, the ship had been equipped with a small armory that contained military style shotguns, assault rifles, and pistols, and all crewmembers had been trained in the use of basic weaponry. There was an abundance of electromagnetic concertina wire which could be used to construct force field fences powerful enough to repel any large predators for planned overnight or extended duration visits.

The landing parties would gather data on Terra Prime and the Providence would gather sensor data from orbit. They would gather as much data as they could in six months and then give it to the science staff. After analyzing the data, the science staff would prepare a final report.

After much thought and prayer, Flynn had decided that Mattie would lead the landing party that would break ground on the base camp. She would lead Team One with five science personnel and five security personnel under her command. The day before they were scheduled to launch, Flynn was sitting in his quarters reading the Sacred Text. He could not get past Psalm 91 that particular morning, as he was praying for the safety of every team member that was to launch that day.

Flynn was not concerned about her personal safety. He knew she could not be harmed and could not die, but he was praying that she would protect the rest of her team who were not as invincible as she was. He still remembered the close call that he had had with the dog-lion on that first landing just over a week ago.

He prayed, "Lord, give her the full measure of the powers of this world so that she may be equipped to protect and serve those under her charge. Give her, and the members of her team, the courage necessary to carry out their assignment and gather as much useful data as possible. In the name of our High Priest, Jesus, Amen."

After his time of prayer, he met with Mattie alone in the Main Bridge conference room. He wanted one more shot at imparting wisdom and advice to her before she embarked on her journey. Team One was scheduled to land in a grassy plain 10 miles west of one of the seas that lay along the equator. As planned, that would situate them equally distant from a small mountain range further to the west. The terrain there looked to be very similar to what they had seen on their first landing, so Flynn felt compelled to warn her to be on guard for the presence of dog-lions. He had no way of knowing that they would be there, but wanted her to know how formidable they were just in case.

"G-daddy," she said excitedly, "I saw it too, remember? I was there and I know what a creature like that is capable of! Besides, dad and I already prayed about it this morning in the Chapel. The Lord is with us. We *will* be OK; don't worry."

"You're right Mattie," he replied, "the Lord is with you indeed. Just watch out for those dog-lions and any other dangerous animal life that you may encounter. Be careful around the sea as well. Who knows what dangers may lurk beneath those waters. For some reason the harmony of nature has not been established on this planet the way that is has been on Earth. It is probably my number one question for the First Born when we return."

She looked at him with a half-smile and said, "G-daddy, everything is going to be all right, I promise you, now let me go. I have to give the final briefing to my team before the PLV insert. We're leaving in two hours."

"OK," he replied reluctantly, "I'll be on the bridge for the launch if you need me." He grabbed her by the shoulders, kissed her on the cheek, and then watched as she walked out the door to meet with her team.

Three hours later, Flynn was following the descent profile of the Falcon from the Main Bridge. Nadia had the bridge for the launch but Flynn was there, nevertheless, as he had promised Mattie he would be. When the Falcon had left the Lower Airlock and started its descent toward the planet, he prayed again silently for Team One's protection.

The descent profile was tracked by the ship's telemetry, and everything went according to the sequence he had experienced on his visit to the planet. During the reentry phase they had lost radio contact as was expected and Flynn was busy counting the minutes that would normally pass before they would reestablish contact.

As he did so, he sensed that same feeling of imminent danger that he had experienced right before the dog-lion attack.

He stood up out of his chair and shouted, "Nadia, stay on your toes, I sense there may be something wrong here with the Falcon. We should have heard from them by now."

"Aye Captain," she replied tersely.

She then turned to the sensor operator and said, "Do we at least have them on radar? Can we track their position and where they are on the profile?"

The operator turned to her and said with all the color drained from his face, "First Officer Habibi, I'm afraid we have lost them. I'm not picking them up on any of our telemetry; we have no way of knowing where they are or the state of their craft."

Flynn jumped on the radio and shouted, "Falcon, Falcon, do you read me, do you read me?"

He repeated the call several times but there was no response. After about a full minute of silence, Flynn was poised for another round of calls.

Just then, they heard the sounds of a faint and crackly radio signal followed by a broken but readable transmission "… storm … out of nowhere … damage … ship … emergency … way off course … will call … land …"

It was the voice of Cory Brown, the copilot of Crew One. Flynn figured that Brian Salley must have had his hands full and had given all radio comms to his copilot.

"Lord help them!" Flynn shouted urgently. "Angels protect them; help them get on the ground safely!"

The bridge crew responded with a collective "Amen!" and then settled in for what would be a long period of uncomfortable silence.

An hour later, the atmosphere was tense on the bridge and Flynn was pacing back and forth, praying under his breath, waiting for some kind of positive response.

Suddenly, the sensor operator jumped out of his seat and exclaimed, "We're picking up their emergency beacon and we have a fix on their location ... they are in the mountains about 20 miles west of the intended landing zone ... I'm picking up signals from eight ... now ten biosensors ... they appear to be alive and well though all their heart rates are elevated!"

Flynn was relieved and said, "OK everyone; let's put our heads together. We're going to find out what happened to them and how they are doing, one way or another.

"Command staff: I'm convening an emergency meeting in the conference room ... now! Sensor operator, keep us posted. Nadia, you still have the bridge. Pardon the interruptions and the breakdown of protocol."

"Not a problem Captain," she replied, "completely understandable."

Half way through the command staff meeting, Ensign Munn came running into the conference room completely out of breath. They had been discussing possible options and scenarios when he burst through the door and shouted, "Captain, they've established contact with Team One. First Officer Habibi requests your presence on the bridge."

Flynn darted out the door in response with his staff hot on his heels.

After a long and protracted exchange of information between Flynn, Mattie, and Brian Salley, the situation had become clear. The Falcon had encountered a vicious storm which had developed rapidly and without prior warning as they lined up for their final approach. Their radios had been damaged and they had lost 40% power on the scramjets due to several direct lightning strikes. Their navigation and automatic landing equipment had gone off line at a critical time and they ended up having to fly the ship manually to keep from crashing.

They had managed to fly it out of the storm but in the process had ended up way off course. They had lost so much power on the scramjets that they ended up using their rocket thrusters to augment their thrust on final approach and landing. As a result they consumed much more rocket fuel than they had planned. When they broke out of the clouds they were at 8,000 feet AGL and only had a few minutes to pick a suitable landing spot. They ended up spotting a small valley near a mountain lake which had just enough flat terrain for them to put the Falcon down.

None of the crewmembers had been hurt, but the Falcon had sustained major damage. No one knew how long it would take to repair or whether they could repair it at all with the tools and equipment that were available to them on site. Mattie's plan was to break ground on the base camp as planned with the Falcon in the center and with a perimeter force field surrounding the entire camp. Once the base camp was set up and secure, they would assess their situation more completely and report back to the Providence.

One week later, Flynn looked down at Terra Prime from the Main Bridge windows and tried to imagine what Team One must have felt like. They were marooned for the foreseeable future on a strange planet with limited supplies and with potentially hostile wildlife and unknown dangers all around them. He prayed under his breath for Mattie and her team and asked the Lord to give them wisdom in dealing with the challenges that lay ahead for them. He had resisted the temptation to just jump down there and take control himself. He did not want to give Mattie the impression that he had no confidence in her leadership.

For that matter, Mattie could have just as easily jumped up to the Providence to confer with Flynn and others on their predicament. But Flynn knew that she would not leave the landing party without the protection that a member of the Brethren could provide.

He remembered the words of Flynn Jr. who had reminded him on more than one occasion that Mattie was more than capable of leading Team One through this crisis. "After all, dad, she's my daughter, she's your granddaughter, and she's a Roberts. She'll do just fine."

On his end, Flynn knew one thing for certain. Their one and only priority was to somehow repair the Falcon. It was the key to everything. They needed it up and running to be able to resupply the base camp and to ensure the safety of Team One. Any further exploration of the planet was secondary now.

After a week of examination, they had determined that the most critical damage to the Falcon was to the scramjet fuel control unit. This unit sent control signals that metered fuel to the scramjet engines in response to throttle settings. The lightning strikes had evidently fried the unit to the point that it could not process enough signal strength to command full power on either of the scramjets. There was no way it could be repaired on site; it would have to be replaced, and no one had come up with a plan to do that just yet. Furthermore, because they had used more rocket fuel than planned during their emergency landing, the Falcon would not be able to fly a standard profile for a return rendezvous with the Providence.

Mattie had recounted in her last contact that Team One had found a source of fresh water that had been tested and was drinkable. There was a small mountain creek that ran into the lake that was about a half mile from where they had landed, and it ran within a few hundred feet of the base camp. Water was not an issue, but they only had a week's worth of food left. They had enough fuel in their portable fuel cells to power the force field fence for another four to five days.

At the end of her report she noted that they had seen fish in the mountain stream and an abundance of birdlike species in the surrounding trees, but had not spotted any dangerous predators in the area. While that last part was somewhat comforting to Flynn, all things considered, he wondered if it might be a longer year than he had anticipated.

The phrase "ad astra per aspera" came to the forefront of his mind. He remembered it from a memorial plaque at Pad 34 where his childhood idol Gus Grissom had died in AD 1967. It was Latin for "a rough road leads to the stars."

He thought of his wife Hannah back on Earth, literally light years away from him, and he missed her now more than ever. Though he and Hannah would live forever in their new celestial bodies, time and distance still had meaning, especially in the First Sphere. As he gazed at the lush and beautiful planet below, he remembered a few lines from a poem he had memorized long ago:

> "Absence makes the heart grow fonder:
> Isle of Beauty, fare thee well!"

*To be continued in book two of the series: Millennial Voyage*

# :TECHNOLOGY APPENDIX

### Ship's Construction and Outer Hull

The entire ship was constructed of fourth generation composite materials that were high strength and extremely heat resistant. The composite plates that were used to form the ship's hull incorporated built-in nanoporous pathways which allowed negatively charged nanoparticles to circulate in swarms and eddies around positively charged nodes that were placed all over the ship. Dielectric shields lined the inner walls of these plates that worked to protect the ship and the crew from any harmful effects generated by the resulting electromagnetic (EM) fields. This shielding caused the EM fields to project outward from the outer hull forming a system of overlapping buffers. These overlapping buffers acted as a force field that was powerful enough to protect the ship from most of the space debris or micro-meteorites that might be encountered along their flight path. It also provided protection for the crew from harmful space radiation.

### Particle Beam Emitter (PBE)

The thing that looked like a fencer's foil was actually a powerful Particle Beam Emitter (PBE) that was synchronized with a state of the art phased array Collision Avoidance Radar (CAR). The radar could see for hundreds of miles out and would detect anything that was too large for the EM buffers to deflect. Even at extremely high velocities, the computer controlled synchronization would automatically fire the emitter when necessary to destroy the debris and protect the ship's outer hull. When the ship was repositioned for deceleration and the PBE could not be used, the designers believed that the plasma plume from the celestial matter drive or the fusion boosters would destroy any space debris too large to be deflected by the EM buffers.

## Ship's Sensors and Communications

A Surface Mapping System (SMS) was housed immediately aft of the PBE and adjacent to the CAR. The SMS consisted of a ground mapping radar that was integrated with LIDAR for surface mapping of any planets of interest that they might encounter on their journey. The ground mapping radar could be used independently of the LIDAR in an airborne mode for flight following during launch and recovery of the Falcon PLV.

There were other sensors that the ship employed that were housed in various places throughout the ship. They included short range and long range electro-optical, meteorological, multi-spectral, thermal, and gravity field sensors. In addition to these sensors, specially equipped sensor pods could be launched from the Lower Airlock which could be sent to the surface of any planet or object of interest.

The ship's communications consisted of the latest technology transmitters and receivers but everybody on the crew realized that, except for short range ship to ship and ship to shore communications, they would be of little use once they reached the outer Solar System. Once you got that far out, communication with Earth would be impractical and extremely time consuming. Once they left the confines of the Solar System, the Providence would be on her own with no contact possible with Earth until they got close to her again on their return journey.

When not wearing their space suits, ship to shore and person to person communications was available through nanostructured transceivers that were woven into the collars and the wrist bands of the crewmembers' flight suit styled uniforms.

The ship was also equipped with state of the art telemetry for command, control, and monitoring functions during launch of the Planetary Landing Vehicle (PLV) and sensor pods.

### Command, Control, and Data Center (CCDC)

The CCDC was where all the ships systems converged into one centralized computer control system via advanced fiber optic and high fidelity wireless connectivity. The CCDC provided a direct connection from the Engineering Deck which relayed all pertinent information about the Ship's Power, Ship's Propulsion and Ship's Pressurization and Life Support systems to the Main Bridge. There was sufficient redundancy housed on the Engineering Deck that it could serve as an Alternate Bridge in the event of complete CCDC system failure.

All the computer systems on board were based on the leading edge carbon nanotube based architecture. In these systems, the number of transistors that were placed on a single microchip was far beyond anyone's wildest dreams and those who thought there was a theoretical limit to Moore's Law had so far, been proven wrong.

Thus, the Data Center portion of the CCDC was able to contain all the star charts within the Milky Way Galaxy that had been mapped out by the Royal Space Flight Academy to date, an incredible amount of data. There was a link to the Navigator Station on the Main Bridge that allowed the Duty Navigator to pull up and examine any star system that was desired.

### Tokomak Reactors

The primary Tokomak Reactor was started with electrical power supplied by the Bethel Space Station. After that, it operated off of ship's power in a sustainable loop configuration. As long as fuel was available to feed the plasma in the reactor it would provide electricity for the ship and for the magnetic containment and compression of the reactor. The back-up reactor was there in case there was a failure of the main reactor. To save fuel, it would not be started unless it was needed. There was a system of high capacity fuel cells that provided a backup source of ship's power if both reactors happened to be offline at the same time. Primary fuel for the Tokomak reactors was stored in the six fuel tanks just aft of the Celestial Matter Drive scoop.

### Maneuvering Verniers

The excess heat from the primary Tokomak reactor was used as an ignition source and a secondary means of thrust for a system of chemical vernier thrusters placed strategically around the ship. These thrusters helped to maintain the stability and control of the ship and to maneuver it as necessary throughout all phases of the mission profile.

# :ABOUT THE AUTHOR

Dr. Scott R. Forrest is a dynamic and engaging author/speaker who has been teaching the Bible for over 25 years. He is a combat decorated military pilot with 29 years of aviation service with both the US Marine Corps and the Air Force Reserve. He earned his Ph.D. in Engineering in 2004 with research and emphasis in the field of micro and nanosystems. He has served as Director of the School of Ministry, the two year Bible School at Word of Life Center Church, in Shreveport, Louisiana, since 2005. His wife Trish serves at his side as Administrative Assistant and uses her organizational gifts to help him run the school. In 2008 Dr. Forrest was appointed as Director of the Technology Transfer Center in Shreveport (Louisiana Tech University). He teaches mathematics, statistics, and research methods with two satellite campuses located on Barksdale Air Force Base, Louisiana Tech and Embry Riddle Aeronautical University. Dr. Forrest regularly uses his military flying experience and his background in engineering and science to offer a unique perspective and complement his teaching of the Bible.

For the latest on his books visit and like his author page: www.facebook.com/scottrforrest

Follow Dr. Forrest on Sunday afternoons at 1230 CST as he hosts The Spirit Dimension on KFLO Shreveport, The Promise 90.7 FM. Available on the internet from anywhere at: www.promisetalkradio.org

*Archived broadcasts can be accessed at the author page listed above.*

Send comments or questions about the radio broadcast to: thespiritdimension@gmail.com

If you would like to contact the author or are interested in having Dr. Forrest come and speak at your church or organization, his contact information is listed below:

Dr. Scott R. Forrest
138 Downing Court
Bossier City, LA 71111

Email: sforrest9123@yahoo.com

Twitter: @DrScottRForrest